NEVER BEEN FOUND

A Tomas O'Malley Story

KENNETH S. KAPPELMANN

Black Rose Writing | Texas

ISBN: 978-1-68433-041-6
PUBLISHED BY BLACK ROSE WRITING
www.blackrosewriting.com

Printed in the United States of America
Suggested Retail Price (SRP) $18.95

Never Been Found is printed in Garamond Premier Pro
Edited by Lisa Petrocelli

This book is dedicated to J.P. Beaumont

NEVER BEEN FOUND

It was a strange November day in Chicago. The normal below-freezing wind and snow had been pleasantly replaced with a more tepid fall day. Jamal walked through the well-manicured grass of the cemetery. He did not know what he was going to do, but he finally found a critical piece of information. As he looked toward his father's grave, he knew the rest of the puzzle was waiting. He saw the man kneeling down in front of the newly placed marker. He held his head in his hands and appeared to be crying. *Crying,* Jamal thought to himself. *What a joke.*

He drew within about fifteen feet of the man and said, "Hey."

The man raised his head and their eyes met. Tears were streaming down his face, making him incapable of speech at that moment. He looked away in shame.

"What are you doing here?" Jamal asked.

Again, the man did not answer.

Jamal's tone became harder as he held back the anger growing within him. "You killed him. You killed my father. I just need to know why."

The man did not look up but his hand moved toward his leg where resting unnoticed previously was a small handgun. He picked up the gun and turned back to Jamal. "Let it go, Jamal. You need to let this one go."

Jamal pulled out his gun and pointed it at the still-crouching man. "I don't think so."

1 *NINE DAYS EARLIER.*

I looked across wet pavement marking the end of the alley and could tell from the smell that what I would find down its dark passage was nothing I wanted to see. The smell of day-old flesh on what would be an unseasonably warm Chicago morning would make anyone's stomach turn. There were several squad cars already in place and crime scene tape had been affixed to block the alley, but none of that kept the onlookers from hoping to catch sight of the gruesome remains. The thought sickened me. All I wanted to do was avoid these types of scenes, and all these locals wanted to do was snap a picture for their Facebook or Instagram friends.

I saw Frank Sullivan. Franky was another detective who, like me, had worked his whole career in downtown Chicago. Our eyes met, and I could immediately tell he felt the same thing—*get these people out of here.* Standing quietly behind Franky was Dr. Elise Gerstenberger, the medical examiner. All of our eyes made contact, and it was clear to us it was going to be a long morning. I wished that I had not stopped at Mr. J's for a Dagwood that morning as I did not think it would be sitting well in a few minutes. A Dagwood is a greasy loaded burger with just about everything on it. They are available all day and night, and after an evening of Wild Turkey and Coke, they usually hit the spot. I had not seen Franky there, but from his green look it appeared he had made the same trip.

"Morning, Tommy. Looks like we have a bad one today," stated Franky motioning to the alley.

"Yep," I replied. "It will only get worse if we don't get it cleaned up quickly. By the looks of the sun, it is going to be close to eighty today. Has to be a record for

November in Chicago."

Dr. Gerstenberger nodded. "Yes, we should get to it."

Dr. Gerstenberger was not at all who you would expect working in the worst area of Chicago. She was tall, in incredible shape, and what most would call extremely beautiful. That being said, her husband, Dr. Alan Grove, was one of the head medical professionals working at Abbunex Labs, a pharmaceutical giant in the North Chicago suburbs. Needless to say, the couple were millionaires, but when you talked to them, you might as well be drinking an Old Style Beer at a Cubs game because you would never know it.

Franky, "Dr. G," as everyone called her, and I proceeded down the alley. Franky and I were not partners, not anymore, but always seemed to catch cases that linked us together, and this was no different. We both had an interest in this body. Franky had an open case involving murdered prostitutes in the old Cabrini Green area, and I had a missing black high school girl who was believed to have been killed several weeks ago. In short, we were hoping the body might provide some answers.

"Any new findings on your missing girl?" asked Franky.

"Nope," I said softly. Her father is back on his deliveries and her brother is playing ball at Kansas, but her trail is cold. I'm thinking this might be her."

He nodded but I do not think he really cared about the answer. As you approach a dead body, you really don't want silence. We all knew that. Franky just took the lead. There were several Chicago PD officers around the body. I recognized most of them. I did not know any of them well, but I knew them well enough. One noticed our approach and stepped toward us.

"Hello, Detective Sullivan and Detective O'Malley." Turning to Elise, "And Dr. G. This is an ugly one. We are working on an ID. No wallet or anything but I think you might know him."

His eyes were fixed on me indicating that his comment was for my benefit. I looked back toward the officer. "Pete, isn't it?"

"Yes, Pete Schram," he replied.

"First, I thought we were talking about a dead girl. You said I might know *him*. Does that mean this is a male?"

That is why I am known as the number one detective in Chicago.

"Yes, sir. Older male, in his sixties. African-American. Appears to have been executed." He paused, then added, "You know, shot in the back of the head."

Really, that is what you mean by executed, I thought. I nodded understanding. "Why do you think I might know him?"

"I think he is tied to your case. The one I saw on TV related to that basketball player at Kansas."

"Jessica Jackson?"

"Yes, I think this might be her father."

My eyes dropped but not further than the sink of my heart. Without another word I pushed by the officer and knelt beside the body. It was covered, waiting for the medical examiner, but that did not prevent me from seeing some of the characteristics that were exposed. I could determine the relative height and weight of the body, another innate ability of being a homicide detective for more than twenty years. A talent to be used at parties like guessing someone's age. I reached out and pulled back the sheet. My eyes locked on the corpse's open eyes and death mask. My body fell just a bit causing Franky to take a step toward me before he realized I had caught myself and was fine.

Franky asked softly, "Is it him?"

"Yes, it is Malcolm Jackson."

•　　•　　•　　•　　•

"Jamal is on fire tonight," Danny Piper said. Danny was the assistant coach of the defending national champions, Kansas Jayhawks. "What's he got, twenty-eight points this half?" As he said it, the sold-out crowd roared again and another three-pointer drained without hitting any rim.

Head Coach Bill Williams nodded and then sent another player to the sideline to replace his young forward before halftime. To a slurry of high fives and a huge smile, Jamal Jackson took his seat on the bench next to Coach Williams. The coach bent down before his player, and although anyone watching knew he was still coaching, this was one of those conversations that was more about "attaboys" verses "this is what we need to work on." As they were talking, the athletic director flagged Coach Piper to the side.

The buzzer sounded for halftime and the Jayhawk players leaped to their feet and headed into the locker room sporting a 52-41 lead over the visiting Duke Blue Devils. Both perennial powers in college basketball squaring off this early in the season was something the colleges loved.

After the ESPN reporter finished with Coach Williams, Piper grabbed his fellow coach's arm and pulled him to the side whispering away from all news media. "Hey Coach, Sheahon just told me something about Jamal. It is about his father." Sheahon Zenger was athletic director at the University of Kansas.

Coach Williams stopped and looked up toward the much taller Piper who not only had an extremely successful career in the NBA, but led the 1988 Kansas Jayhawks to the National Championship under then coach Larry Brown. "What happened?"

Danny could hear the concern in his voice as Coach Williams had to assume if the AD was coming in the middle of such a big game, the news had to be significant. He leaned even closer to his head coach and whispered, "His father has been murdered. They found him today and his mother positively identified him."

Bill's eyes dropped, but it was Danny who continued, "Do we wait to tell him?"

Coach Williams shook his head. "No, have Sheahon stay outside the locker room. When we head back to the floor, I will keep Jamal back and talk to him. Then have Sheahon take him to his office and help him arrange to get home. He needs to be with his family now."

Danny nodded understanding. "I can't believe it. First his sister, now his father." His voice trailed off as there was nothing more to say. Bill thought about the first time he ever met Jamal's father.

●　　●　　●　　●　　●

Three years earlier.

"Damn, J, I can't believe what you can do in the air."

"Shut up, Tiny," Jamal replied. You could do the same, you just need to shed a few hundred pounds."

The smile instantly faded from his friend and some laughter came from the others on the court. The court they played on was in the heart of the South Chicago projects. It was concrete and the nets were chain, but the talent level on any given afternoon exceeded most colleges. The players were mostly black as was the neighborhood, but occasionally a white boy would show up and as long as he had game, there were never issues.

Tiny was Jamal's best friend, and had been since they were kids. Their birthdays were a day apart, they lived on the same floor in their apartment building, and they were both athletes. Tiny—his real name was Tyrone Nielson—is the stereotypical person to be nicknamed Tiny. He was easily 350 pounds and had been since he was in the eighth grade. Although he had an unbelievable basketball shot, at 350 and only 5'10" tall, football was going to be his sport of choice.

Moses, another player who would most likely go to a top Division 1 college in basketball but a year behind Jamal in school, pointed and said, "Hey, J, another one coming to visit. Who is visiting today?"

"I don't remember. I think Dad set up Kansas, but if they were like Coach K, they won't come to this area."

Jamal looked over to two men parked about half a block down the street who were now walking toward their court. Jamal's dad had been sitting on the side watching the boys play, as he did almost every afternoon, and now stood to intercept the two men. One man was shorter, white, and in basketball shape, but the years had added a few pounds. The other was tall, African-American, with a mostly shaved head. If not walking toward a basketball court, an onlooker would have thought this was a businessman with his bodyguard. In this area, the bodyguard was needed. But because it involved basketball, all were safe.

Malcolm greeted the men who he recognized from their pictures. "Hello, Coach Williams, Coach Piper. It is a pleasure to meet you."

●　　●　　●　　●　　●

The men returned the greeting and all shook hands. Coach Williams was about to speak when Jamal's father continued. "You know, my son has been recruited by nearly every major basketball school in the country. I have asked all of them to meet here on the court where Jamal learned to play. They have all wanted to meet at hotels, or airports, or somewhere else. You are the first to show up here. How come?"

Coach Williams smiled. "I can't speak for any other schools or coaches, but if this is where he learned to love the game, then this is the Jamal I want to know."

Malcolm seemed to like this answer, but he did not intentionally let it show. He turned to the court. "Jamal, come here and meet these coaches."

Jamal tossed the ball to Tiny with a firm chest pass and jogged over to where the three men stood. They shook hands and gave brief introductions, though they all knew each other even before a word was spoken.

Coach Williams took the lead. "I am not here to feed you any lines or tell you something is better than something else. You can get a great education at all the schools you are considering. You will be a premier basketball star no matter where you play. If you want me to tell you why a Kansas program is better, I would be glad to, but I also know that every coach has the same speech about their school. That is why I am here. I don't want to talk. I want to watch. This is your home. This is your Lawrence, Kansas. Show us what you can do here. Coach Piper and I want you in Kansas, but above all, we love basketball, and I have seen enough to know that some of the best basketball I will ever see might be today on this court—*your* court." He paused, smiled at Jamal, and then motioned to Coach Piper and Malcolm. "Come on, let's see what these boys can do."

They began walking to where Malcolm had been standing against a chain-link fence. As they walked, Coach Williams turned back to Jamal and loud enough for all to hear, he said, "And Jamal, make sure your friends know that even if you opt to not come to Kansas, we will be watching for anyone else who might be a fit for us as well." That created a stir among the boys who had continued shooting the entire time since Jamal had left. Tiny fed the ball back to Jamal as he walked up, and immediately he released an NBA range three-pointer that swished, though the sound of a basketball on a chain net is far from a swishing sound.

The boys broke out into teams, and in street-ball fashion just short of the Harlem Globetrotters, they proceeded to tear apart the court in some of the best street basketball the two coaches had ever seen. Jamal was the center of attention, and some of his monster dunks even brought his opponents to their knees with shouts and jeers. Moses seemed to have a magic hand to feed him passes by the rim and with one thundering dunk that shook the backboard to the point of breaking, the pick-up game ended. Claps from both coaches were all that answered the exchange of high fives on the concrete surface before them.

"What do you think?" asked Malcolm.

Coach Williams flashed his charismatic smile. "It has never been about what I thought, Mr. Jackson. It is about what you and your son think." He stood and shook his hand and began to walk away, giving a short wave toward Jamal and the others who had stopped to watch the discussion.

"Is that it?" asked Malcolm. "Aren't you going to tell me how great Kansas is?

How by coming to Kansas, you will pave the way for my son to play in the NBA? Aren't you going to sell me?"

He stopped and turned back still smiling. "Mr. Jackson—"

He was interrupted by Malcolm's raised hand. "Please, call me Malcolm."

"Malcolm," he continued. "You have raised an incredible young man. He has a discipline and skill that only a father who cared and was involved in everything regarding his children could have created. Your son will get those things you just referenced no matter where he goes. I don't need to sell you. You have worked forty years in the same job selling your business every day. There is nothing I can say that you have not heard a thousand times over the last forty years. I am not going to lie, we want Jamal at our school. I will promise you that I will carry on the same guidance level you have given him. I will never replace his father, but I will be that father five hundred miles away. The only word I want you to hear from me when you think about Kansas is *trust*. Other than that, you have all the information you need."

Malcolm nodded as Jamal came jogging over. "Coach Williams, Coach Piper."

They both turned to the young man, though it was Coach Piper who answered as he was closer. "Yes?"

"I just wanted to thank you for coming. This is the first chance I've had to show any coach where I grew up playing. I like meeting at the Drake and all. I mean, the hotel is beautiful, but in my world, this is where I find the most beauty." He paused then added, "And my friends like you being here too."

Both coaches reached out and shook his hand. "You are talented, Jamal, as are many of your friends. Have them stay in touch with us, and I hope to see you in Kansas sometime soon." They turned and headed back to their rental car with Malcolm and his father talking quietly in their wake.

Coach Piper looked back to Coach Williams and whispered, "Is that it? You don't want to talk any longer, meet his mother or anything?"

Williams smiled. "Nope. We just did something no other school did. We gave Mr. Jackson what he wanted—appreciation for the job he did as a father—and we did it in his home."

"Are you saying we are going to sign him after being here for thirty minutes?"

"No, I am saying we have as good a chance or better as any school because we just spent this thirty minutes here in Chicago, on this court."

•   •   •   •   •

The noise of the crowd at the game brought Coach Williams out of his momentary thoughts. He felt a small tear form in his eye as he thought about speaking with his star sophomore forward. It was one of those talks you hope you never have to have, but as an adult you end up doing it more and more as the years go on. He did not know how Jamal would take it, but he knew if he had to miss the rest of the game to help his player, he absolutely would.

2 "CAN YOU DETERMINE the cause of death?" I asked Dr. G.

She looked up and pinched her lips together like I had seen her do numerous times when she was interrupted. Dr. G was easy to work with, brilliant, and in my experience was yet to be wrong. However, she did have one rule which I typically ignored much to her chagrin. She would tell me the results only after she had them, and asking during her workday usually only proved to be a negative. In this case, however, time was short and I wanted to know how the father of my missing girl ended up dead in an alley in a crappy part of Chicago.

Her voice was slightly cold, but I couldn't tell if that was because she was annoyed with my question or because she was working on a dead body, both of which I assumed would bring out the coldness in a woman. "Typically I would withhold a determination on cause of death before examining the victim in my lab, but in this case, I can say with a high level of certainty it was the bullet through the back of the skull."

"So the officer was correct. He was executed."

"Again, based on what I can see here, yes."

"Is there anything more you are willing to share with me now? I accept it is with only a certain level of confidence because your examination is not complete." I smiled ever-so-slightly, which she caught.

"You really should not patronize me, Tommy. It tends to make results take much longer." She smiled back knowing she really held all the cards.

"Okay, Doc, you win, just let me know as soon as you have anything."

Elise held up her hand. "Wait, it may be worth it to you to know that your victim was not shot here."

My eyebrows raised. "Dumped?"

"I can't get into specifics, but I believe he was shot at least twelve hours ago and was dumped here sometime overnight."

"Thanks, Doc, anything else?"

She smiled and knelt back down to continue her work. "No, not yet, but as I said, I'll know..."

"More after you get him into your lab," I finished for her. "Yes, I got that."

She smiled. "I have your number. I will call. You will want a family member to make a positive identification, won't you? You have them come any time after four or so this afternoon."

"Thanks, Doc, I will call before we come."

After brief nods between us, I turned to go meet Franky who had left to search for and possibly interview any witnesses. I had worked this area my entire career, including when Cabrini Green was actually the definition of the problem of public housing. Gang violence, prostitution, crime, and neglect defined this impoverished area of Chicago. Over the last decade, however, the city had worked to demolish the buildings and begin something new. It was by no means the upper echelon of class, but it was greatly improved. Franky was walking toward me, and I could see the look in his eyes as he approached so I did not need to hear his response.

"Funny, and you may not believe this, Tommy, but nobody saw anything."

I shook my head and issued an exaggerated voice in response. "Really. Nobody saw anything? Unbelievable."

We turned and began walking together, and I filled him in on the information Doc G was willing to share at this time. Franky considered walking back and asking if she had any additional information, but upon further thought, we agreed that direction would not end well for either of us. Although we were no longer partners, both choosing to officially work alone in our careers at this point but supporting the other essentially 24-7, we still were best friends and had been for nearly twenty years. Franky was ten years older than me, and his body showed it. He had fired his gun only four times in the line of duty and never killed a perpetrator. I could no longer count the times I had been forced to use mine, and my death toll was greater than twenty.

It was interesting how our careers had gone the same direction, but we had both faced such different events over the years. Franky had always remained clean and free of controversy. I, on the other hand, seemed to be chased by controversy.

From Internal Affairs' investigations to trauma counseling and the most painful experience—recovery. I had been shot four times, stabbed twice, beaten, and tortured once—all in the line of duty and all taking a toll on my mental state. Franky said if I could just keep my nose clean for a few years, Captain would be in my future. That was twelve years ago and the only "captain" in my future had Crunch Berries with it.

Franky was single and had been since his wife passed away from breast cancer five years ago. He had not been the same since, but I understood. They had never had kids despite trying, so now he was alone, other than me and Darth Vader, his 187-pound Newfoundland that rivaled the movie star dog Beethoven in size and drool-ability.

I too was single, but the mother of my children had not died of cancer, though if I could arrange her death, I probably would. In my opinion, she put the heat in hell, and her and her new husband could collectively kiss my big butt. That being said, we do have two wonderful children who are all grown and in college and since that change, our lives have improved. Still, if some tragedy did happen, possibly a chainsaw accident or a lightning strike her direction, I am not sure I would cry. I had to check myself to make sure I was not speaking out loud.

"You heading back to the station?" I asked.

"No, I need to connect with my confidential informant on Lower Wacker. I'm still working the dead hooker case."

Typically we don't mix confidential informants, as the more people who know them, the less confidential they become. That being said, this CI was also my CI and tagging along may prove useful. Possibly a question about Mr. Jackson may spark some information. "Hey, you care if I tag along? Perhaps he may know something about last night's murder."

"I don't know, Tommy. Quinton has been more skittish lately. I don't want him to vanish on me."

I looked toward my friend and saw he was reaching. The hooker case was eating at him. He essentially had no leads and four dead hookers. He caught the case from the start and was the first to link the initial two deaths, but since then two more had died and he was no closer to solving it. He and the whole department were feeling the pressure. I placed my hand on his shoulder. "Tell you what. I'll go. Quinton knows me. I will stay in the car and not say anything. If the situation allows it, then you can signal me or ask a question yourself. I need whatever help I can get."

Franky nodded and as we approached his car, he motioned for me to get in. He was driving his own car today, a 2005 Ford Taurus. No flash, no babe magnet, and no air conditioner. I took my suit jacket off and loosened my tie. Meeting with a CI often required dressing down. Lower Wacker, where we were going to meet this one, would be fine, a drive-up. For all the onlookers, we were drug dealers or drug buyers. How we looked was immaterial. "Let's pick up something to drink on the way. There is a White Hen Pantry around the corner, then we can head to Wacker. I texted him I would be a little late anyway."

I nodded agreement, and we were off. I would need to circle back to get my car, but for now this was the best option. Franky's relationship was stronger with this CI than mine was, and I did not want to lose the opportunity. I only hoped when we did talk, it would prove beneficial. Regardless, after that, I needed to speak to Malcolm's wife, notify her of her husband's murder, and then escort her to the morgue, all of which were duties I dreaded. How do you tell a woman you met when her daughter was missing and presumed killed that her husband was just found executed?

"Thinking about talking to Mrs. Jackson?" Franky asked, obviously sensing my thoughts.

"Yep," I replied. "She hasn't been the same since Jessica. Her son is away at college. Her daughter is missing. Now her husband is dead."

"Maybe if a tornado hits her apartment her luck will improve?"

I did not answer, but part of me hoped I would hear tornado sirens before the day was out.

We arrived on Lower Wacker in the designated place and waited. Sometimes we would wait for hours, but usually it was about ten minutes or less. Today, there was a lot of activity which usually meant it would be longer. To our surprise, Quinton, who most everyone called "Q" on the streets, showed up minutes after we arrived. He was jumpy, more so than normal. It could have been drugs but seemed like something else. I wasn't going to speak so it would be in Franky's hands if we were going to pursue his current state.

"Hey, man, I got nothin' to say to you today," issued Q, his voice hyped up and speech broken.

"Relax, Q, I just want to ask you a few questions. I can make it worth your while."

"No, man, and why do you have your boy with you? You said it was just going to be you."

Franky leaned out his window slightly and lowered his voice to speak softer. "We had an issue this morning. He joined me because we thought you might be able to help with that as well."

"No, man, can't help today. Too many eyes." He paused and looked around. "You know what I'm sayin'?"

"What eyes?" I asked, to the quick glare from Franky as I had not kept my mouth shut.

"You know, the man. The man is watching."

Franky replied quickly not giving me the opportunity to continue. "What man, Q? What man is watching?"

"No, man, can't say. Just give me the normal."

"You haven't answered our questions yet," Franky said.

"Listen, man, I got to go. You know what I'm sayin'? I got to go."

"Wait, Q," Franky said louder. "Do you know about the murder last night? Over by the old Projects?"

Quinton stopped walking away and turned back toward the car. "Listen, man, just give me the normal, and I'll tell you."

This was strange. Quinton always just told us the info, we paid him, then he took off. What was going on, I wondered? Why was he acting so different? I wasn't going to let him drive this. "Q, a man was killed last night. The man was the father of a girl who disappeared in the same area months ago."

"Jessica," Quinton said. He did not say it as a question. He said it as if he already knew it.

"Yes, did you know her?" I asked.

"No, man, I don't know her. I got to go."

He turned when Franky added trying to get him back on track, "There was another murder of a hooker two nights ago. Did you know about that?"

Quinton suddenly calmed. "Word I hear is that the hookers are payment that gets out of hand. Big boss man has some debts he is building and uses the hooker to pay. Then big boss man cleans up the mess."

Now we were talking. I looked toward Franky, then back to Quinton. "Q, how about the murder last night? Jessica's father? What is the word on her?"

"I never hear nothin' 'bout that." He stopped, appeared somewhat paranoid again, and then looked around all directions. "That's all I know, man. Just give me the normal and I be gone."

Franky pulled a hundred dollar bill out of his pocket and slipped it to Q like he was slipping him drugs. "Be careful, Q. The big boss man is not someone you want to be messing with."

Quinton did not say a word. He crumbled up the bill, jammed it into his pocket, and turned and ran back down Wacker.

"You think he was talking about Polino?" I asked.

"I don't know anyone else who fits that description." He paused a long time then added, "But I can't see Joey Polino getting side-down with anyone. Whoever Joey owes has to be a huge player."

I nodded. "It begs the question. Why don't we know about him?"

Franky turned his head to face me. "We need to talk to Clark in Vice. He will keep our questions quiet but he is definitely in the know."

"He's under right now?" I asked.

Franky nodded. "Yeah, I think he hangs out at Kroney's most nights. We can go there."

I half-smiled making only one side of my lips turn up. I raised my hand curling it into a fist and put it in front of my friend. "Drunk and Wild?"

Franky bumped my knuckles with his own. "I am thinking Oklahoma Cowboy Drunk and Wild."

Franky smiled but it was somewhat predictable. Franky was 100% Italian but truly he was an American cowboy and anytime we had to go undercover for any reason, even if it was just to protect someone else who was undercover from being identified, he always wanted to be a cowboy. I shook my head and replied, "Sounds good. I will dig out my hat, but first I need to do the ID on my victim."

"I will drop you by your car and then head back to the station. Come by my desk when you are done." He paused again then added, "And Tommy, good luck. I don't think this one will go well."

●　　●　　●　　●　　●

I stood outside the Jackson's front door for several minutes before I knocked. I was sure Andrea was home. She had not worked since her daughter went missing, and the family car was in the driveway. I was also sure she knew there was a problem.

The coroner had said the murder happened the night before which meant Malcolm had not been home all night. Knowing what I did about the family, I would say that Malcolm staying out all night without calling had never happened before. I raised my hand to knock, and I remembered the last time I stood before the door bringing news of this nature. I could see my knuckles striking the wood door causing the hollow echo inside. I could see Malcolm opening the door in earnest hoping it was news that we had found Jessica. I could see his jaw drop when he saw my expression.

At that time I had only found a clue to the whereabouts of Jessica. However, it was not the girl, it was the back seat of an Oldsmobile Delta 88. Significant bloodstains showed someone had lost approximately 10-15% of their blood in that car. DNA testing had confirmed it was Jessica's. Her body was no longer there, and to date still had not been found. Although theoretically she could have lived through that level of blood loss, nobody believed she could have lived without significant medical attention, and none of the hospitals had received any patients fitting the bill. Jessica was dead. I just could not prove it to them without the body.

I don't know which was worse—having the final proof that your child had been murdered or having the door slightly left open that she could be alive. What I had seen of Andrea Jackson since that afternoon told me that it would be better to keep the door shut. More than likely, we were never going to find her body and for Mrs. Jackson, that door would always remain slightly open, eating at her every day and every night. Today, however, was not a day that a door would be left open.

Andrea was a strong woman. She was tall and probably responsible for Jamal's height. Her hair was average length, and her skin was smooth and soft in appearance. She was an absolute beauty in her day, and although nearing sixty now, the years had not taken much away from her. She was the mold that held the family together, but also respectful that Malcolm was the father in the house. You honored his word, no exceptions. She and the kids understood that. But this was a family full of love. They had four people living in a two-bedroom apartment. Many in the area were run-down, but this building was better. The tenants, like the Jackson family, were proud of where they lived and wanted it to stay that way. As other buildings were being torn down, the belief out there was that this one was going to make it. It might be given a small face-lift, but families would not have to move.

I raised my hand and knocked lightly on the wood frame. Rustling was heard and then footsteps approaching the front door. I heard the dead bolt get released and watched the handle turn, the movement almost appearing in slow motion. When Andrea's eyes met mine, I could see she had been crying. When she took in my expression, the burst of tears exploded and she fell into my arms.

"He's dead. He's dead. I know he's dead," she screamed through her tears. "I have called all night. He never called back." Still crying as her voice trailed off, "He's never not called back."

"Let's go inside, Andrea. We need to talk."

I stayed with Andrea for the next hour and tried to provide comfort. There is a fine line for a detective on how close you can get to people, victims' families especially. However, that line becomes clouded when either the crime is never solved or multiple tragedies happen. Detectives, police officers, or anyone in similar fields never want to feel responsible, but when they cannot solve the crime or give any peace, those feelings of responsibility always creep up. The fact was, I liked the Jackson family. I liked them a lot. Malcolm was a truly good man who worked at an industrial laundry for forty-five years delivering uniforms five days a week in some of the worst parts of Chicago. The neighborhood knew him. Nobody, and I mean nobody, messed with his trucks. I heard him tell a story that a new drug dealer had moved into the Green and arranged to have his truck hit during a delivery. The other dealers in the area got everything stolen back and the new dealer ended up in the hospital. Malcolm was respected that much.

At some point, I am not sure when, Andrea had calmed to a point where I could tell her what I knew and what we had to do. She took her mind someplace cold and distant. I could see it in her face. She stood, walked out of the living area for a few minutes, and came back in a black dress with a veil that fell down from her classy black hat. I stood and she took my arm. Her voice was frail, and I could still hear there were tears behind them. However, unless you were looking for it, you would have never known.

"Detective O'Malley, would you mind if I keep hold of your arm as we do this? I will be strong for you and Malcolm, but I just don't know how strong."

"Well, ma'am, it would be an honor to walk with you under my arm."

She smiled slightly but the smile was short-lived. The pain carried within her completely eclipsed any chance for a true smile, but the effort was not lost. We walked to my car which she had been in only one other time—the day we headed to where the only clue we have ever had in regard to her daughter was found.

After turning the ignition on, the big Chevy 350 motor fired up with an explosion, and my 1974 brown Camaro was ready to move. I sent a quick message to Dr. G that we were on our way, and then with a push of the gas, we headed to the morgue.

3 "HOW YOU DOING, Tex?" I asked as Franky approached my car.

In a southern drawl that would make, well, nobody proud, he replied, "Y'all be looking good in this Camaro."

I shook my head in disgust. "Next time we go Irish. We can pull off Irish."

We fired up the Camaro and headed up the Lake Michigan shoreline toward the bars where we thought Clark would be. Tom Clark was probably as close to Franky and me in his career path as any. He could have promoted numerous times and each time it came due, he pissed someone off to a level that the idea just died right there. That being said, since joining Vice some fourteen years ago, he had never wanted to leave. Every cop is good at something. Some are good at traffic, some are good at murder, and some, with especially thick stomachs, are good at Special Victims, and in Chicago, the division of SVU included Vice. Clark was that guy.

Franky took off his Stetson cowboy hat and placed it on the back seat. Clark won't be out for several hours. We should hit J's for a Dagwood and then hang out in the area for a while before he shows up."

Mr. J's was a hole-in-the-wall burger joint that nobody outside of a four-square block area of downtown Chicago had ever heard about. However, you only had to go there once to know you would never order a burger again in your life if it wasn't a Dagwood. I gladly agreed to the Dagwood since it had been about eight hours since I had had one for breakfast. Moments later, we were ordering at the counter. From Mr. J's, we walked down to Flapjaws bar near the university. We were not officially on duty so having a beer would have been appropriate, but with all that had happened today, club soda was the drink of choice. To play our roles with Clark, we would be ordering several drinks later.

We left Flapjaws and headed toward Kroney's. We did not know for sure if Clark was going to be there, but if he was going to be anywhere, he would be there. Clark had been under for over six months. He was trying to get inside a high-class prostitution ring involving Loyola University students. It was a far cry from the hookers being killed on Franky's watch, but just as serious to the girls. Clark did not want the girls, he wanted the corporation organizing it. The time of pimps and hookers had long since passed, and now white-collar, high-end Internet prostitution was moving in, with much higher payoffs as it was reaching a much wider clientele.

I found a spot at the bar while Franky went to the head, but then my phone rang and I saw it was Dr. G.

"Hello, Doctor, to what do I owe this pleasure seeing as how we just talked a few hours ago?"

"I wanted to tell you some more about my findings, but not with the spouse present," she replied, with a matter-of-fact tone that sparked my interest.

"What did you find? Something to help identify the killer?"

She gave a short breath which was meant for me to understand she only reported the facts. She did not find killers. That was *my* job. "Your murder victim was tortured. I put his time of death right around one a.m. but he was tortured for hours before that. His wrists were bound and he had faced electrocution, what looked to be some sort of burning—possibly hot oil—but I am having it checked out at the lab to be sure, and a general beating. He took it all."

"Damn," I said to myself instantly visualizing what she was saying. "Anything else?"

"No, that's it. Just wanted you to know."

We bid each other good-bye and I could not help wondering what in the hell Malcolm had gotten himself into. Torture? Execution? I was sure it had to do with Jessica, but what? *What had he found out and why didn't he come talk to me?*

Then, Franky appeared from the bathroom. I had gone with standard jeans and a button-down shirt for my "cowboy" attire, but short of wearing chaps, Franky was all Texas ranch hand. His belt buckle could double as a hubcap, and I assumed his trip to the head was longer as he fought with figuring out its workings. He eventually returned and was pleased to see a Goose IPA in front of an open seat at the bar next to me.

"You boys having a good night?" a particularly young and attractive bartender asked.

"Yes, ma'am," Franky replied. "Even better now that I lay my tired eyes on you."

I threw up a little in my mouth. Now Franky was double her age and he had no interest in meeting up with a girl, woman, or anyone else for that matter. However, he sure did like fishing. He called it fishing, not flirting, because flirting did not allow for the catch. Fishing allowed you to catch one, stroke the ego that you still had it, but you could still release it with no harm. My friend Franky knew how to fish.

The bartender smiled and said, "My name is Lori if you need anything."

I interjected, "Why don't you bring me a Wild Turkey and Diet to go with this beer and my friend here another IPA? After that, we will see how things go." She smiled back to me and soon after returned with two more drinks and laid a menu at the edge of the bar in front of us. I didn't mind beer, but usually just one was good. Franky would have IPA all night.

I looked to Franky who was smiling at the woman trying to continue to make eye contact. She saw his gaze, smiled, reached her hand out to his on the table, and added, "You are so cute." Then she disappeared back to her other customers along the bar.

"Get a life, Franky." I said, much to his pleasure.

Franky smiled but then his smile faded. "Say, Tommy, I forgot to ask you how things went with Andrea Jackson?"

"She is an amazing woman, Frank, but the visit itself sucked."

He nodded understanding. "Is she going to be okay?"

"I don't know," I replied. "We placed a call to Kansas and spoke with the athletic director. It was actually during Jamal's basketball game. I think he is set on a Southwest Airlines flight to Midway tonight." I stopped when I saw something on the TV above the bar. "Hey, Lori," I hollered waving her over. "Is there any way you can turn the sound up?"

She grabbed the remote in time to hear the end of the ESPN story. The announcer said:

"Going into half with the lead, the Jayhawks were poised to give Duke its first loss. Then, to the surprise of all the fans and his teammates, star Sophomore Jamal Jackson did not return from halftime. Only weeks after tragedy struck this Chicago

family with the loss and potential death of Jamal's sister, Jessica, ESPN News has learned that Malcolm Jackson, long-time Chicago resident and father to Kansas forward Jamal Jackson, was found murdered in downtown Chicago this morning. As reported earlier, Jamal was informed during halftime when the athletic director learned of the event and immediately found a flight to Chicago. The Kansas players opted to forfeit the game in support of their teammate. Coach K of the Duke Blue Devils has expressed an interest to play the remainder of the game at a later date if the NCAA will allow it. Regardless of the direction the NCAA takes, let me be the first here at ESPN to say this transcends any basketball game, and all our thoughts are with the Jackson family during this time of loss."

"That Bill Williams is good people, you know?" Franky said.

"Yes, you know before Kansas he was over Illinois? I can't believe he forfeited the game."

Neither of us spoke as we sipped our drinks and continued half-listening to the highlights on the television above. As a homicide detective you see things no human should ever see. As a man at a bar, you drink some of those things away for at least a few hours. The wash-out rate for homicide, SVU, and Vice in Chicago is about 70% before three years. I guess Franky, Clark, and I are the exceptions.

It was about an hour and three more drinks later, when a bearded, scraggly male sauntered up to the bar and sat on the stool next to us. He was right by Franky making him two down from me. I barely even looked at him other than to wonder if he had money to pay for whatever he was going to order. As my eyes scanned closer, I saw the ever-so-slight wink. "You boys doing all right tonight?" he asked in an all-too-familiar voice.

"Why, things just picked up a bit, I'd say," I replied.

"Good. I am just grabbing a quick drink before I head out. Good night to be drinking."

"That it is," added Franky.

There was a pause while Lori brought over a beer for the newcomer whose order she did not even need to take. "Good to see you, Nick. I didn't think you would be in tonight."

"Well, you know, Lori...I can't go a night without laying my eyes on your sweet body."

"That is not the message you gave me when you left with Diane last week. Seems looking at my sweet body wasn't in your top ten."

"Now don't be silly. Diane just needed a ride home. My eyes were still on you."

"Get a life, Nick, and while you're at it, why don't you pay down your bill. Your credit is running out here."

He smiled and blew her a fake kiss before she turned to us in a huff. "Stay away from this loser."

Both Franky and I smiled, and I knew beneath his beard he was feeling fairly proud of the exchange. Male ego thing at work. "Maybe I should buy you a drink if your credit is no good, stranger?" asked Franky.

"That would be mighty fine of you."

"I'm Bo and this is Luke. We are from Oklahoma."

We both reached out hands and as Clark shook mine, he slipped a paper in my hand which I in turn slipped directly into my pocket. "You boys in town for a conference or something?"

"No, just a vacation. Anything you want to recommend for us to do?"

Clark looked around questionably. He leaned closer and in a much softer tone said, "I can get you some company, if you are interested—if you know what I mean."

I looked at Franky and tried to imagine how I would react if I knew this wasn't a game of making things look right. I shook my head. "Why, that does sound intriguing but probably not my thing. I assume you feel the same way, Luke?"

"Yeah, I think we are good here. I like the view." He said that last part loud enough for Lori to hear which she returned with a smile and hair flick.

"No problem. Thanks for the drink, boys, but I think my welcome here is about to end."

Franky was about to protest as he did not know Clark had passed me the note, but I placed my hand on his shoulder. "Nice meeting you...Nick, wasn't it."

"Yeah, Nick. Take care, boys, and don't worry, Lori doesn't bite, unless you ask her real nice like."

She heard that and threw a bar cloth at him striking him square in the back and leaving a wet mark in the center of his shirt. "What an ass," she stated to herself.

Franky turned back to me with a flat stare which clearly stated, *what the hell, Tommy, we needed to talk to him.* Without missing a beat, I slipped the wadded-up paper into his hand under the bar. His eyes softened and he looked down, taking both hands to open the note. It read simply: *"Not here. Ten minutes, the alley behind Pippen's".*

"Well, Bo, I guess we need to go see what this downtown has to offer."

We waved to Lori and did the air gesture that appeared to be writing on a receipt to signal we wanted our bill. In moments she was back. Although I was paying, she seemed to only pay attention to Frank. Damn fisherman. I threw two twenties on the table which she did notice and noticed it even more when I said we did not need change. A minute later we were walking back down the street toward Flapjaws which happened to be on the way to Pippen's. Most non-Chicagoans thought Pippen's was named for Scottie Pippen, but us old-timers that knew the bar was in town long before either MJ or Scottie graced us with their presence, knew better. Pippen's put the "dive" in dive-bar, and similar to Mr. J's and the Dagwood, this place was a staple in a few-mile radius. We reached the front of Pippen's and the large bay windows were open which allowed people to both sit on the sill and step through to get from the front walkway to enter the bar. A patron who had already had too much—and it was only about 8:30 in the evening—jumped up and gave us both high fives as we walked by. He then stumbled and fell to the ground trying to make it back to his chair. His friends picked him up and just like good buddies, threw another beer down in front of him laughing.

We turned down the narrow back alley and I became instantly aware of the location of my gun. We both knew we had downed a few drinks and should not use our guns for any reason. However, when walking into a dark downtown Chicago alley, having a gun within reach does provide some level of confidence. There was literally no light other than the bit that made its way from the sidewalk back toward the bar. We heard the sound of a bottle being kicked ahead of us but could not see anything. We couldn't call out a name because if we called the wrong name, we risked putting his cover in jeopardy. Therefore, we walked.

"I hate this," Franky whispered.

"You and me both," I replied. "What the hell are we walking into?"

At that moment a flashlight blinded us from the end of the alley. "Stop there!" a voice demanded.

My hand moved into my pocket to rest on my gun. Neither of us spoke. We were waiting to let whoever this was make the next move. When the individual spoke again, it was clear that this was not our undercover friend.

"Who are you?" asked the same voice.

"I'm Bo and this is Luke. We are from Oklahoma." Franky lifted his hat.

There was an eerie silence. Franky and I understand how silence can be a powerful interrogation technique resulting in extreme stress for those being interrogated. So Franky and I waited in silence. Breaking the short silence, the voice from the alley spoke again. "Turn around and walk away."

Nothing else was said. No ultimatum. No threat. It was actually worse than if a threat had been issued. A spoken threat helps determine what you are dealing with. Open leaves all possibilities out there. If we really were Okies from Muskogee, we would have turned tail and run. However, for all we knew we had a comrade in trouble at the end of the alley. We couldn't leave, but what reason would we have to stay?

Just then Franky did the unthinkable. In a drawn-out and drunk cowboy voice he said, "Well, all be, is that you, Jesse, trying to mess with us? What the hell you doin' scaring us half to death? Get your cowboy ass out here or so help me I am going to come down there and rope your butt back to Oklahoma." He took several steps down the alley as he spoke. I matched his pace.

"I am not Jesse and I am telling you, get your ass out of here. If not, you will be carried out of here in an ambulance."

Ah, I thought to myself. Now we had a limit. Taken out in an ambulance. Could mean killed, but usually if someone was willing to kill you, they would say it, or at least they would say leaving in a body bag. Taken out by ambulance was a good thing.

Franky continued, "Damn it, Jesse, let it go. You already got us. Now, come back to the bar. We have more whiskey to drink."

We took a few steps closer when we heard some rustling and the flashlight went off. We were cast into total darkness. It is strange, before the flashlight was on, it had been dark. Now that it was off, it was pitch black. Going from dark to flashlight-in-the-face to dark again made the last dark exponentially more opaque. Franky let out a groan as a man brushed by him punching him in the stomach as he passed. I turned in pursuit but Franky grabbed my arm. "Let him go," he whispered. "We need to look for Clark."

We heard moaning ahead of us causing us to pull our guns, though we knew if we fired them it would be the end of our careers, even if we hit our mark. "O'Malley? Is that you?" The voice was weak but clearly from Tom Clark, our friend and the person we were supposed to meet.

We holstered our guns and ran toward the voice. We still could not see but it sounded as if he was in trouble, injured, or both. He had called us by name so I was no longer worried about his cover, but I still didn't use his real name. "Nick? Nick? Are you all right?"

Just then another flashlight came on ahead of us pointing at the ground where the voice had been. It illuminated the figure of a man on the ground in a slumped position. He appeared to be trying to evaluate his condition and was not attempting to stand. He waved as a signal he was okay, but with the broken half-hearted level of his wave, he had seen better days.

"What happened? Are you all right?" I asked as we arrived.

"I am fine, but a bit surprised."

"Surprised? What do you mean?" asked Franky, reaching out to help him up.

"To put it simply, I was just mugged."

I didn't mean to but I laughed out loud. It was involuntary and could not be stopped. "Mugged? You?"

"Shut up, Tommy!" he exclaimed, pushing himself up. "I thought it was you in the alley. I walked right up to the jerk and out of nowhere he clocked me. I think I was hit with a large flashlight or nightstick."

"Mugged?" I repeated again.

He looked right at me. "Yes, mugged, and you should keep this to yourself if you know what's good for you."

"Lay off him, Tommy," broke in Franky. "He is just building up street cred. He needed a few hits put out on him to show the man he is tough. You know, this professional hit man who lingers in a dark alley waiting for a possible target to come in. You faced the best of the best." Franky's sarcasm was clear, as was the smile on both our faces.

"Whatever," he replied, now brushing himself off. "I was here to help you, and look what it got me."

"Speaking of that," I started, "we do need your help."

"I figured as much when I saw you at the bar. Things have been tense lately. Everyone is jumpy, and I don't want any reason to be linked to the police. People keep coming up missing."

That statement caught me. "Missing? People? Who?"

"Drug dealers, their girlfriends, some of the professional girls. Basically, anyone involved. This is big, Tommy, real big."

I nodded understanding. "Is it Polino?"

A cat rustled and let out a scratchy meow causing us all to jump. Clark continued, "That's just it. Word is there is somebody new in town. Somebody Joey Polino brought in but has started to move around him. Joey is into him for something so he is letting it happen. That's all I know. Word is he is also responsible for the changing of rank. He is moving up and Polino and his guys are moving down."

"What's his name?"

Clark leaned in a little closer. "I don't know, but I heard he is buying up the strip clubs down south, in your neck of the woods. He is using them for moving money and girls. I also heard he has some heavy hitters with him. Big guys that kill first then ask questions. He is using Polino to clean up the mess."

Franky looked back to me and then to Clark. "How big does this guy have to be to put Joey Polino to the level of clean-up? What does all this mean, Tommy?"

Clark shook his head. "I asked that same question, how big? But I can't get anywhere, and I don't want to ask too many questions."

"Are you still good?" I asked, and before he could answer, I added, "I mean with your cover."

"Yeah, but I am being careful. I am in too deep to get out clean now and not deep enough to get what I need. With this change, I am having to start over with whoever the new guy is, which probably doubles my time under."

"Keep your head on a swivel, Tom. This one is for keeps." Franky put his hand on Clark's shoulder which Clark took as it was meant—a serious warning to pay attention.

"You guys did not look for me to talk about Joey Polino and this new boss though. What did you want to know?"

I lowered my voice to match the others. "There was a murder and body dump last night. Black man. He was the father of my missing girl, Jessica Jackson. He was shot, execution style. Dr. G said sometime after midnight. She also said he was tortured. Do you know anything about it?"

Clark looked back, all humor from earlier was gone, and he could not have been more serious. "I saw the story on TV tonight. The son who plays at Kansas, right?" I nodded before he continued. "Until that story, I had not heard anything."

"That normal?" asked Franky.

Initially I did not understand the question, but when I heard the answer, it made more sense. "Exactly. I hear about every murder, from professionals to laborers to hookers, and everyone in between. If a bum is killed in an alley and his grocery cart is stolen, it is talked about in my circles. But this, I hear nothing. Whoever is behind this one is powerful enough to keep everyone quiet about it."

"Yeah, our CI didn't know anything about it either," I replied.

"I will nose around a bit, but asking too many questions may get me more noticed than I want. Give me two days then come back to Kroney's. We can play with Lori some more." He turned to Franky. "I think she likes you."

Franky smiled. "I am sure she does, but I have a firm rule of never going anywhere you have been."

I nodded. "Definitely a good rule."

4 I TOLD ANDREA JACKSON I would pick up her son when he arrived. The extra time spent downtown with Franky made that promise a tough one to keep. I did not have time to drop off Franky before heading to Midway Airport so Franky got the added thrill of joining me. We walked through Security without a ticket which you can do as a police officer, but it is still a hassle. I'm not one to take shots at other individuals who have sworn to protect and serve, but airport security guys are simply assholes. There is no other way to describe these guys. Many could not cut it as police officers and either had to join independent building security firms or join the TSA. These guys love it when detectives come through. It's the only time in their lives that we get to be their bitches.

We got through Security and in Southwest Airlines fashion, the plane was on time. The flight attendants were singing in the jetway, and the passengers disembarked in great spirits. When my eyes met Jamal's, all that good cheer vanished. Had we not been there when Jamal walked off Southwest Airlines Flight 544 from Kansas City to Chicago Midway, he would have been greeted by a wall of press. It only took one ESPN story to alert every freelance reporter to come in droves. The days of a reporter catching an exclusive story were just about done. Because we were there, we were able to get TSA security to escort the majority of the reporters away for not having a ticket. How the media got through that "extremely tight" security was beyond me, but after advising them of the breach, TSA's most elite force went crazy.

Jamal greeted me with a locked handshake and wrists bent around back. It was the young man's handshake that fortunately, with my time on the streets of Chicago, I knew and preferred. We turned and walked. We did not speak much as we walked. A little small talk but for the most part quiet. I knew when we left Security there would be that same wall of reporters waiting to pounce. Therefore, instead of leaving, I pointed Jamal over to Harry Caray's restaurant where we could order food and sit peacefully at the tables until most of the reporters left under the assumption that we'd found another exit. We ordered, and then sat somberly.

Jamal looked up at me. It was clear he hadn't spoken because he knew his emotions would get the best of him and that would not be "cool." His voice cracked ever-so-slightly when he asked, "What happened?"

I was sitting next to him and across from Franky. I put my hand on his shoulder. "We don't know much, Jamal. Have you spoken to your father recently?"

"No." He paused. "Well, I mean yes, but only about basketball. We had not even mentioned Jessica in weeks. I tried not to ask about her because I knew there was no news or I would have heard about it."

"What about basketball had you discussed?" I asked, trying to keep Jamal emotionally calm. I had not done well with his mother and left without asking key questions I needed to ask as early in the process as possible. With Andrea, those questions would wait until tomorrow. With Jamal, I wanted to talk to him now.

"Just my play. This week's preparation for Duke. How to defend and who I could drive against. That sort of thing."

"Did he say anything about his work? Anything new he was working on?"

"No, nothing to me," Jamal answered. Then he paused and his eyes changed. As an investigator, you learn to look for those things—eye movements, twitches, and "tells" if you will. In this case, his tell told me that he remembered something. Franky saw it too.

"What is it, Jamal? What are you thinking?" I asked.

"Well, I don't know if it is important, but he did have some issue on one of his deliveries the other day. It was at a strip club. He asked me if I had ever been there."

"Did he say what the problem was?" asked Franky.

Jamal shook his head. "Not that I remember. It was said in passing, and he always talked about problems on the route. He was a route driver delivering uniforms and mats in one of the worst parts of Chicago. Half his route was cash only. He was always getting in arguments. As much as everyone liked him, when he cut them off for no payment, they fought back. He refused to carry a gun because he said by having one, his chance of getting killed increased by like a hundred percent."

"He was right on that account," I said. "Think though, it is important. Do you know what strip club? Are you sure he never mentioned any issue out of the ordinary?"

"Like I said, I really don't remember him mentioning any problem." Jamal carried a slight annoyance in his repeated response, then softened. "He was only concerned about one thing. It was the only reason he brought it up in the first place. He asked if it was the club where Tiny worked as a bouncer. He wanted me to tell Tiny to get a new job. It was someone's name—Rich, or..."

"Rick's Cabaret?" Franky interjected.

"Yes," Jamal replied quickly.

"Is that where Tiny works?" I asked.

"No, he works at the Red Carpet."

Franky and I looked at each other. We weren't familiar with the clubs other than by the crime that took place around them. Both clubs had had shootings in the past and both clubs were high on the Vice list of activities. We did not know who owned them or how they were run. However, it was the second time in less than two hours that strip clubs were mentioned. In my line of work, coincidences didn't happen. I made a mental note to thoroughly investigate both clubs and to ask Clark about them in two days when we met again. Something about those clubs was tied to Malcolm, I was sure of it.

I turned back to Jamal. Our food had been delivered and he was pouring into his meal. I assumed he had not eaten since his basketball game which had been almost seven hours earlier. "Is there anything else you can remember about your conversation with your dad?"

"No, that's it." He seemed to be looking for something from me, so he added, "Was any of that helpful?"

I smiled. I could see he really wanted my answer to be yes. "Absolutely. All information is helpful because right now, all I have is a dad that did not come home one night and was found murdered the next morning. We have to retrace his steps, and any help in doing that is critically important." I stopped, looked to Franky to see if he had any questions, and by his appearance, I thought he did. "Franky, anything you want to ask or add?"

"Just one question, Jamal. Your friend, Tiny, how did he end up at a strip club? I thought he was going to play football."

"He tested positive for drugs over the summer. Lost his scholarship and everything. His folks can't pay for college so he didn't go."

"Is that when he took the job at the club?"

"No, he took that over the summer when we graduated—about a year and a half ago. He tested positive right after that."

Franky's phone rang. "Sullivan. What? Where?" He paused and listened intently. "Okay, O'Malley is with me. We are at Midway now but will head that way immediately. Keep everyone away until we arrive."

I looked at him and already could guess the answer. He hung up his phone and nodded. "Another dead hooker with the same M.O."

"Does this have something to do with my dad?" interrupted Jamal.

I placed my hand on his shoulder. "No son, different case. This is Sullivan's case. I am working your dad's, but it does mean we need to leave." Turning back to Franky, he said, "Let's drop Jamal at his mom's and head over."

The drive to Jamal's was quiet. There was no more discussion on the situation. I spent the time trying to review everything I knew for sure compared to the theories in my mind. I ended up with a big pile of squat. I had a missing girl, a dead father, a mob boss who was openly letting his turf get taken, some dead hookers, which may or may not be related, and the dead father's concern over a strip club. Yep, squat.

"What did they say about the body?" I asked after Jamal was in his house.

"Nothing more," Franky replied. "Just that she was about the same age, same area, same level of beating, and appeared to be the same cause of death."

"Strangulation and stabbing?"

"Yes, sir. Left in the hotel on Blackhawk, between Cleveland and Mohawk."

"In the heart of the old Green. It is the same M.O."

Franky's voice dropped. "That's five, Tommy, and I am not one step closer than when I first started."

"We'll figure it out, Franky." I paused while at a stop light and turned to my friend. "You think your case and my case are related?"

There was a long silence as the light changed and I started forward. Eventually Franky let out sigh and answered, "No, too far a reach. What would Malcolm and Jessica have to do with dead hookers? I have a crazy pervert who is getting off on killing girls he doesn't think will be missed. There is no ESPN special report on my murders. Most times reporters don't even show up at the scene. The perp you are after is a professional."

"A professional? Why do you say that?"

"Think about it, Tommy. A girl vanishes without a trace but there was no attempt to clean the car or hide it. The killer did not care because he knew it was not traceable to him. What did you find with the car?"

"Nothing," I replied. "A complete dead end."

"Right. And the father was tortured, killed execution style, and left in the middle of the street. Again, no fear of capture."

"I see your point, but..." my voice trailed off.

"But something is still bugging you, isn't it?" he asked.

I didn't answer but he was right. I felt like I was missing something. Maybe nothing I could have found yet, but when I did find it, it might tie all this together.

●   ●   ●   ●   ●

We arrived at the scene and contrary to before, only police were here. There was no crowd or photographers. The few people that were around were those who were temporarily evicted from the hotel, and they were not pleased with the delay. Several were probably paying by the hour.

I walked into the hotel room expecting to see the same scene we had witnessed at the previous murders, and I was not disappointed. Dr. Gerstenberger was already present and close to completing what was needed at the scene. She saw us walk in and came over to meet us.

"Same as the others. Strangled with some sort of rope to near death, but the cause of death is stabbing. As before, the areas where the weapon penetrated are precise. The killer only required one stab here,"—she pointed—"and the girl was dead within seconds, so the need for the pattern is not related to the act of the murder."

"How long has she been dead?" I asked.

"According to body temp and state of rigor, I put her dead for at least twenty-four hours." She pointed to a young street cop who was doubled over in the corner looking a bit green. "The officer who took the call and arrived first on the scene said they don't have maid service here so until the room was rented again, nobody found her."

I initially was caught by the twenty-four hours to find the body, but when she said they did not have maid service, I actually thought I might throw up. I had not put my gloves on when I entered the room, but now they went on immediately.

Franky scanned the room, saw the lab boys doing their work, and then glanced back to Dr. G. "I don't suppose the lab is going to find anything useful. Probably a DNA nightmare in here. Is there anything else you think is useful?"

"No. My work here is done, and if you don't mind, I have court in the morning."

Franky nodded and I reached out to grab the inside of her arm when she turned to leave, stopping her briefly. "Yes, Tommy. Something else?"

"Doc, you didn't happen to see any similarities between any of the hooker killings and my dead father, did you?"

She stopped and immediately appeared surprised by the question. "Why do you ask, Tommy? Do you think they are related?"

I coughed and lowered my voice as I did not really want Franky to know I was still pursuing this angle. "I don't want to skew your work. I simply want to throw the question out there. Were there any similarities in the deaths?"

She hesitated before answering. The silence seemed an eternity in that room with a dead body and a conversation I wanted kept confidential, but was probably only ten seconds or so. "Other than they were tortured or beaten before they were killed, no. The torture was different and the method of killing was different, but both methods of killing were immediate."

I shook my head but did not say anything.

She added, "I can see this is eating at you. I'll tell you what. Tomorrow, once I finish this autopsy, I will review my notes from all the hookers and your case. If I see anything by looking at them together, I will let you know."

"Thanks, Doc, I appreciate it."

It was rolling on one a.m. when Franky and I left the hotel. There are plenty of bars in downtown Chicago still open at that time, but in our world, there was no reason to go anywhere other than Flapjaws. We arrived after the kitchen closed but the drinks were still flowing. This was not a cop bar, but a few of us old-timers always seemed to find our way here on those days that called for it. A dead father of a missing girl and a fifth hooker was one of those days.

• • • • •

I walked into the precinct at 7:02 a.m., two minutes late for our case meeting. Sergeant Craig Carter was, shall I say, not understanding of my tardiness. There is really no way to describe Carter other than to say he is a pompous, arrogant jerk. That being said, he was an honest cop, and since he was my boss, the words I used were, "Sorry, Sergeant, ran into some trouble on the case last night. It was a late night."

"Was the problem at Flapjaws, O'Malley? Heard you were there till three a.m."

This asshole knew exactly what to say to set me off. It was like his crabby little mind could get inside me, find the one thing that would irritate me to an unhealthy level, and then exploit it. He was like a wife.

I had been walking by him to take my seat with the other detectives when I stopped and stared him down from about three feet. "Yeah, Sergeant, after seeing one of the parents of my missing girl with his brains all over the sidewalk and then another dead hooker in a serial killer chain of dead hookers, I thought I might grab a beer with a few friends. Seeing as how we are the only ones on the street doing real police work anymore, maybe being two minutes late can be accepted every once in a while."

"O'Malley, goddamn it. In my office. Sullivan, run through the meeting."

I proceeded without stopping directly into Carter's office. I knew this was where it would end up. Carter was a prick, and he was also a prick that would never stand for disrespect in front of his subordinates. "Goddamn it, O'Malley. Do you have to be such an ass all the time?"

"Me, Sergeant. I was two minutes late. I spent the evening at a hotel in the old Green looking at a seventeen-year-old girl's cut up and beaten body. Sorry I was a few minutes late but Jesus, cut me some slack."

"Sullivan wasn't late. He was with you. How the hell could he make it here on time?"

"Because he is better than me."

Carter did not know what to do with that one. He was about to protest then realized he had nothing to say. "Damn it, Tommy. I don't care if you are on time or twenty minutes late, just don't be disrespectful if I call you on it. I worked hard to become Sergeant and I am not afraid to remind everyone that is who I am."

"I get it, Sergeant. It is just the wrong day. You want me to kiss your ass out there in front of everyone to make up for it?"

"Maybe I do, you asshole."

"Then let's go back out there. I need everyone to hear the report on the hooker case and the Jackson case. They are bigger than what we thought."

Sergeant Carter was intrigued with that comment, but what stuck in his mind was my offer to kiss his ass in front of the team. We left his office and returned to the group. Sergeant Carter took the lead at the front and I took my place in the front row.

"All right, sorry about the delay. We will finish running through the cases, but first, I want to turn it over to O'Malley." Carter was actually grinning as he spoke.

I stood, turned to face the other detectives, and then without a word, walked up beside the sergeant. I was also sporting a smirk when I bent down and laid a big kiss right on the side of his ass. Without another word, I retired back to my seat.

The bulk of the detectives laughed. The others wore a "holy shit" look on their faces.

Carter stepped up to me, leaned down with his lips right next to my ear, and whispered two short words.

The rest of the meeting was uneventful, though all the necessary information I needed passed throughout the ranks was done and everyone broke up. It took Franky less than ten seconds to ask me what the sergeant had said. I smiled. "All he said was, 'traffic duty.'"

"Oh, damn, Tommy, do you think he means it?"

"Who knows," I answered, but froze when I saw who was walking into the precinct. "Jamal? What are you doing here?"

Jamal walked up to Franky and me and there was not one ounce of softness in his step, his demeanor, or his tone. "I want to find my father's killer. I want to help in the investigation."

I motioned for him and Franky to follow me into one of the nearby interrogation rooms. "Jamal," I began, "I understand your feelings but you have to let us do our job."

"No, Detective O'Malley, you do not understand my feelings. You can never understand my feelings. Unless you have had your sister disappear and probably be dead, your father be murdered, and your mother be in a place no human should ever go. Unless you have experienced that situation, then you have not felt what I feel."

As a detective, I do my best to never make comments like, "We will find the killer," or "I understand your feelings," because the fact of the matter is I never know if I will find a killer and I definitely cannot match the feelings family members are going through facing their loss. Today, I failed. "You are right, Jamal, I can't, but that does not change the fact that you are too close to this. You need to focus on your mother and helping her. I will handle the investigation."

"I am on it too, Jamal," added Franky.

"Listen, Detectives, I can respect your jobs, but my dad was killed in the Green. He was executed. He never did anything to anyone. He worked that area for more than forty years, driving that white truck with a red star on it delivering laundry every day. Somebody shot him. He was shot in cold blood. I trust you will do everything in your power to find that killer, but I have contacts you don't have. I am going to find the killer, and this discussion is over."

Stealing a line from Sergeant Carter, I yelled, "Damn it, Jamal, we can't do our job and protect you. Your father was not killed. It was a professional hit. Do you think these guys will think twice about killing you too? They won't. Don't mess with this, Jamal."

"I came to tell you so we might be able to work together. It is clear you won't work with me so I will work alone. Good-bye, Detective O'Malley." He turned to Franky. "Detective Sullivan."

He stood up to leave and I put my hand on his shoulder to keep him in place. "Don't, Jamal. I don't want to have to knock on your mom's door again to let her know her only son is dead." I paused and then in a lower tone added, "Please don't do this."

"Good-bye, Detective O'Malley," he repeated again, pushing through my hand.

"Damn kid," I said to myself, though I said it plenty loud enough for Franky to hear.

"Can you blame him, Tommy? I would do the same."

"Me too, but he better not get in over his head."

Franky nodded. "He already is, Tommy. He already is."

•　　•　　•　　•　　•

Franky and I had to go separate ways today. I needed to speak with Andrea Jackson about the days and nights leading up to Malcolm's death. Then I wanted to hit some of the strip clubs in the area starting with Rick's and the Red Carpet. Franky needed to get with the coroner on the most recent dead hooker and see about an identification. Then he was going to do a little investigating into who was buying these strip clubs and where the money was coming from. I had skipped breakfast because I was running late and did not much feel like eating, so I went without food. I did not set up a time to meet with Andrea Jackson, but I assumed she would be home all day regardless. Sometimes a surprise visit made the questioning go better.

Knowing Jamal wouldn't be there was probably also good, though I was concerned where the boy was going. I was sure the conversation with Andrea would be horrible for both of us, but I needed to know everything about Malcolm in the days leading up to his death. The only person I thought could help me with that was his wife. I would check out his job too, but the wife was usually the best option.

I arrived at her building around ten a.m. and spent a few minutes just surveying the area. It was still the Projects, but with each passing year the area was improving. The city had chased out much of the gang crime years ago, but now the more sophisticated and organized crime had moved in. Still, this building looked untouched.

Her door faced the outside and was on the first level so it made for easy access. They had lived there longer than I had been alive. They had probably seen things you should never see in your home. Now, at a time when things were finally turning clean, their whole family was decimated. I raised my hand to knock and the door swung open before I could even make contact.

"Hello, Detective O'Malley. I heard you on the steps."

"Hello, Andrea. Would you mind if I talked to you for a bit?"

"Come on in, Detective." She was in what I would call lounging clothes. She clearly had not been out of the house other than to visit the coroner since Malcolm disappeared. Further, the house was in shambles with dishes stacked everywhere and everything in general disarray. She saw my look and added, "Jamal is going to help me clean when he returns. I thought he was going to see you."

I coughed slight embarrassment on being caught by the appearance of the place, but her question kept me on track. "He did come to the precinct and I did talk to him. That is one of the things I wanted to talk to you about. He needs to keep his distance from this case. He wants to assist in the investigation, and I need you both to understand that I believe the individual who killed your husband is dangerous—very dangerous. I do not believe this was some random crime. His murder was professional. Do you know what that means, Andrea?"

She did not respond immediately. Her face was long and sad. Wrinkles that had not been there yesterday now appeared like leather. She had aged fifteen years overnight. Now I was telling her that her only son was putting himself in danger. I was piling on more things to worry about, but I needed her to talk to Jamal. When she finally broke the silence, her voice was cracked and almost unrecognizable. "Silly me, where are my manners. Could I get you some tea?"

I heard the pot boiling in the kitchen but the only way I would drink tea is if it was mixed with Wild Turkey, and I did not see that as an option. "No, ma'am. No, thank you," I corrected. "Will you talk to him? Will you talk to Jamal about staying away from this investigation?"

"Detective O'Malley, do you have any children?"

"Yes, ma'am. Two kids, both older and have moved out on their own." I already knew where this was going. I did not have young kids and had not lost one so I could not understand this situation like she could. I had to agree. I could not understand what she was going through, but for her well-being, she needed to say it and I needed to let her.

"Well, I had two children, Jessica and Jamal."

"I know, ma'am. I..."

She cut me off with her raised hand. "There is nothing in this world I wouldn't do to protect my children. I would walk through fire for my children." She stopped, took a small drink of tea that she had poured and left on the table, and then continued. "However, I can't stop Jamal right now. I have a wonderful relationship with my son, but not the bond he held with his father. Do you know Malcolm would start work at four a.m. to ensure he was done in time to go watch Jamal every day on that river court? All the boys knew him. All the boys respected him." She paused again and wiped a small tear from her eye. She spoke more softly now, "All the boys loved him."

"I'm sure they did, ma'am, but please help me protect Jamal now. Today he needs his mother."

"I will talk to Jamal, Detective, but I don't think it will do any good. I have never seen him like this. He would give up basketball forever to find his father's killer. He said that, and I believe him."

"To be frank, Mrs. Jackson, basketball is the least of my concerns. I don't want you to have to go to the morgue to identify his body." She looked up with eyes almost in terror, and I knew that one got her. I may have bordered on crossing a line, but I needed her committed to change the boy's mind.

"Is there anything else?" she asked curtly.

I rose from the couch, recovered the teakettle, and poured her another cup. "Yes, I am afraid there is. I need to talk to you about your husband's last few days. Did anything out of the ordinary happen at home, at work, or any time for that matter? Was he working on anything? Had he received a strange call or threat?"

She shook her head. "Not that I am aware of. A few days ago he was very distant when he came home. That happened a lot in his job. Usually it meant someone he had been servicing for years couldn't pay, and he had to cut them off. Sometimes customers that had been his friend for so long would yell at him and blame him. It was hard on him, but not out of the ordinary."

"Did he say if that happened recently?"

"Like I said, nothing out of the ordinary. It happened every week. He did not say anything this time either. I could just tell."

I jotted a few notes on my pad before asking another question. "Mrs. Jackson, I am sorry to ask, but I have to rule out everything. Was your marriage going well? Were there any problems?"

She smiled. "No problems, Detective. We loved each other like the day we met. He may not have been a great catch to a lot of women, but he was perfect for me."

I smiled in return, and I could see the love in her eyes. I spend a great deal of time looking for clues in people, and this clue was easy to see. Malcolm and Andrea Jackson were a strong, healthy couple. "I can see he was," I responded. "When was the last time you saw him?"

"It was that night, the night he..." her voice trailed off.

"The night he was killed?"

"Yes," she replied softly. "We had just had dinner and were settling down. He wanted to watch ESPN because they were doing a special on the Kansas–Duke game the next day. He got a call from his boss, Steve Jewel, the general manager of the uniform plant, because someone left the gate open at the plant. An alarm went off or something. Steve lives down in Tinley and it is a forty-five minute drive for him. He asked if Malcolm could swing by and make sure it was closed tight. Something like that happened a couple times a year so it was really no big deal."

Maybe it was no big deal to her, but definitely a big deal to me. I did not want to lose this discussion by making any comment, so I jotted down more notes including the general manager's name and to follow up on this security issue. "And so with that call, he left?"

"Yes, and I expected him back within forty-five minutes tops."

"Did he ever come back?"

Her face grew very solemn. "No, that kiss good-bye was the last thing I have to remember him by."

I gave her a moment or two to revel on that memory. "About what time was that?"

She thought a minute more, and then answered. "Maybe 7:45 or 8:00 p.m."

"Okay, so he came home from work at his normal time. He was acting normal, although a few days before he appeared to have had a rough day at work. You have a regular night until he gets a call to go to the plant. He leaves for the plant and that was the last time you saw or spoke to him?"

"Yes, well, other than the text he sent me."

"What text?"

She picked up her cell phone and began pushing buttons to get to the right screen. "Here it is." She handed the phone over to me.

I read it out loud. "I love you and I will be home later because I found..." And then it just stopped. I turned the phone back over to her. "What does that mean? What does, 'I found' mean?"

"I am not sure. Until you asked me the question, I had forgotten about the message. I assumed at the time it simply meant he found the problem with the gate but his text got cut off."

"And you had no other calls or texts?"

She shook her head. "No. I mean, I tried calling and texting him, but he never responded."

"Did he have any friends or other family members, a brother or sister maybe, whom he may have talked to either that night or before?"

Again she shook her head. "No, his only brother was killed in Vietnam, and as for friends, we really just had each other. He had people he talked with at work, but he did not do anything with them or talk to them about stuff." She paused and added, "At least as far as I know." She turned away and immediately spun back to face me. "Do you think it is important? Do you think he was talking about fixing the problem at the plant when he found something?"

I did not know the answer, but I did think it seemed odd. Maybe it was nothing. Maybe his text did just get cut off. Or maybe something cut it off. "Mrs. Jackson—"

She quickly interrupted me. "That is now one too many times you called me that. I am Andrea and I trust you, Detective O'Malley, like a friend. And so did Malcolm, so please call me Andrea."

"Yes, ma'am," I said slowly. "Andrea, have you seen your husband's phone? I don't remember it in evidence from the scene. Did the police give it back to you with his other belongings?"

Her head tilted. "No, I have not seen it."

"Can you give me his phone number? I think I have it, but it would be safer, to make sure I have it correct, if you can confirm it for me. Then, with your permission, we can run a trace on the number and see where it has been and what calls or texts were made the night he was killed."

She confirmed the number and I entered it in my notes. I assumed Franky would be at the station, and he could run this to IT and begin the trace immediately. I placed my hand on her shoulder. "Andrea, I know this is a difficult time and I cannot pretend to understand, but above all else, get your son back with you. Keep him here. Let me do my job for you. Let me do my job for you both."

She smiled, and a tear came back to her eye. "I will try, Detective O'Malley, but I do not think I can stop him. The cut is too deep to heal with just me. He needs to go out and find the healing on his own."

"The funny thing about cuts—they can be torn open further if you are not careful."

We did not speak anymore. She retired to a recliner and stared at a blank television screen. I put my hand back on her shoulder in an act of support, but then left her alone. As I walked out of her house, I noticed how deathly quiet it was. I wondered if it was always that way, or if it had suddenly gotten quieter since her husband died. I have seen hundreds of spouses left alone in the world. However, there was something about Andrea that struck me deeper. As I thought about it, the only answer I could come up with was that I had not seen hundreds of women left alone whose husbands were such good people.

I walked out of the apartment hoping I never had to go back there with news of another family member's death. My fear was, I would.

5 I WAS BACK at the precinct an hour and a half later. I had thought about going straight to my next stop, the strip clubs, but I wanted to grab a bite to eat and I wanted to touch base with Franky, in person if possible. I was going to grab a Dagwood but when I left Andrea's apartment, I realized I was only a few blocks from having an El Famous burrito. If you have never had an El Famous, then you really have never had a burrito. Known for football-sized burritos, they are everything and then some. Folks with me usually frown, but I don't even get meat, just beans and cheese. It often makes for a rough night, but the pleasure while eating it makes everything worthwhile. You know, most people think of Gino's East or one of the other major pizza spots when they think of Chicago food. For me, why stray from an El Famous and Mr. J's. If something works, stick to it.

As I rounded the corner toward my desk, I noticed my partner in crime was not back. I figured I would call him shortly and see if we could meet, but first I wanted to do a little research. I had authorization to do some minor searches for phone activity, with the owner's permission of course, so I started there. I would be able to tell if the phone was active and if so, where it was. Finding previous numbers dialed or text message information would be up to the IT boys.

I entered Malcolm's phone number into the system and within seconds I knew that the phone was off, and the last time it had pinged a tower was where we found his body. In a word, I had crap.

"What are you doing back here?" Franky asked, actually causing me to jump from my seat.

"I wanted to run this phone number and then find out what you learned today."

Franky leaned closer showing interest. "What phone number? You got something?"

Deflated when I realized he must have thought I had a hot lead, I replied, "No, just Malcolm's number. His wife received a questionable text message from him the night he died. Possibly about the time he died. He also went to his place of work late that night. I wanted to find out if he really went there."

"What did you find out?" Franky asked.

"Nothing yet. I need the boys in IT to run it down. I need to see the other text messages and find out his path for the whole night, maybe even the last few days. I need more than the last place the phone pinged." I changed my tone and turned toward my friend. "What did you find out?"

"Not too much. I researched the strip clubs in the area. Two have been bought in the last five months by an outfit whose financials are based out of Costa Rica."

"Costa Rica?" I questioned.

"Yeah, and the movement of money from the overseas bank to the local bank is all via electronic transfer so it is easy to track, but also somewhat invisible in the real world. The bank and the accounts appear to be legitimate. They are owned by a conglomerate of businesses under the name of Bad Boy Services. They own businesses in New York, Atlanta, Chicago, Los Angeles, Kansas City, Minneapolis, and Dallas. Their businesses range from strip clubs, to gold purchasers, to pawn shops, and to paycheck cashing."

"All businesses known for moving a lot of cash under the radar," I added.

"Exactly, and do you want to know what two strip clubs they recently bought in Chicago?"

I shook my head. "Ah, would it be Rick's and the Red Carpet?"

"It is. Funny, those are the two names that just came up in our conversation with Jamal."

"I think we should go visit those two locations."

Franky moved and sat down at his desk. "Let me do a little more work on their background. I want to see what crimes, if any, have been recorded on the premises since the new owners took over. Also, we should throw a call into Vice to see if there was any prostitution moving through them."

"Right, do that and I will run this number down to IT. I want to take it there in person. I need the results today if possible."

"Sounds good."

As I walked away I turned back to Franky and said, "Hey, Franky, nice work."

"No problem, Tommy."

"Did you find out anything on the autopsy of the hooker?" I added before leaving.

"Just her name, or at least her professional name. Star Light. She had it in her belongings on business cards with her picture. Other than that, nothing."

I shook my head as I saw the disappointment in his face. "Can you check out one more thing while you are at it? Malcolm worked at a uniform industrial laundry plant in downtown Chicago. They had some security issue the day he died which the general manager asked Malcolm to check out. Something just doesn't seem right about it. Why would a GM send a route driver down to the plant late at night for a security issue?"

"You want me to run the GM's name through the system and see what comes up?"

"Yes, and check out the business too. See if they have a security company that monitors the business and if there truly was an alarm that night."

"Will do, Tommy. What's his name?"

"Jewel, Steve Jewel."

"Got it. I will have it by the time you get back. Maybe we should run by this laundry plant before the strip clubs." He raised an eyebrow and added, "Maybe say hello to Mr. Jewel directly."

"Sounds like a plan, Franky. Give me twenty minutes." I paused then smiled at him. "I should warn you though, I had El Famous for lunch today."

"Damn it, Tommy, you knew we were going to be together this afternoon. What the hell were you thinking?"

I smiled and added, "Bean and cheese only." Then, I walked off lifting my leg to one side in imitation as I did. Franky got the message.

•　　•　　•　　•　　•

Fifteen minutes later I had dropped off the number and explained its urgency. The IT guy smiled and said no problem but then threw the form I had completed to the bottom of the stack. IT guys in the police system are similar to TSA guards at airports. They can't get a real police job so they have to make every cop feel beneath them whenever they can. My position was simple. There is a reason they were not real cops, and it was not worth my time to explain that to them.

We got in my Camaro and headed toward A-Tas Uniform Services. This was one of the largest uniform companies in the country, and you could see the white trucks with red lettering all over town. I think they did food vending of some kind too because I always saw their cups at Wrigley and the Cell. And no, I am not a White Sox, Cubs, or Bears fan, though I will go to the games when tickets fall my way. I have lived in Chicago since the sixth grade, but my dad was from White City, Kansas, population a few hundred. He fed George Brett and Len Dawson to me my entire life. If I were anything but a Royals and Chiefs fan, I would be disowned. Therefore, my blood flows royal blue and arrowhead red and that is the way it will stay. Adopting a team because you move into the town where they play is weak, end of discussion.

"What is Mr. Jewel's story?" I asked. "Any priors?"

Franky pulled out a stack of papers that clearly showed this guy was not Mr. Clean, as the laundry job would have implied. "There are a lot of small crimes. Drunk and disorderly at a ball game, smacked around his wife, indecent exposure, he peed outside a park, and such. The interesting one is that he was physically removed from a club and beaten to a level requiring emergency transport to Rush. The emergency room called the police but Mr. Jewel refused to press charges. Do you want to guess the name of the club?"

"The Red Carpet."

"Bull's-eye."

I was not entirely sure where the A-Tas facility was, but my GPS was talking constantly so I knew I was getting close. I glanced at Franky who was still turning through the pages but did not add any more of Mr. Jewel's sordid history to our discussion. "So we have this slimeball who drinks, hits women, and frequents strip clubs. He gets the crap beat out of him but refuses to press charges. This piece of work calls Malcolm Jackson, a forty-year-plus employee with a stellar work history to come fix a security issue at the plant. There must be people further up the food chain of this business that should be called first, don't you think? Why did he call Malcolm? Was there even a security issue?"

Franky added, "Did he even call Malcolm?" I swung my head to him but did not add any comments. The truth is, Andrea had not said she saw his phone or anything. Until we pulled his records, we really did not know if Jewel actually called him. Maybe the call came from someone else, but who would make Malcolm drop everything and leave on a moment's notice? All good questions, I thought.

If the old Cabrini Green was the worst area of Chicago, A-Tas Uniform Services was located in its close cousin. I am sure the land was cheap to build a plant there, and that is most likely attractive to a company such as A-Tas, but it's not really a great place to bring customers to visit. The security was impressive at first look. A tall fence with barbed wire angled outward at the top. It looked like we were trying to enter a prison, not an industrial plant. It had an electronic key entry gate and camera with intercom system for those coming without a badge. We watched a delivery van pull in and the gate close immediately behind it. We could have tailgated in, but not without the delivery guy seeing us, and we weren't here to test the system anyway, just understand it.

We drove to the gate entrance and pushed the intercom. "Hello, welcome to A-Tas, this is Donna Dodge, how can I help you?"

I cleared my throat. "Hello, Donna, I am Detective Thomas O'Malley with the Chicago Police Department. With me is Detective Frank Sullivan. We would like to have a short discussion with your general manager on a security incident the other night. Would Steve Jewel be available?"

There was a long pause on the system. We even heard it click completely off so no background noise was coming through. We both knew she was checking with Mr. Jewel to see if she should claim he was in or not. A slime like that probably had steps in place in case wives, girlfriends, the law, or anyone else made a surprise visit. Franky pointed ahead. "I ran his DMV information. That is his car parked right there. Plates match."

Just then Donna came back on the line. "Mr. O'Malley..."

"Detective O'Malley," I interjected.

Donna paused then corrected herself carrying a slightly annoyed tone with her. "Detective O'Malley. Would it be possible to make an appointment for tomorrow? Mr. Jewel is tied up for the rest of the day."

I pressed my lips tightly together. It was not my place to be put off, especially by a receptionist. We were not exercising a warrant. We simply wanted to speak about an issue, especially since it involved the homicide of one of his employees. "Listen, Donna, I don't know what Mr. Jewel is so busy with that he can't speak to us about the murder of one of his employees, but I would highly suggest you buzz open this gate and inform Mr. Jewel we are here and wish to speak. It will only get worse if you do not."

Again there was a click and dead silence. Eventually, the gate made a loud squeak and began to slowly move open. Franky turned to me. "I guess we are invited in."

"I guess so," I replied, smiling along with my counterpart.

We entered the lobby of the laundry facility, and in all honesty, it was quite nice. The company had spared no expense when they built the factory. Through large bay windows leading into the plant, you could see a highway of rails and conveyors moving garments like magic. There were large washers, dryers, and all sorts of people moving about in an organized fashion. To an onlooker who did not know what they were looking at, it appeared pretty cool.

Although captivated by the site of the equipment through the windows, it was not long before the not-so-cheery voice we recognized from the intercom grabbed our attention. "You will both need to sign in and while you're at it, why don't you produce some ID?" Her tone was cold and hard, as if we were really causing her great hardship.

"I'll be glad to, and you must be Donna. Might I say you hear someone through an intercom and their voice often depicts them so well you can picture them before you first actually meet, and I can say you have a beautiful voice and the voice is carried in the person."

Although my intended sarcasm came across genuine, she rolled her eyes and barely looked at my ID. However, her crabbiness vanished and she now seemed pleased with our presence. "You can have a seat over there. I have already called Mr. Jewel. Can I get you any coffee, water, or tea?"

Franky actually raised his hand as if he were addressing a teacher. "I would love some coffee." He coughed a bit. "Black, if possible."

"And you, Detective O'Malley?"

"No, thank you, ma'am. I am trying not to drink so much,"—I paused—"coffee, that is."

She brought the coffee over to Franky and then turned to me. "Well, are you trying to avoid all kinds of drinks, or just coffee?"

"What do you mean?" I replied.

"I mean, if you would like to grab a drink after work, I know a little place in LaGrange that would be nice. That is where I live, just off the city."

I smiled broadly and was completely caught off guard. This is a woman that hated every square inch of us not three minutes earlier and now we were having drinks? I stumbled over my first few words then found the right path to take. "I, I, uh, think that sounds great, but it will have to be sometime in the future. This case is going to require all my attention for the next several days."

"Weeks maybe," Franky added.

Although I had stumbled a bit, she seemed to take the words as sincere and smiled as she returned to her seat at the receptionist desk. Donna was not ugly, in fact she was very cute. However, I really did not date much. I may have a friend or two that I spend time with on occasion, but my life was complicated. It always had been. Furthermore, meeting someone on a case never worked out for me, never.

At that moment a small man approached from an office at the far end of the lobby. He had light brown hair and was wearing a button-up shirt with the top three buttons open, revealing a few gold chains and a hairless chest. To say he was not built would be an understatement. I am sure with one hand tied behind my back and one foot in a cast I would be able to take him down in less than two seconds. If I were a woman, I could guarantee this guy would not be my type. You could tell when he walked that he thought his shit didn't stink. He made two or three jokes with the ladies working in the office before he decided to grace us with his presence, which was most likely further posturing that he was not concerned about two detectives insisting on speaking to him.

"Steve Jewel?" I asked as I stood to face him.

"Yes, sir, that is me," he replied.

I waited a moment for him to say, *"That's my name, don't wear it out."*

"I'm Detective O'Malley and this is Detective Sullivan. We need to speak to you in private, if you don't mind."

"No problem, boys. Come on back to my office."

Boys, I thought to myself. This guy is a prick.

Franky motioned to the factory floor. "That guy looks like maintenance. Could I spend a few minutes talking to him? I love plants like this. It must be really hard to manage such a big place. I would love a quick run-through of the equipment."

This caught Steve, and me for that matter, off guard. Franky no more knew anything about laundry equipment than I did about being an astronaut. He knew how to investigate though, and the more people we talked to, the better. Steve tilted his head but clearly liked the ego stroke Franky had given. "Why, yes. That gentlemen's name is Jay. He is my maintenance manager and he would be glad to give you a quick tour." He turned to me. "As long as your captain doesn't mind."

"I'm a detective, just like Frank," I interjected. Turning to Franky, I added, "If he is available, then go for it. I can handle Mr. Jewel on my own."

Steve flagged down the maintenance manager, introduced him to Franky, and then waved back to me. "Come along, Officer O'Mallen, we can talk in here."

What an ass. "It is Detective *O'Malley*, but I think you already knew that."

"Oh yes, my mistake. O'Malley."

We continued into a small conference room next to what I believe was his office. The conference table would sit six people and each of us sat on one side. There was a small mini refrigerator in the corner which he immediately motioned to. "Can I get you something to drink? Water? Soda? I also keep something stronger in my desk, if you know what I mean?"

Again I thought, *loser*. "No, Mr. Jewel, I am fine."

"Please call me Steve."

"No, I believe I will stick with Mr. Jewel," I replied. He seemed a bit taken by this response but it was clear to me he just wasn't getting it. I did not like him. I did not like his kind, his personality, or anything about him. This guy was a Class A scumball. I knew it, and somewhere deep inside he knew it as well. "Listen, Mr. Jewel, and let me be frank. One of your employees was murdered, and the last person he spoke to was you, so I've been told. That makes you my number one suspect. So if we can cut through all the bullshit, we can determine if I am going to keep you as my number one suspect or if by chance you might be able to help me, and in the process clear yourself. For starters, where were you two nights ago?"

Immediately an expression of defense slid across Steve's face. "Wait a minute, Detective. What are you talking about?"

"Don't play dumb with me either. I don't have the time or the energy to deal with assholes like you." My voice was raised and I was clearly agitated. If Franky had been in here with me, he would have put his hand on my shoulder to calm me. However, because he was not here, I did not let up. "Two nights ago a route driver of yours received a call which his wife said was from you. We are pulling his and your phone records to verify, or you may simply confirm it for me now. Either way, I will get it. He was told there was a security issue here at the plant and that he was the closest to go fix it. He left immediately following the call. Then, four hours later he was murdered, execution style. Now, I ask you again and for the last time, where were you two evenings back following that call?"

"Okay, okay. I came here. After I called Malcolm, I thought I should come and make sure everything was all right. I got here about an hour after I called him. I am coming from Tinley, you know. I took the tollway in. When I arrived, the gate was closed and locked and the alarms were off. I assumed Malcolm had fixed it and was already gone."

"Did you see anything out of the ordinary? Did you see anyone?"

"No, like I said, the place was locked up. I don't like being here at night so I did not poke around too much. I checked the gate, got back in my car, and did a quick drive-by before heading back home."

"Did you take the tollway home also?" I asked.

"Yes, right back the same way I came. No stops."

I thought a second then asked, "Do you have an I-Pass for the tollway?"

"Of course I do. I drive the roads too much to not have the pass. Not just for the toll reductions, but the fly-through lanes make a huge difference."

I was starting to calm down and also knew verifying his story would be easy because the same way we could pull phone records, we can pull I-Pass checks. We could tell where and when he went through each toll.

"Was anything stolen?"

"What do you mean?"

"I mean, you had a security issue. Your gate was opened or forced open or something. People don't just come along, open a gate, and then leave. What did the people who broke in do?"

He turned a little red, like he was starting to tell me information he did not want to reveal. "No, nothing was stolen. We came in the next day and everything was exactly as it should be. It may have been the gate not closing tightly when the last person left, or kids or something."

"I doubt it, and you doubt it too or you would not have come in. Did you talk to Malcolm again that night?"

"No."

"Wait a minute. You call a route driver, not a supervisor or manager, but a route driver, to come in and fix a security issue, and he has enough moxie that he does not even call you back to let you know he fixed it?"

"Listen here, Detective O'Malley. I do not know what you are implying, but I don't think it is appropriate, and I don't like it."

"Appropriate! *Appropriate*!" I yelled. I opened my folder and pulled out the crime scene picture of Malcolm with his head blown off. "Do you think this is appropriate?"

He looked at the picture and then turned away in disgust.

"You listen to me, Mr. Jewel. Your whole story stinks. Maybe you are just a slimeball who really just sent his forty-year employee in to take all the risks of a possible robbery in progress, or maybe you had some reason that you wanted Malcolm gone. Either way, I am going to turn every aspect of your life upside-down until I find out. You can count on that."

Steve was now squirming down in his chair wanting to be anywhere but there. "I didn't do anything. You check out whatever you want, but you won't find anything on me. Now, I want you gone. If you want to talk to me again, talk to my lawyer."

"That is not what an innocent man would say—*talk to my lawyer.*" I stood up and put both hands on the table leaning down to bring my face as close to his as possible but still be on opposites sides. "I don't know if or how you are involved, Jewel, but when I find out, I am personally going to bring you down. That is something you can bet on." I paused, stood to leave, and then turned back. "And you are still my number one suspect."

"Get out of my plant, Detective O'Malley."

"At least you got my name right this time," I stated. As I stepped out of the room the ladies at the various desks all turned their heads back down and began typing or shuffling through papers. It was obvious they had heard everything as neither of us had restrained our voices in the least. Franky was making his way back up from the plant and Steve went over, opened the door, and flagged him over. "You get out of here too. Now!" he exclaimed.

Franky reached out to shake his hand but Jewel ignored it. "You must have had a good talk with Detective O'Malley," Franky said.

Steve Jewel did not reply. He pointed to the exit.

●   ●   ●   ●   ●

We got back to the Camaro without speaking, but I could see Franky was chomping at the bit waiting to ask me what in the hell took place at my meeting with Mr. Jewel.

"What in the hell took place at your meeting with Jewel?" Franky asked.

Still the best detective out there. I knew what people were going to say before they said it. "He is a slimeball, and I let him know that is what I thought of him."

"That's great, Tommy, but did you learn anything useful or just piss him off?"

"Nothing much. He claims to have an alibi, which we can check out. He did claim there was a security issue that night, but the whole thing just doesn't sit right. Why would he call a route driver? Why would he come in himself after he took the strange direction of calling the route driver in the first place?"

"And why would he call anyone when the maintenance manager I talked to, Jay Aksamit, is automatically called by the security company?" Franky added.

"What? The maintenance manager was here too?"

Franky shook his head. "Yes, and he was the one who fixed the gate."

I turned the corner and saw the sign for the tollway in the distance. I thought about Jewel's story and tried to tie everything together. "Did your maintenance guy see Jewel or Malcolm?"

"Nope. He came here, saw the gate was open about two inches causing the sensor to alarm. He closed it, locked it, and left." Franky paused then added, "And he called and left a message stating as much for Mr. Jewel, who did not answer."

"Wait a minute!" I exclaimed. "He called Jewel and told him it was handled? Jewel never mentioned that. Further, why would Jewel or Malcolm have even come in?"

"Jay said he did not call Mr. Jackson to let him know it was fixed. He was not aware that Mr. Jackson had been asked to come in. Apparently, there had been rare times in the past when Mr. Jackson had been called, but not since the security system was upgraded to automatically call Jay."

I stopped the car and turned to Franky. "We need to follow up more on Mr. Stephen Jewel. He is involved. After we run by these clubs, I'll do a full background on the slimeball and check out his finances. Something is off with him. We need to find out what happened to Malcolm when he came to fix the issue at the plant."

"If he was called to fix the gate," Franky added, carrying the same idea forward.

"Jewel confirmed he called," I replied.

"Right, he was called, but was it to fix the gate or was that simply what he said or what Jewel told him to say to his wife? What if he used that as an excuse to protect her? What if he never came to the plant? Nobody can place him there."

I nodded. "Interesting. He does get a call from Mr. Jewel, but Jewel knows the maintenance manager is going to fix the issue automatically. He calls Malcolm to meet somewhere else or to do something else. But what? And why? And why would Malcolm go?"

"Jewel's the general manager, Tommy. If the chief called you for a meeting, wouldn't you go?"

I nodded, but I still thought we were missing something. "Let's check out the Red Carpet. It is not far." We drove the rest of the way in silence, turning the facts over in our minds. I do this when I know I am onto something but there are still gaps. In this case, the gaps were too big but they were coming together. I just needed a few more pieces. We had several things already lined up which might help fill those gaps. First, the strip clubs, then get everything we could on the finances and background on Mr. Jewel, then back to Tom Clark, our undercover vice cop whom we were meeting the next night. Between those things, I believed key information might be identified to fill in some of the gaps.

●　　　●　　　●　　　●　　　●

"Tommy O'Malley, it's been a long time."

"Hey, Joey, it has been a long time. You know Franky."

Joey Polino stood tall but did not reach out to shake either one of our hands. "Yes, I know Franky. Tried to bust some of my girls not that long ago. Had to explain the law to him and his sergeant." Joey was grinning. He liked to highlight the small victories he could claim. "What do I owe the pleasure of two of the city's most noted homicide detectives to grace the doors of my humble establishment? Someone die I don't know about?"

Franky replied. "No, Joe, if someone died, I am sure you would know about it."

He smiled showing his near-perfect teeth and then retook his seat behind the desk.

I had known Joey Polino since he and I were in the sixth grade. I had just moved to Chicago and joined the school, and instantly Joey and I were friends. Kids are blind to their friend's families and because my dad was new to the area, he did not know the history of the Polinos. Joey's dad was killed when Joey was in the eighth grade. He had been murdered outside a bar in Cicero. At the time, I did not realize it was a professional hit. I thought it was just a random gang shooting. From that point on, Joey moved up the crime world ladder. At eighteen when he wiped out those responsible for the hit on his father, Joey put himself on top of the ladder. Our friendship ended in high school when I saw the things he was doing.

"I want to understand what is going on with you," I asserted.

"What the hell does that mean, Tommy? You want me to open my books?" He laughed and in the background his three-hundred-pound henchman issued a small chuckle as well.

"No, I want to know what has you so scared that you are selling off your establishments and kissing some new guy's ass?"

Instantly his smile vanished. He stood and took a step closer, as did the "gorilla" behind him. His voice was slower and deeper. "Listen here, Tommy, don't let our old friendship sway your judgment. Nobody scares me."

Franky reached his hand forward placing it on my shoulder to make sure I kept things in check. I tilted my shoulder down causing his hand to slide off. I took a step closer to my old friend. "That is not what I hear. I hear you're working with someone big. You have essentially become his bitch and have sold some of your businesses to pay off your debts. Further, you are providing him anything he needs and are cleaning up his messes." I paused then added, "But what do I know? I am just a cop."

The redness in Joey's eyes burned like fire into mine, but I did not flinch. Gorilla moved another step closer and appeared to be reaching for something in his pocket. Joey's lips tightened. "Listen to me, Tommy, and it is only our friendship that allows this. Never speak to me in that fashion again in my own place. If you have anything you want to charge me with, then do it. Speak to me however you want at the station, but you know as well as I do that you have nothing on me, nor will you ever."

"What's going on here, Joey?" issued a female voice from the side. "Anything we need to be aware of?"

Unseen by me as my focus had been on Joey were two incredibly beautiful women. The shock of the voice almost caused me to reach for my gun and draw it in response, but fortunately I did not. I did turn to face them and was taken by the sight.

"Sorry to startle you, officers. I just get a little concerned when I hear yelling by the police where I do run a business. You know, in this line of work, police are not the best for business." The woman who had spoken walked over with an outstretched hand. "I am Brit, and this Michelle. We are sisters and we subcontract space here for our girls to dance. Basically, Mr. Polino owns the building, and we run what is inside. Do you have a problem with what is inside?"

Her hand was delicate and soft to match her complexion. She was by all accounts gorgeous, but she was not a dancer or entertainer. Neither of them were. I could tell just by looking. This was a businesswoman, hard and decisive, and if my initial thoughts were correct, she did not want Joey messing up her business and was going to do what was needed to end whatever the issue was.

Releasing her hand, I replied, "I am Detective O'Malley and this is Detective Sullivan. We need to ask some questions tied to our murder investigation."

Michelle smiled. "That sounds fine." She stepped forward reaching out what I thought was her hand to shake, but instead she was handing me a card. "Here is the name and number of our attorney, Staci Lambda. She will be able to answer any questions you have." The two girls smiled softly as if they were giving me exactly what I wanted but in actuality, they knew they were shoving my questions down my throat. "Now, since you have gotten what you needed, I assume that means you may be on your way."

Gorilla took a few steps back still smiling broadly, and Joey held a very satisfied stare on me. "Ladies," I began, "thank you for this card. This is exactly what I needed. But more than a thank you, please be careful. You might be playing with fire on this one."

"Get the hell out of here, O'Malley," Joe said.

I turned without another word and then stopped as I saw something out of the corner of my eye. "Franky, please walk over and pull that minor off the bar and escort him out of the building. I have one more thing to say to Joe and my new friends, Brit and Michelle."

Franky turned his gaze to the bar and saw Jamal Jackson staring back at him. "Jesus Christ, what is he doing here? I will go get him, Tommy."

I turned back to Joe, causing Gorilla to step forward and stand right beside me. In one quick move, I jabbed my finger into his throat, kneed him in the crotch, and sent an uppercut across the bottom of his chin. Any one of them alone would have incapacitated him for a few seconds, but together, he was down for the count. One thing I may have forgotten to mention, though Joey knew it all to well as I had saved his ass numerous times in high school, was that I was a fourth-degree black belt and trained whenever I could. Very few things scared me, especially the size of my opponent. The gorilla was on the ground unable to breathe or speak. I moved to be only inches from Joe's face and to his credit, he held his position strong.

"Do not touch Jamal Jackson. I do not know why he is here, but if anything happens to him, you will wish you did not know me."

Joe did not flinch. "If you mean the boy, he came to see me about a job. He might be a good investment. Just think if he gets to the NBA and is on my payroll."

The comment was left hanging on a female voice from the side. "Yes, 911. There is a man posing as a police officer who just assaulted one of my employees. I fear he may be armed."

I turned away to greet the smiling face of Brit speaking into her phone. My eye caught Franky escorting Jamal out of the club and I softened slightly. I glared back at Joe, and as he waved a good-bye and mouthed the words without speaking, I turned to head out. "Okay," the woman's voice continued. He appears to be leaving on his own, but I will try to get the vehicle information. I think his name was O'Malley, but who knows if he is really a police officer."

I knew I would have to sort this one out, and Sergeant Carter was going to rip my ass again. However, my first priority was to rip Jamal a new one.

I made it to the car shortly after Franky had delivered Jamal, tossing him into the Camaro's back seat, which, for a D1 college basketball player, was no easy feat.

"Just what in the hell do you think you are doing here?" I asked.

"Better than you, O'Malley. I was about to get a job there. I could have seen things from the inside."

"Damn it, Jamal, you do *not* want to mess with these people. They will dig into you for what they can get and spit you out the back door. Don't you get it?" My voice cracked a bit as the anger grew within me. Part of me wanted to pick up the kid and shake some sense into him, although I knew it would not work.

"I will not fall into it. I will keep myself safe, and I will only be there to catch who killed my dad."

I thought I saw a tear forming in his eye and heard the pain in his voice. I let out a frustrated grunt but pursued the conversation no further.

Franky asked, "How long were you there, Jamal?"

Jamal's head had fallen down, and he lifted it slowly to respond, "I don't know. Long enough to interview for a bouncer job and look for Tiny a bit."

"Your friend Tiny works there? I thought you said he worked at Rick's."

"Nope, he works at the Red Carpet. He sometimes goes to Rick's to help out if needed, but his main job is at the Red Carpet."

"Then we have our guy on the inside already?" I said, more as a question than a statement.

"I don't know. Maybe." He paused, thought about his words then continued. "I mean, I like Tiny and trust him, but he is not the same guy I went to high school with. Maybe he has bought into the lifestyle promoted by Mr. Polino, or maybe he is still using. Regardless, he may not want to cut off the hand that feeds him. He does provide for his mother."

I shook my head in understanding, but I was still pissed I found him in there. "Who did you talk to when you interviewed?"

"The big guy brought me in to meet with Mr. Polino. We talked about basketball more than the job, but I think he liked me."

"Mr. Polino likes you a lot, because he sees a payoff with you. He wants to get you caught up and tied to him somehow and then use that to push you in certain directions." I was trying to be as blunt as possible without having to come right out and say it.

"What do you mean? It would just be a job. It is good money too. I actually thought I might consider it in the summers except that I don't know what the NCAA allows with my scholarship. He offered me money to help with the funeral. He said very nice things about my dad. Said he knew him well from all his deliveries. Said he always came in the early morning so nobody would be here as he did not like coming to a club like this during normal business hours."

Jamal had said so much there in those few sentences that my head was spinning. I started to ask a question but Franky shot in first. "I thought the place was open twenty-four hours a day?"

"Nope, I just learned they close down from two a.m. until six a.m. Dad always delivered before six a.m. He still liked getting done early. Even without me there, he went to the River Court almost every afternoon."

I now spoke. "Jamal, he wants to own you. He wants you to owe him so you will pay him back. His big payoff would be the NBA."

Jamal looked stung and confused. "What do you mean? I would never use that guy as an agent or anything."

"No, he doesn't want to represent you. He wants to *own* you. Let's say you get on the Bulls and the Bulls are favored to win by fifteen over the Timberwolves. He may suggest to you that the Bulls only win by fourteen. You don't take anything away from your team. The Bulls still win, but the big winner is the guy who bets against the spread."

I saw the look change in Jamal's eyes. "Point shaving? Seriously. I would never do that."

"Just understand the end game, Jamal. That is all."

Jamal nodded some level of understanding, and I could tell he was troubled by the possibility and had not previously placed himself in that position. He changed the subject. "Hey, Mr. Polino did tell me Tiny is over at Rick's right now if you want to go meet him and stop by that place. Mr. Polino says he owns both of them but a friend runs Rick's. I can introduce you to Tiny. I drove my mom's car. It is parked over there. I would prefer not to leave it here."

I glanced to Franky and despite my judgment to not involve Jamal, I could see in his eyes he agreed. Jamal could give us an *in* that we did not have without him. Having Jamal go with us would be better than him going alone, which I also knew he would do if we cut him loose now. So with a very slight nod only I saw, Franky and I agreed.

"Very well," I began, "you can come with us. Follow us in your car and do not talk to anyone other than your friend. Introduce us, get us a tour if you can, and maybe we can meet the man in charge, Mr. Polino's friend."

Jamal actually smiled at this and got up to leave the back seat of the Camaro, but Franky did not open or unlock his door so he was trapped. "I mean it, Jamal. No funny business. We are not including you in the investigation. We are trying to find a killer. That killer may or may not be linked to these clubs. Let Franky and me do our job."

"You got it, Detective O'Malley." Franky released the door lock and the boy jumped out.

Franky shook his head and that is when I noticed the face in the office window. Joe Polino was watching us. I waved in his direction and he waved back. "He doesn't fear us at all," Franky said.

"Not yet," I replied. "Not yet."

●　　●　　●　　●　　●

The two clubs were only a few miles apart, but with all the short stop streets eating into our time, it probably took us about ten minutes to reach Rick's. From the outside, Rick's was much nicer. I would call it a gentlemen's club and the Red Carpet the blue-collar strip club. Rick's offered valet parking, included a twenty-dollar cover just to get in, and escorts to a seat. Shorts, sweats, and T-shirts were not allowed in Rick's, which meant Jamal could not go inside. Further, a large sign clearly stated anyone under twenty-one would not be admitted and subject to prosecution should they try. But when Tiny saw his friend, all rules seemed to be thrown out the window.

"J, I am so glad to see you. Sorry 'bout your dad, bro."

"Thanks, T. I wanted to stop by to see how you were doing. Everything going okay?"

"Yeah, fine. How's your mom holding up?" Tiny asked.

"You know, she is hanging in there, I guess." Jamal paused. "It is tough with my sister still missing and nobody knowing anything."

Tiny slumped at the mention of Jamal's sister. I assume Jessica and Tiny were close as well with the boys being such good friends, going to the same school, and growing up together. It made sense Jessica would also be friends on some level with Tiny. I had interviewed Tiny once during Jessica's investigation but he did not know anything. I would have recognized him with his size as that is something you just don't forget. I assume he would not do the same in return. There is nothing memorable about me, to say the least. That is why I was surprised when he called me by name. "Detective O'Malley, good to see you again. You working on J's dad's case as well?"

"Yes, Ty, I am. That is what brings us here actually. We are trying to retrace his steps on the day he was murdered. Were you working then?"

Tiny seemed to be uncomfortable or disconnected. I could not place it, but I thought I would ask Jamal and Franky if they felt it or if it was just me. Sometimes as an investigator you see things in people nobody else does, and sometimes you see things that are not there because you are oversensitive to it. If a second person sees the same thing, usually it has some teeth. Tiny waved us into a separate area before answering. The noise from the music was loud but the parking lot only had about four cars in it. They were not busy but it was only four p.m. I often wondered about the afternoon clientele at strip clubs. What type of guy goes to a strip club ·

after lunch? Today I might get some answers.

We entered a small office near the front. Tiny pulled out a few folding chairs that were stacked on the wall. "This is where I lead people who I know have a fake ID or are not dressed appropriately. We can sell clothes to these losers, hold them for the police, or scare them and take their IDs. It is much quieter than the front entry area. To answer your question, I never saw Mr. Jackson when I worked here, and I was glad for that. He was always a dad to me, and I was afraid he would be disappointed. I mean, I know he knew I worked here and all, but knowing it and seeing it are two different things. It would be like thinking your kid was a prostitute would be bad enough, but seeing them do it would be devastating."

A bizarre analogy, I thought, but maybe that was in his line of logic to help us understand his point. "So you were not here two days ago?"

"I worked that day, but not here, and I don't come in till four p.m. usually. I work four until close, usually two-thirty or so by the time we get everyone out and everything cleaned up."

"When did Mr. Jackson do his deliveries?" I asked.

"He came in early. Like I said, I never saw him, except for one time when I got stuck doing a major clean-up and didn't leave until close to four-thirty in the morning. He was coming in as I was leaving and I was so glad he didn't see me."

"When was that?" I asked, building conversation not because I thought it was important, but I wanted to keep him talking.

"Maybe two months ago. I don't know, awhile ago, and it was at the Carpet, not here."

"Who did see him? I mean, he had to check in with someone, didn't he? He had to see someone if the place was closed until six a.m."

"No, he had been delivering to both places since they existed. Everyone knew him. He had a key. He would come, drop off the towels and kitchen uniforms and bathroom stuff, and go."

I looked at Franky, and he looked back to me. I know both our thoughts were the same. Are you kidding me? A mob boss let some route driver have full access to his place. No way. "Are you telling me, Tiny, that Joe Polino gave Mr. Jackson access to his clubs while nobody was here?"

"Well, not the full club. He had a key to the back kitchen. To get from the kitchen to the main club required a different key."

That made more sense but still left a question or two in my mind. Suddenly, a beefy African-American man entered the room and stared Tiny down. "T, Mr. Moretti would like you to return to the front." His tone was hard and although the words were harmless, I got the impression this was not a good thing. Beefy turned to us without changing his tone, "Gentlemen, please accompany me to the main office."

Tiny did not hesitate and did not even bid us farewell other than to nod to Jamal as he left. Beefy was staring hard at us, and although I knew I could take him, he was easily 350 pounds and possibly pushing 400. This was not a person I would choose to get mixed up with. We all rose collectively and turned to leave. As we stepped by, he placed the back of his hand on my chest. "I sense you do not fear an altercation with me. That would be a bad idea for you."

What can I say, the guy could read people well. I pushed his hand away. In a tough-guy voice straight out of *The Sopranos*, I replied, "It would be a bad idea all right. Just not sure it is a bad idea for me."

He smiled broadly showing some of the whitest teeth I had ever seen, other than one gold one next to his canine. "I guess we will see what happens."

Without another word I followed Jamal and Franky through the door and into the main strip club. There was a woman dancing in front of two men who appreciatively threw dollar bills toward her. She was one hundred percent naked which automatically drew Jamal's eyes, as well as Franky's and mine. What can I say? If you see an accident, you can't help but stare. You see a naked woman, same thing. Beefy walked at a slightly quicker pace to get in front and lead the way. I believe he actually brushed by my arm to make contact to prove he could. I wasn't impressed.

We came to the side of the club near a large door that said "VIP." I have never been a VIP, and I did not think I wanted to be one here, but it did not mean I didn't wonder. The door we went through had been locked but Beefy had the keys. It took three dead bolts each using a different key. "I guess the person in here really does not want visitors," I offered.

Beefy turned around still with that huge white-toothed smile. "Nah, it is more to keep people from leaving than to prevent entry."

Actually, to his credit, that comment had some teeth, no pun intended. We walked into one of the most lavish offices I had seen in my life. There was a glass wall that appeared to be a one-way mirror allowing those on this side to see directly into what I believed was the VIP room. There was a small bar in the corner loaded with the most upscale liquors available, there was a fireplace, a conference table, and extremely plush carpet. Another wall was finely carved wood shelving which included pictures of numerous famous people, books, and other memorabilia. In the center but toward one of the far walls was a large desk. Behind that desk was a man I had never met before. Beefy left us alone shutting the door behind him, and all three locks clicked tight from the outside. When I turned for a clearer look I saw the locks were not standard ones that you could open by turning the handle from this side. The locks on this side were simply flat plates. An eerie feeling crept over me.

"Welcome to Rick's. I'm Ross Moretti. I received a call you would be stopping by. You must be Jamal." He reached out for a quick handshake with Jamal and then turned to me. "And who is Franky and who is Tommy?"

"I am Detective O'Malley and this is Detective Sullivan." Ross Moretti reached out his hand to shake which neither Franky nor I took. We had seen slimeballs like this hundreds of times, but this guy was different. This guy was so overbearing in confidence he would make Bill Clinton look confused and weak. Without another word, this creep was at the top of my list of suspects. "Can I ask why we are in your office?"

He slowly took his hand back but made it clear he was not pleased. "Well, let me see…Detective O'Malley, was it?"

His speech stopped as if he was waiting for me to confirm. As if…

He coughed to cover the momentary silence and then continued. "You come into my club. You take my doorman away from his post so any loser can enter. You have a private conversation with him about my business, and all this after you placed a similar visit to my sister club. However, over there, you send an underaged minor in before you to see what you can gather instead of coming right in and asking."

I interrupted. "Isn't underaged and minor the same thing?" He pressed his lips together and I could tell I was really starting to piss him off.

"So tell me, Detective O'Malley, have you spoken to Sergeant Carter yet? Because you should know, I have."

In hindsight, I should have stood up, forced them to open the locks, and walked out right then, but alas, I rarely make the right decision when dealing with someone who obviously wants to posture in front of me. I smiled and I believe Franky even yawned. I leaned just a bit closer before I spoke. "Is there a problem,

Mr. Moretti? My friend here wanted to see his high school friend to tell him his father had died. Oh, wait, you know his father, don't you, because he had keys to your club and your sister club."

"If that is why you are here, then why did you not say it to him when you spoke?" He stopped and pushed a button on his desk which turned a TV on the wall to a security camera feed in the room they had been in with Tiny. In that feed stood Beefy with what appeared to be a patron who was sitting in the same chair I had just been in, but this guy appeared scared to death. Through the TV we heard Beefy speaking: *"What do you mean, you thought the age to enter was eighteen? Do you know what we do to minors here? This is not just a bar. This is an adult business. Do you want to find yourself in the alley out back naked and missing most of your teeth?"*

We could hear every word clearly and the boy appeared as if he was going to soil his pants. The TV shut off and the point was made. Every word we had said with Tiny was heard by Moretti. I tried to remember everything discussed but it really did not matter. My direction was not going to be different. "How well did you know Mr. Jackson?"

He smiled, stood, and walked to his small fully stocked bar. "Can I get either of you a drink? I know cops love Scotch. I have some of the best here. Imported directly from Scotland."

I ignored the question. "Mr. Jackson. The man who delivered uniforms, towels, and mats. You gave him a key. How well did you know him?"

He walked back to his desk, reached under, and pushed another button. We heard all the locks open automatically on the door. "Good day, gentlemen. Send Sergeant Carter my best."

As he spoke the door swung open and Beefy was back. I turned back to Moretti. "Afraid of something?"

Moretti did not answer. He simply nodded to Beefy who had moved to stand beside me.

"That was quick," I said to him as I turned. "Do you always go so fast?" Sexual intent implied.

"It doesn't take long with pussies."

He one-upped my sexual innuendo. I liked that. Beefy escorted us straight back through the club and out the front door. As we passed, Tiny and Jamal gave each other knuckles, but I could see the fear in Tiny's eyes. Beefy scared him, just like the boy we saw on the camera.

Once outside we saw that boy again. He was walking fast with a clear limp heading to what we assumed was his car. "Hey," I shouted. "Wait."

The boy glanced back and then pushed himself through the limp toward his car even faster. When he looked back, both Franky and I saw the same thing. "Stop!" Franky yelled. "Police."

The boy wanted to keep going but when he heard the word *police*, he hesitated, seemed to think about options, and then stopped.

We ran to him with Jamal in tow. "What happened to you? Did they do that inside?"

"No," he said firmly. "I fell when I tried to run."

"Your face is beaten. Your nose appears broken. If that man did that to you, we can handle it."

"No!" he said firmly. "I fell. If you want to arrest me for trying to enter the bar underage, then do it. Otherwise, I am leaving."

I was about to protest more but I knew it would not do any good. The boy was scared beyond belief. He had urinated in his pants, and he was going to have to explain a broken nose and two black eyes to his family and friends. Beefy had literally scared the piss out of him, and made it clear that to speak anything about what happened would only make things worse for him and most likely his family. I leaned in closer. "Take care of yourself, and do not mess with these guys. They are bad news."

He nodded, turned, and continued to his car. I turned back and saw a look of terror on Jamal's face. His voice cracked a bit as he asked, "What has Tiny gotten involved with?"

"I don't know," I replied placing my hand on his shoulder as we turned to head where we parked. "Let's hope he is only a doorman."

Nothing more was said. Jamal needed to head to his mother's house, and he promised he would make no more stops on his own tonight, though he would not commit to letting things drop altogether. Franky and I needed to get to the station. Carter had called me numerous times, and talking to him in person was always better than the phone. I did not want to talk to him at all, but sorting out this crap with the strip clubs was necessary. Who knows what Moretti and Polino said to him? Nothing I could not fix, but letting it stew too long would only make it worse. Franky said he would join me at Flapjaws later if I was going to be there. I told him it was almost guaranteed I'd be there knowing what was going to take place at the station.

●　　　●　　　●　　　●　　　●

5:50 p.m., Tuesday

I arrived at the precinct and as I walked through the door all I heard was, "Is that damned O'Malley here yet? Somebody find his butt and bring him to me now, damn it!"

I walked toward Sergeant Carter's office while another detective patted my shoulder as I walked by. "Sergeant Carter, you wanted to see me?"

"Shut that door, O'Malley, and sit your ass down because when I am through with you, you won't be sitting in this office or any other law enforcement office again."

I shut the door and found a chair in front of his desk. About forty-five minutes later I emerged from the office feeling as if I had been through a prostate exam. Although I believe everything was fine with my position, I did learn that Mr. Moretti and Mr. Polino were in some sort of relationship with the police commissioner. This smelled bad to me, but it definitely was not worth investigating at this time. Carter's position was simple—he did not care what I did or who I messed with to solve this case, but if it came back to him, he was going to take action. In no uncertain terms, I would be the fall guy. He had no love for either of the slimeball strip club owners, but he also knew they were deeply connected, and unless we had something ironclad, messing with them would not end up well for anyone.

I walked back to my desk and nobody spoke to me, not that there was anyone around. It was going on seven p.m. and most everyone had headed home or to the bars. Cops more than any other professionals hid in the bars after work. The things we see sometimes need to be muted before going home to our families. In my case, that family left a long time ago. My wife left with the kids because she was tired of living alone. Yes, I lived with her, but she was alone. My mind was always on a case. I could not separate the dead body in the gutter with having a normal discussion about the PTA. Eventually, she left and I couldn't blame her. I saw it again and again with homicide detectives. That is why Franky and I were so special. Somehow we had withstood the test of time.

I sat at my desk and knew tonight was not going to be a good night. Something about meeting someone who very well might be a murderer and not being able to do anything about it tore at me. It had been almost forty-eight hours since Malcolm had been murdered. The funeral was going to be sometime this week, and I was feeling the pressure. I only had a few days left to find the killer if my goal of solving this murder before the funeral held true. Although I had some suspicions, I really was no closer to solving the crime than I was when I walked down the alley toward his body. I stood up and threw my hands across the top of my desk pushing everything to the floor. The stapler made the loudest crash as it popped open and threw its belly of staples across the wood floor. Carter stepped out of his office to see what the noise was. He saw me, nodded, and went back to his desk. Carter was like me. Single not by choice, by abandonment. He had nothing to go home to either.

6

I WALKED INTO FLAPJAWS an hour later. I had left my desk in shambles and figured I would pick it up tomorrow. I expected to see Franky sitting at our normal spot at the bar and instead saw Jamal with a seat open to the left next to him. He was talking to a man to his right that I had never seen but had the look of toughness.

"That better be a Coke, young man," I stated as I walked up.

Jamal was startled and turned quickly to face me, the look on his face clearly showing he knew I would not be happy he was here. "Hello, Detective O'Malley. I am sure you are surprised to see me, but I wanted to talk to you further."

The man next to him reacted slightly to Jamal referring to me as Detective, enough of a reaction to catch my attention. I wondered what they had been talking about. That could be pursued later. Now I wanted to know what in the hell brought him out here tonight, at a twenty-one and over bar no less, after he promised he would stay with his mother. I motioned for him to move to the open seat on his left and I took the one Jamal had vacated next to the man. As I sat, I noticed a small plaque sitting in front of the man now on my right. Next to the plaque was a full glass of ice water. He took a drink of his water when he noticed my gaze.

At that point, the bartender, Roy Pura, who I knew well, walked up and smiled. "Good to see you, Tommy. I was going to kick your friend out for being underage, but since he was waiting for you and talking to another detective, I assumed he was okay to be in here."

My ear caught the "other detective" comment. I glanced to the man who nodded, and then I replied. "Thank you, Roy. I will keep an eye on him and get him out of here as soon as possible."

I sat down, and he threw me a water. "You want your usual, Tommy?" the bartender asked.

"What are you drinking there?" I asked the man next to me.

He looked over. "I'm drinking water, but when I used to drink from a full menu, it was always McNaughton's. Now, however, after several years of using a limited menu, I stick to water."

I nodded understanding. If he *was* a detective, I completely understood. "Roy, I'll have a McNaughton's." As the bartender moved to gather the Canadian Whiskey bottle, I reached my hand out to the man. "Tom O'Malley. As you might have heard, Detective Tom O'Malley, but my friends call me Tommy."

"Glad to meet you, Tommy. I am E.Z. Zimmerman. Detective E.Z. Zimmerman from Minneapolis, and my friends call me Zimm."

"Glad to meet you, Zimm. What brings you to Chicago?"

He smiled slightly, and it appeared he did not want to continue. I was not sure what to make of that or what to say during the uncomfortable pause. With a long sigh, he finally finished his thought. "Well, for whatever reason, the APHF gave me an award for a case back in Minnesota. I had to come down here to receive it at a banquet tonight. Not really my cup of tea, if you know what I'm saying."

"The American Police Hall of Fame? Well, congratulations, Zimm. That is really impressive." Roy set my drink down in front of me. I left the McNaughton's sitting alone and grabbed my water. "Zimm, I raise a drink to that. To be recognized at that level means your life was on the line, and there is no way not to be appreciative. I am sure it is well-deserved."

Jamal, hearing the conversation, lifted his glass of soda in respect as well. "What was the case? Can you talk about it?"

He grumbled a bit again, but I think he could tell Jamal was truly interested and impressed. "Nothing too deep. A drug ring and gang business being regulated and shaken down by cops. I think because my partner got shot and I got shot at, the award came my way. To be honest, I wished they had given it to my partner. He took the bullet. However, he had been pulled from the case because he knew one of the victims well."

I leaned back to allow Jamal and Zimm to see each other more clearly. Jamal seemed satisfied with this answer and went back to his drink. I continued to probe further into our new friend. "I saw you both talking, but I don't know if you were formerly introduced. Jamal Jackson, Detective E.Z. Zimmerman, Zimm."

"Very nice to formerly meet you, Jamal. It was a pleasure hearing your story."

"Thanks for listening," Jamal replied shyly.

I shudder to think what all Jamal told him, but I assume the kid just needed someone to listen. E.Z. Zimmerman struck me as someone who had heard a lot of stories in his days. I nodded to Zimm as my way of acknowledging his time with Jamal, and he returned the gesture with one of his own. I turned to Jamal. "So tell me, Jamal, what brings you down here after I instructed you to spend this evening with your mother?"

He leaned in closer and did not mix words as he started. "Those guys today were dirty. I know they were. Do you think they had my father killed?"

"What guys?" I asked, trying to stall so I could think of the answer I wanted to give.

"Those creeps at the Red Carpet and Rick's."

"Jamal, I don't know how to answer that." My voice trailed off just a bit before I continued. "Those guys are dirty, but that does not make them killers. The truth is, I don't know who or what your father was involved with. Maybe he drove up and saw something completely unrelated. We just don't know yet."

Jamal looked down. He desperately wanted me to provide some answers, but I really had nothing to offer. He looked up again. "What is our next move?"

"Your next move is to get home. Your mother needs you now, Jamal, more than she ever has before. And you need her. Don't get caught up in the mess of this. Let Franky and me do our job. We will do everything we can to find your father's killer and find out what happened to your sister."

"I know, Detective O'Malley, but I want to help."

"The best help you can give me is to take care of your mother." I don't think Jamal was buying what I was selling, but I also think he did know his mother needed him. If I were in Jamal's shoes, I would do exactly what he was doing so I could not blame him, but I could not accept his help either. Dealing with where I thought this was heading was troublesome. This was going to be dangerous. The people the case had led us to so far were exactly how Jamal described them—dirty. What I did not know was *how* dirty.

Jamal stood. "It was a pleasure meeting you, Detective Zimmerman." Zimm nodded again and sipped his water. Jamal turned to me. "I will go stay with my mother, but I will be in touch tomorrow. I won't let this go completely."

With that he left Flapjaws. I looked down to the bar and let out a long sigh. "You don't drink, or just being polite to me?" Zimm asked.

I turned back to Zimm. "No, I drink."

"Then pick up that McNaughton's and enjoy. It looks like you need it."

I lifted the glass and sucked some in. The initial burn was real, but I let it soften slowly on its own before speaking further. "Yeah, I don't know what to say sometimes. The kid lost his father two days ago and his sister has been missing and is presumed dead. What do you say to someone going through that?"

"He told me about his father and a little about the guys he thinks are responsible. Sounds messy. Sounds like his father got involved in something he shouldn't have, whether he meant to or not."

"You got that right, Zimm. I just feel like I am missing something."

He smiled. "You want to bounce it off me. I *am* an award-winning homicide detective, you know."

I smiled in return. "Yes, you are an award winner, aren't you? I was going to ask what department you were in. Homicide is my guess."

Zimm nodded. "Yes, homicide." His voice trailed off a bit catching my attention.

"You mentioned your partner got shot. Is he okay?" I paused and when he did not answer immediately, then filled the void with a follow-up. "You guys close?"

"Yeah, as close as partners can be. I have had several partners over the years. In fact, the reason I left the force was tied to the fact that no other detectives wanted to work with me because bad things seemed to happen to all my partners. That, and the asshole they made Captain had a hard-on for me. No matter what the situation, I still feel responsible for each and every one of them. My first got injured in the line of duty and has had to transfer to a desk job. After that, my partner on the case that brought me here was Big Al Munk. In fact, Al should be here by now. He was leaving the hotel before I was." Zimm paused as if he was remembering something and then continued. "You know, we had not worked together for a long time and when he heard about the award, he said he wouldn't miss this night for anything. I think he was happier about the award than I was." Zimm paused again and took a long slow drink of water before changing the direction of the conversation. "How about you?"

"I have had a partner or two, but none of them have stuck. Although I work alone, my old partner, Frank Sullivan, who should also be here by now, works with me or I with him. We are the old-timers, just not officially partners." It was my turn to take a drink, but I did not choose the water. "We always have each other's back," I added softly. Zimm showed he understood. "I am starting to think this case is tied to an old case I have been working, and an old case he has been working. My fear is it is much bigger than we expected."

Zimm tilted his head slightly. "You mean you have three open murder cases that are all tied together?"

"Officially, one of the cases is a missing persons'. I took over the case when the victim's DNA in the form of liters of blood was recovered in the back seat of a car. From that point forward, the case has been cold. Another case is a serial killer, so the body count is even higher."

"What changed?" Zimm asked. "What brought them together?"

Why was I talking to him? I thought to myself. *Why was I sharing this information with someone I just met?* My mind trailed off which I think he sensed.

Zimm broke the silence. "I am overstepping my bounds. Sorry, I—"

"Nonsense," I interrupted. "I could actually use the sounding board."

He smiled in return. "Then please continue."

"The girl's father was found executed in an alley about a half mile from where her blood was found."

He pressed his lips together tightly, shaking his head. "So that is the sister and father of Jamal?"

I did not answer, but just grabbed my drink and finished the McNaughton's. We sat in silence for a few minutes and then Zimm turned to me. "You know, what helps me sometimes is my attorney."

"Your attorney?" I asked questionably. What is a police detective doing with an attorney, I thought?

"Yes, he is my attorney, but moreover, my friend, confidant, advisor—all of those in one. My point is, he is someone I trust that I bounce things off of. He is rarely tied to my situation personally so he gives me unbiased views. He usually asks the right questions to help me open my mind."

"Okay, are you offering to be 'my attorney' tonight?" I asked.

"I am no replacement for Ralph Cowan, my attorney, but I would be glad to give it a shot."

I proceeded to tell this man I had only known for fifteen minutes the specifics about the case. I kept anything that was truly confidential out of my story, but I included some gray areas in my description. I had not asked for a badge or verified anything about him, but there was something about this guy. To me it meant simply that if we worked in the same precinct, we would be partners. As I went through my summary, he sat amazingly quiet. He never asked a question, asked for clarity, or anything along those lines. He listened. I needed to find a Ralph Cowan or an E.Z. Zimmerman of my own. When I was done, he reached out, grabbed his water, nodded to Roy to take my empty glass away and bring two more of the same drinks, and then turned to me.

"The easiest answer is usually the most simple."

"What do you mean?" I asked.

He swiveled his barstool to face me more directly. "Let's look at each case. The missing girl. She was not like her brother. She was into drugs and different things. She was mixed up in something that the family does not want to admit. Either by choice, or she got in over her head and ended up there. Something went bad and she got hurt."

The drinks were delivered and Zimm took a drink of his water, coughed a bit, and then continued. "The father could not let the loss of his daughter go. He continued to search. He was tied in deep with the bad part of Chicago through his job. He knew everyone and everyone knew him. He asked questions and got some answers. He became the detective. He asked too many questions, or his questions started to get too close. Someone found out and became concerned, and despite this man being a staple in the area, the person ended his questions for good. The prostitutes, possibly linked to this whole thing, or possibly a serial killer. The link would only be tied to organized crime—the same organized crime that the daughter got mixed up in and the father found out about. If it is the same, then something is going on within that crime group to be this reckless. Maybe two groups fighting for territory. Maybe one boss owes the other something big, but regardless, the situation is unstable at best."

He finished without another word and then went back to sip his water. I thought about what he had said and was surprised how defined it was with so little information. He immediately went to Jessica being not the good child compared to her brother, something I had not really considered. How well did I know Jessica? I had never met her. I had only received information about her from her family and friends. A family is going to paint their daughter or sister the way they wanted her seen. I would need to investigate that further. And as for the rest, I could not argue his points. Zimm did not tell me anything I did not already have in my head, but much of it had yet to be admitted.

"I can't argue with you, Zimm. It doesn't mean you are right, but in just a few minutes you have made me rethink a few steps in my investigation."

He smiled just a bit. "Good. Again, it is just an unbiased perspective. It works and I use it on every tough or complicated case."

Just then a large man approached Zimm from behind. "Sorry to keep you waiting, Zimm. I had problems finding a cab."

"In Chicago?" I asked.

"I think it was more they did not want to give me a ride," he replied, though he had no idea who I was.

Zimm interjected. "Tommy O'Malley, this is Big Al Munk, my old partner on the case I mentioned."

Big Al reached his hand out. "My friends call me Chip."

I stood up and shook his hand, and I can tell you his grip fit his body, but I had to pass on the obvious—Chip Munk. "Glad to meet you, Al. Your partner has been kind enough to provide some new perspective on my case here in Chicago."

"You a detective?" he asked.

"Yes, homicide," I replied.

"Been at it long?" Al asked, almost as if he was sizing me up for my abilities.

"More than twenty," I replied. This seemed to lend credibility to my existence.

Al motioned to the table behind them. "You guys want to move to a table? I could use a place to sit with a backrest, and I could use a drink."

Zimm picked up the tab at the bar. I told him he did not need to, especially since his tab was zero, but he equated it to hitting a hole in one on the golf course and buying everyone in the clubhouse a round. He got this award and wanted to pay. It gave me the impression that money was not a big issue for him, but knowing he was a lifelong detective and may be retired, I wouldn't believe he was swimming in green. To be honest, I didn't care. I just liked the company. I didn't realize until that night that I really don't talk to many people that are simply my friends, not that E.Z. Zimmerman was either, but maybe that is what made him so different. Before long, Franky joined us at the table, and the four long-time homicide detectives talked until two a.m. Normally, if I left a bar at two a.m., I would hail a cab for sure. Tonight, however, other than those first two drinks at the bar, not another drink with alcohol was poured. We just didn't need it.

We were just breaking up to leave when my cell phone rang with a blocked number appearing on the screen. I answered. "O'Malley."

"Tommy?"

"Yes, this is me. Who am I speaking to?"

"Tommy, this is Clark. We need to meet before tomorrow."

I motioned to Franky. "Clark, what is it?"

"How well did you know Malcolm Jackson?"

"What? Where are you?" I paused and tried to get my mind right and back on the case. "What about Malcolm?"

"Tommy, we need to meet. First thing in the morning, like seven a.m. The alley behind Pippen's."

"Clark, I can meet but what about Malcolm?"

"Seven a.m., Tommy." And he was gone.

I clicked off my phone and lifted my eyes to be met with six other eyes locked on me. Franky asked, "That was Clark? It sounded like trouble. What's up?"

"I don't know," I replied. "He said something about how well I knew Malcolm and that we had to meet first thing in the morning."

"Where and when?" Franky asked.

"Seven a.m., the alley behind Pippen's."

"I'll pick you up at six," replied Franky.

Zimm nodded. "Be careful, gentlemen." Then, turning mostly to me, he added, "Remember what I said. Don't make things too complicated. If someone appears dirty, then there is a good chance they are. Don't force actions to fit into your theories. Let the facts direct you."

I nodded understanding. We all shook hands and were about to go our separate directions when Zimm turned and handed me his card. "Why don't you call me and let me know how this one goes?" He paused and finished, more to both of us, "And if either of you are ever in Minneapolis, look me up as well. I would love to get together again. I have a place you can stay downtown as well, so don't worry about a hotel."

"And the same goes for you. Give us a holler if you are back this way."

"Will do," he replied as we walked out.

7 SIX A.M. CAME way too early. As a cop, I never get enough sleep. Even if I have the time, which is rare, my mind will not let things go. Four to five hours is normal. Three hours is nasty. Franky came to my apartment, and fortunately, since I gave him a key, he did not have to pound on the door as he had in the past. He had a cold Diet Dr. Pepper waiting and a Dagwood dripping grease through the brown bag.

Franky smiled when he saw me emerge from my room. "You look like hell."

"Thanks," I answered, my voice deep and cracked. "Is that a Dagwood I smell?"

"Yep, with a forty-two ounce Dr. Pepper by its side."

"Damn, Franky, if you were a woman, I would marry you."

"You couldn't have me," he replied. His voice turned more serious. "I tried contacting Clark through his captain, and he said that he had not had any contact with Clark in several days. He said that was normal, but I think my questions sparked his interest. He said he would call if he heard from him."

"I have a bad feeling about it, Franky. Clark's call was cryptic and short, like he didn't have time to speak, and whatever he had to say, he wouldn't say it over the phone. I thought all night about what I believed he was trying to say...that Malcolm Jackson was dirty. We checked his finances and there was nothing. The guy lived paycheck to paycheck and used every free minute to help boys on the streets learn to play basketball. Including Jamal. He paved the way for at least three others to make it to college."

"I know," Franky replied. "I don't know what it means, but I think we need to get there early. We should check the area out. If something is not right, I want to know about it before it happens."

"Let me throw this burger down and we can go. It is only about fifteen minutes to Pippen's. We will be there by six-thirty."

"Sounds good," Franky replied.

We headed that way in my Camaro because Franky always said that my car blended better in alleys and drug areas, and I am not sure if that was a compliment or not. Regardless, when we did not want to stand out, which was most of the time, we drove the Camaro. We arrived at Pippen's about 6:35 a.m. The streets were empty as would be expected, except for the one or two homeless that were wrapped in cardboard blankets on the pavement in any corner they could find. The temperature was unseasonably warm for November so the life on the streets was still prospering. In the next few weeks, the cold chill of Chicago would arrive and the downtown streets would change. For now, however, any corner or alley was fair game for a bed.

The morning light had just begun to show, making the alley that was dark the last time we were here start to show how unkempt it was. There was debris of all types around and another homeless man shuffled in his sleep causing a liquor bottle to roll free from his covers. The smell of urine did bite the air, but for the most part there was no movement or sound. Franky and I looked at each other and I noticed Franky was unbuckling his shoulder holster. Although I did not know if it was warranted, I did the same because something did not feel right. My hope was Clark would bound around the corner, we could talk, and then go about our separate business. I knew we were early, but something made me feel like Clark would be early also. With as many eyes that I believed were on him, he would not leave himself short on time for any meeting.

As we moved around the dumpster, we saw him. "Clark!" Franky shouted, now drawing his weapon.

"Jesus Christ," I said.

Franky was on his knees shooing a rat away from the body. Blood soaked the ground but somehow Clark appeared to be alive. The amount of blood was significant, and we could not tell where it was coming from. As I looked closer, I saw his hand was pressed against his throat with the weight of his body holding it in place.

"Don't move him, Franky. His position is the only thing keeping his blood flow blocked. Call it in, *now*."

Franky grabbed his phone and called for an ambulance and backup. I did a quick glance around the alley and when I saw nothing, I knelt down beside Clark. "Clark, can you hear me?"

Clark raised an eyebrow but did not, or could not, speak.

"Who did this, Clark?"

He opened his mouth causing blood to spew out mixed with words that were impossible to understand. "Clark, hang in there, buddy. Help is on the way."

He appeared agitated at this but could not move without causing his injury to become much worse and most likely fatal.

I placed my hand on his leg. "What, Clark? Do you know who did this?"

He blinked his eyes one time.

"Does that mean yes? One time is yes?"

He blinked his eyes one more time.

"Did it involve Malcolm Jackson?"

He blinked his eyes one more time.

"Was it Moretti or Polino?"

Just as I asked, Clark coughed hard spitting a volume of blood forward that must have been pooling in his stomach or lungs or both. The dark, almost black, blood drained from both sides of his lips and his head fell to the side. His breathing stopped and I thought about CPR but knew it was no use. He was dead.

The alley was lit with activity for the rest of that morning. Although this was the death of a police officer, because he was undercover, we had to treat it as just another gang hit or drug death. Clark had worked his way deep into the underground world of Chicago. Drugs, prostitution, and organized crime—he was involved in all of them. That is how we treated his body and the news story that would follow.

Dr. G walked up and placed her hand on my shoulder. "I heard you and Franky were the ones who found him. I am sorry, Tommy. I know you worked with Clark a long time."

"Thank you, Doc. Now I just want to find who did this."

"I know," she said softly. "Tell me, can you walk me through what you saw when you arrived?"

"He was alive, but barely. He wanted to talk but couldn't. I think he was shot through the throat or mouth. He coughed once, which caused a major amount of blood to come out through the mouth, and he died." My voice trailed off as the emotion of speaking about it came over me.

Her voice was still soft and caring. "He was dead already for all practical purposes. His lungs were most likely filled with blood. Even if you had been a paramedic, there was nothing you could have done."

"Find some clues to who did this. Make sure you do not miss anything. You are the best for a reason. Please show it again."

She understood, but as always she would let her work decide what she found. No request from me would change how she performed her job. She went right to work, starting with photographing the area and then with the medical steps of inspecting the body on the scene. She had her assistant with her, as she did on all the high-profile cases. Together they were a fine-oiled machine of medical expertise. Every time I saw her work, I knew why she was in her position.

An hour later they were taking the body to the morgue. I saw Franky talking to some men near the front of the alley. I recognized one as Clark's captain. The other two looked vaguely familiar but I couldn't place them, at least I could not place them then. My mind was jelly. It was almost noon and we had been there for over five hours. I wanted food and I wanted to regroup. This case was already nasty, and it had just taken the nastiest turn imaginable—a dead cop. If Sergeant Carter was on my ass before, now the ass-ripping would reach the mayor. Nobody would allow this one to go unsolved. Nobody.

Franky saw me heading that way and separated from the group to meet me. "You ready to get out of here?" he asked.

I did not reply, only continued walking out of the alley. When we were out of earshot of anyone else, I asked, "What is going on here, Franky?"

"I don't know, Tommy, but it isn't good."

"Killing a cop? That just shows they have no fear."

"Everything about these cases shows no fear," he replied. "They kill during the day or night. They leave bodies in the open not worrying about who finds them or when, and they don't care who they kill."

"We have to solve this one, Franky. We have to."

"I know."

There was a pause as we walked down the street adjacent to Pippen's Tavern. Franky broke the silence. "Where to now?"

My voice was cold and low when I answered. "We are going to see Rosalyn Clark and her two boys."

"Ah shit. We are giving the notification?"

"Do you know anyone else who should do it? We were there when he died."

He nodded. "No, we are the best for the job. Do you think she knows anything about what he was working on or what he was close to?"

"For her own good," I stated, "I hope not. And If I know Clark, he did not tell her a thing."

"How long have they been divorced?"

I thought a moment. "At least ten years. I know he asked me about divorce when he was going through it so it was after mine, but other than that, the years flow together."

"Didn't they reconcile for a while?"

"Yeah, got another kid out of it." My voice dropped. "Another kid without a dad."

●　　　●　　　●　　　●　　　●

Jamal sat with his mother. "Mom, what was Dad doing that night?"

Andrea's eyes rose. She had been drinking some wine while she sat with her son, and her tone probably depicted it more than she would have preferred. "Jamal, don't you worry about that. Your father is gone. He was a great man that gave everything."

"I know, Mama, but I can't let this go."

There was a knock at the door. Jamal rose and walked to the door and pulled it open without checking through the peephole to see who was outside. "Hey, T, what's going on?"

"Nothing much," answered his large friend. "I just hadn't seen your mom since all this happened with Jess, and now your father. Thought I would stop by and at least say hello."

"Who's at the door, Jamal?" Andrea Jackson's voice had a note of happiness at having a visitor. As she turned the corner, her lips turned directly upward. "Why, Tyrone Nielson, how long has it been? She reached out her arms to embrace her son's longtime friend, which he returned. "It has been too long, son. Malcolm said he kept seeing you on the River Court but since you don't live with your mom all the time anymore, I don't see you as often. You know, Malcolm never said whether you were going to try to make another run at college?"

"It has been too long, Mrs. J." He paused and his voice choked a bit. "I am sorry to hear about your husband. I know all the boys on the court will miss him, but not like I will. As for college, I don't know but I am going to try."

She placed her hand on his shoulder as they separated. "I know, Tyrone. I know." Her voice trailed off and she slowly moved back into the living room. She found her chair with the footrest up and she gingerly sat down and turned her head away from the boys, hiding the tears that had begun to form. Both Tiny and Jamal saw it but knew not to ask or even bring it up to make the pain even worse.

Jamal motioned with his head for Tiny to follow him. They both took seats on the old hide-a-bed couch that served as a bed when everyone was home so Jessica and Jamal did not have to share a room. The cushions were old and worn but molded well to almost everyone's body. Anyone who used it complimented its comfort, though the appearance left much to be desired.

There was an uncomfortable silence that filled the room for what seemed like minutes but probably only lasted seconds. Tiny tried to make his voice uplifting as he broke the reverence. "Mrs. J, you asked about football. I think I am going to try to get on in Coffeyville, Kansas. They have a community college and the people there have been talking to me. They say I have to show that I am clean and remain that way, but if I do, they can get me on with a scholarship. It is not Texas or Alabama, but at least it gets me back to playing. If all goes well, maybe my junior year I can transfer."

Again Andrea's eyes lit up. "Oh, that is great, Tyrone. Mr. Jackson would be so happy to hear that. He saw so many positive things in you and had goals as high for you as he had for Jamal."

Tiny appeared saddened by this exchange in a way beyond normal loss of a friend's father. Jamal believed in many ways his father served as Tiny's father, but only Tiny really knew how deep. Jamal turned toward his friend. "That is great, T. I don't know how far Coffeeville is from Lawrence, but maybe I can come down and catch some games. Who knows, Kansas is not a great football school, but maybe your junior year I can make sure the coach at KU sees you play."

T nodded appreciation but his mind seemed to be locked on the words Jamal's mother had said.

Jamal continued, "Mom, can I get T and me some lunch? I think we have a frozen pizza in there."

"Absolutely not," she replied firmly. "You are both now officially in training for college. I will make a healthy lunch including vegetables and protein. You both stay right here and I will have it out shortly."

"You don't have to do that, Mrs. J. I will…"

"Nonsense," she stated sharply then immediately softened. "Listen, boys, I want to do this. You boys are all I have left right now, and if I can find a few minutes to feel useful, then I will gladly do it."

Jamal and Tiny could both feel her words more than hear them. She needed anything to take her mind off her losses. If making a healthy lunch would do that, they both knew they would eat like they had not eaten in days. If they had to run to El Famous afterward, then so be it.

When his mom had left, Tiny looked back to his friend and his tone was much more serious. "J, do the police know anything about the murder?"

Jamal was caught a bit by the abrupt question, but he was happy to hear it because he wanted to speak to Tiny about what was going on. "Well, it is good you asked because I want you to quit your job."

"I can't quit," he replied immediately. "I need the job and Mr. Polino is helping me get back into college."

"That is just it," Jamal replied. "Mr. Polino does not care about your college other than how it can help him. He is going to get you into college and then claim that you owe him something. Maybe it will affect your college and maybe it will affect you as a pro if you are lucky enough to make it, but regardless, you need to do it on your own."

"You are wrong about Mr. Polino. He has helped me and my mother. He was there when I lost my scholarship. He is just a good person."

Jamal appeared agitated. "He is not a good person. Is he a good person when he has underage kids beaten up when they try to enter the club? Is he a good person when he extorts money from people?"

Tiny's voice showed defensiveness. "He has a business to run. Maybe it is not the best business to some, but it helps me and my family."

Jamal saw where this was going and softened a bit. "Listen, T, I am just worried about you. You have the talent to make it. My dad saw it and so do I. Don't let it fall short because of greed or taking the easy path."

Tiny was still defensive. "What do you know, Jamal? You are part of the best college basketball program in the country. You have a cakewalk to the NBA."

"And I have worked every day for everything I have, just like you did." He paused then added, "Before the job at the Red Carpet. Before the drugs." His voice had trailed off slightly on that one, still carrying a cold tone which Tiny heard but did not respond to. With no response, Jamal added, still with short tone and coming across as if asking the question proved he was better, "Are you clean now?"

Tiny did not answer. He stood, paced the floor a bit then turned back to his friend. "What do the police know? Something about the Red Carpet or my boss?"

"I don't know for sure. I know they think there is some relation there to some crime, but if it is related to my dad's murder, they are not sure."

Tiny appeared relieved. "Good. Let me know if I can help. I will keep my ears open for anything suspicious."

"Thanks, Tiny," Jamal replied. "I talked with the detectives about you being on the inside for them. We agreed it would be too dangerous, because if Polino suspected something, he could take action on you. But if you simply do it in passing, not looking for anything, maybe something will come up. I really want to find my dad's killer."

Tiny shook his head. "Maybe you should just let things go. What if they come after you or your mom? Nothing can bring your dad back, J."

"I know, but this is one I can't let go."

"Come on in, boys," echoed a voice from the kitchen. "Lunch is ready."

Both boys looked at each other and Jamal may have even rolled his eyes on what food they were about to eat. A frozen pizza sounded so good, but time with his mom and best friend might make up for the option he was about to be given. When he looked at Tiny, he was sure his friend felt the same.

•   •   •   •   •

I lifted my hand to knock on the door. I had given hundreds of notifications, but as I thought about it, this was only my second notification for a cop's wife, or ex-wife as the case may be. I knew the minute the door was opened and she saw my face, I would not have to say a thing. You never know about ex's. Sometimes an ex is even glad that their former spouse had been killed. What they don't realize is that attitude often takes them to the top of the suspect list. Most of the time, however, even though they were no longer married, the love held deep inside a marriage does not ever truly go away and instantly upon notification, tears fall. I believed that would be the case here. Clark and his wife did not divorce because of infidelity, abuse, or any other core reason. It was because of the job. No woman should ever marry a cop. It just isn't right.

Franky stood next to me as I raised my hand to knock. The door swung open before my hand hit the surface.

"It's Tom, isn't it?"

I was so caught off guard by the unexpected question that I gave my token, *buy time*, answer. "What are you talking about, Rosalyn?"

"I have been listening to the police scanner all morning. The murder victim behind Pippen's. That was Tom's regular meeting place. I even met him there before. It is him, isn't it?"

At this stage there was no point in trying to soften the blow. As I've often found, the wife of a police officer is as good a detective as the actual detective. "Yes, Ros. Tom was killed this morning."

She immediately exploded into tears and fell into my arms. As I had said before, I had known Tom Clark for much of my career. Like Franky and me, we were the old dogs of the precinct. Sure, there were others that had the tenure we did, but not in the same positions. We were not up for any promotions nor were we looking for any changes. We simply came to work five days a week for fifty-two weeks a year and tried to make the Chicago streets safer. Today, however, the streets won. Without speaking further, I held my arms in place around Rosalyn Clark as I maneuvered inside the house. I leaned down to her ears and whispered, "Are the boys home?"

Through her tears and in a high-pitched whisper she replied, "No, school till three-thirty."

"Good. Let's sit down to talk. I know the time is hard, but to wait could make finding who did this even more difficult. We need to ask some questions now."

Her voice became stronger. "I know. Please, ask anything. If I can help find his killer, I will do it." She placed her head back onto my shoulder. "But the boys. What are they going to do without their father?"

"They are going to do what all Clarks do. They will survive knowing their father gave everything in the line of duty." My words meant little to the frail woman who had seemingly lost everything. She clearly still loved Tom, but as I thought, that love did not replace the damage this job does.

"What happened to him, Tommy?" she asked.

"We don't know much yet. He was murdered by gunshot. Franky and I were to meet him this morning at seven. He called us yesterday and seemed agitated. He did not tell us why we needed to meet. I was hoping there was a chance he had spoken to you yesterday."

She smiled as she thought about her husband. I immediately could tell from her reaction that she had spoken to him. Her voice was soft and caring. "He came by yesterday afternoon. It was such a nice day for November, and he wanted to play some catch with the boys. They played for a couple hours. It was like the old days, when he had come back. When Marcus was born, things had been different for a while. He was home more and spent time with both boys. I actually thought we might make it. Then the big undercover job, and the fear he had for us. That is why he left the last time. It had nothing to do with our marriage. He was afraid for me and the boys."

Franky broke in as she finished. "Did he say anything about his job? Who he was working with? What was happening?"

Her smile on her memory faded and she looked toward my partner. "No, but he never did. He did not want me and the boys involved."

I understood. I did not think we would gain anything here anyway, so my number one job was to make sure she and the boys were all right. "Why don't you, Marcus, and Jamie all come to my house tonight? I will cook up some steaks and I might see if Jamal Jackson can come over with his mom. They are also going through a rough time and I know Jamie likes basketball. He may like meeting Kansas's star forward."

She smiled. "Thank you, Tommy. That would be nice. I can guarantee you that I don't want to be alone tonight."

"No problem," I replied.

She softened her voice and asked, "What loss did the Jackson's face? Is it like ours?"

"It is the same as yours," I said in return. "Jamal's father, Malcolm, was killed a few days ago."

Immediately her eyebrows lifted. "Malcolm? Malcolm Jackson?"

That caught our attention. "You know him?"

"Yesterday, when Tom was here, he came in and said he was going to leave soon. He got a call. I don't know from who but he reacted slightly. Nothing too much, but it caught him. I am sorry I did not say anything previously but it really was not out of the ordinary for him. But I remember him saying the name

Malcolm Jackson. He said it twice. I only recognized it when you said it because Malcolm is not that common a name."

Both Franky and I were all ears at this point. "About what time was the call?" I asked.

"I don't know. He left by six p.m. so sometime before that."

"Did he have more than one phone?" Franky added.

She nodded. "He always had multiple phones. This was the same phone I call him on, however. I recognized the ringtone. It was the theme from *Star Wars*."

I was puzzled by the phone being his personal phone, but maybe he used the same ringtone on multiple phones. Most cops who have multiple phones set different ringtones for a reason, to know who is calling without having to check each phone. Therefore, he used his personal phone in this case for a reason. *What was this call about?* I thought. Then turning back to Ros, I said, "Ros, this is important. Can you give me that phone number?"

"I can do one better. He left the phone here."

"What? Why?"

"My phone had died and he did not want me without a phone in case of an emergency with the boys."

Both Franky and I were actually excited. At a time that had to have been one of the worst in this woman's life, she was providing critical information that may help solve her husband's death, as well as shed some light on other cases. "Can I have—"

"I will get it for you," she interrupted.

Shortly thereafter she returned with one small black Samsung phone. It was an older phone but still a smartphone by definition. I pocketed the phone without looking at it. My primary goal right then was to ensure she was going to be okay for the time being. "Thank you, Ros. Are you sure you will be okay, or would you like to go get the boys and head over now? I can give you the key."

"No, I will wait for the boys. I need the time alone." She paused then continued, "And you are welcome, Tommy. Do you think this will help the case?"

"I guarantee it."

"Then the boys and I will be over tonight. Maybe you can tell me then who called him yesterday."

I smiled. "I look forward to having the boys over, but I don't think I will share any info with you until I know it is safe. Somebody already killed at least one person for this information."

"I knew that would be your answer." Her face dropped slightly and I could see a tear again forming. "Do you mind if I have some time alone now? I need to get the boys from school in a little while and I will need to tell them what happened. I don't want them hearing about it on TV or from their friends."

"Of course, on one condition. You call me if you need anything, and come by my place whenever you are ready."

Franky pulled a phone out of his pocket. "Do you still need a phone?"

"No, I picked up a new one this morning after the boys went to school. I had been calling Tom all day after I heard the report."

"What number were you calling?" I asked, as I knew she had his main phone.

"He gave me his burner phone number." She grabbed a sticky-note off the table. "708-555-3380."

Franky jotted down the number while I pulled her into my arms. Whispering, I said, "You will all make it through this. Your boys are strong."

She did not reply. We broke arms and I followed Franky out the door hearing the dead bolt lock after the door shut behind us.

"That is a pretty amazing woman," Franky said.

"She is," I replied. "And she gave us one really great clue."

8

MY FIRST CALL was to Jamal.

"Hello."

"Jamal, this is Detective O'Malley."

"Hello, Detective. What do you need?"

"Why don't you and your mom come to my place tonight? We can talk a bit more, and I have another friend coming over who is going through the same thing you guys are. Sometimes there is support in groups."

There was a short silence on the phone. "I don't know, Detective. I don't think Mom feels much like going out to visit anyone, and I have to say I probably agree."

"I understand," I replied. "But I think this will be good for everyone, plus we may get to share some information." I thought that would get him.

"What do you mean? Is this related to my dad's case?"

"It might be. That is why I need both you and your mom there."

"I will get her there. After Tiny leaves we will get cleaned up and head over. Text me your address."

"Will do," I replied. Before hanging up, one thing he said did catch my ear. "What is Tiny doing there?" I had no concerns for Tiny, other than he worked for one of the biggest mob bosses in Chicago history. However, I think that mob boss was after Tiny for his potential. Therefore, right now he was in no immediate danger, but why would Polino or Moretti send Tiny over?

"He stopped by to see me and my mom. Wanted to check in with everything going on."

It made sense, and I nodded. Then I smiled when I realized he couldn't see through the phone to see my nod. "Okay, tell him I said to be careful. The fact he was just associated with us through your friendship should not mean anything, but you never know. Tell him to keep his nose clean over there."

"Will do, Detective. I will see you later."

"Later, Jamal."

•　　•　　•　　•　　•

"What is the number?" Franky asked.

"It says 312 then a bunch of stars." I replied looking at the call log on Tom's phone.

"That is good news," Franky replied.

Franky was more knowledgeable about cell phone tracking than I was. "Why? What's it mean?"

"It means it is not a burner phone. It is most likely a business that simply has its name and number blocked."

"Can the IT boys find the missing numbers?"

Franky smiled. "I would bet this week's salary on it."

I turned my smile down a bit. "Won't you put more on it than that?"

"Just give me the phone."

I handed the phone to Franky who scanned down numerous different things I could not see. He used the phone as quickly as I had seen Jamal use his, which surprised me. He jotted down five or six numbers and then opened the GPS. "Look here."

"What?" I replied.

"Do you recognize that address?"

I looked at the address and immediately recognized it from last night. "I bet he wasn't there for a lap dance."

"Yep, everything keeps coming back to those damn clubs." Franky let me mull that over for a few minutes as he continued to peruse through the phone. He saw a handful of missed calls this morning but none of the numbers came up known on his phone so they were not in the address book. He set the phone on the seat of the car and asked, "What is our next move, Tommy?"

"Let's get the phone to IT and see what they can dig up. I want to know who called Tom to talk about Malcolm Jackson. Once we know that, we will need to pay that person a visit."

"Don't forget, you have dinner plans tonight."

I smiled at my longtime friend. "No, *we* have dinner plans tonight."

●　　●　　●　　●　　●

We arrived at the precinct and saw our flag was already at half-mast. Although we would not advertise why, because Tom was undercover, it still sent a nice message. I delivered the phone to IT. When they learned it was Tom's phone, it was pushed to the front of the line. I expected to have an answer as to the source of that number before I left for dinner. Carter was in, as he always was, and with the death of Tom, even Carter would not open any new wounds between us. He knew how long we worked together. Carter had come in after us and moved up and around us but that did not mean he did not respect us. He gave me the needed space, only nodding one time as he passed by and patted my back in the process.

Franky was sitting at his desk when his phone rang. "Sullivan. Yeah, he is up here. Already? Great, we will be right down."

He hung up the phone and stood up to look for me. "O'Malley," he shouted. "Where the hell are you?"

I poked my head around the corner of the vending machine. I did not speak, but he could tell what I was going to ask.

"Yep," Franky added. "They got the number. They want to talk to us about it in person. Said they tried your desk but you did not answer."

"Maybe I was doing something important," I replied smiling.

"You're right, getting a king-sized Kit Kat is probably more important than catching a cop killer."

I walked around the corner with two king-sized Kit Kats in hand and did not offer one to Franky. He fell in behind as we darted down two floors to IT.

Officer Calvin Wayne Call waved to us as we approached. I had known Calvin for about seven years. He had transferred here from a small town in southern Illinois. He wanted to be on a police beat but the bottom line was he was just too big. Forget the fact that he could not pass the physical. He could not fit in the cars. In southern Illinois he was fine. There were three cops in the town and they drove SUVs. Here, things were not his pace. His wife moved him up here so their children could be near her family. In his younger days he played a lot of golf.

Today, he simply watched it on TV. Exercise of champions. "Good to see you, CW," I said. "You have some info for us?"

His voice was deep, and I was not sure, but there may have been part of an Egg McMuffin on the corner of his lip. "Well, I found your number. It is one of three numbers from the same business establishment. That is why the end digits are blocked. This call came from the phone ending 637. Other numbers at the business end 636 and 638."

"Great," I said. "What's the name of the place? Let me guess, Rick's or Red Carpet?"

"No," he replied surprised. "Those are both good places, but this place is in downtown. Near the water tower. It's a great steak place. The Chop House."

I about fell over. The Chicago Chop House is one of the premiere restaurants in Chicago. The steaks there melt in your mouth. Who in the hell was Tom Clark talking to at the Chop House that was involved with Malcolm? "Are you sure? The Chicago Chop House?"

"One hundred percent," Calvin replied. "I can't be sure, but I would guess the 636 number is the main office or front desk and the other two are at different places in the restaurant. Anyone who calls any of the numbers will go directly to that phone or may be transferred to any of the other phones. However, if they called the second number, you can sometimes assume that the call was specific for wherever that phone was."

Franky looked toward me. "I doubt you have time to go there now. Do you want me to check it out on my own while you go get set up for your dinner?"

"No, let's go there later, after dinner. Fewer people and possibly the right people."

Franky continued. "You know what else? That restaurant is state-of-the-art. They have to have cameras in every room. I bet if we correlate the time of the call with the phone location in the restaurant, we can find out who made the call to Tom."

"Damn, Franky. If we could do that, we might see Tom's murderer on video. We would take a huge step forward in this case."

Franky looked back to Calvin who had been listening to the whole conversation. "You get me the camera footage, I will get you every minute of who was on that phone."

"We need a warrant for the video," I added. Franky pulled out his phone as I continued. "What are you doing?"

"Calling Carter," he said. "When it comes to a murdered detective, no judge in Chicago would refuse a warrant. I want it signed and in my hands by the time you are grilling your hamburgers."

•　　•　　•　　•　　•

There was knock at my door. All heads jumped up from the table as additional guests were not expected. Furthermore, those who knew me pretty well, Franky and to a slightly lesser extent Ros, also knew I never got visitors. To say Franky and I were a bit jumpy was probably an understatement. When I saw it was my boss, Sergeant Craig Carter, although my initial anxiety subsided, my concern grew.

"Hey, Sergeant, what brings you here?"

He handed me a folded paper. "Here is your warrant. I want to join you when we serve it."

"Seriously? I don't think it is necessary. We will gather the video and head back to the station. We won't see anything until Calvin gets ahold of it."

"I know," he replied flatly, then stopped when he noticed I had company. "Sorry to intrude."

"No, please come in. It will be good for you to meet these individuals and good for them to know you are involved."

We walked in together and Franky rose nodding to the sergeant as we approached. The others remained seated with the large plate of burgers and grilled chicken now down to only a few remaining pieces. "Rosalyn Clark, this is Sergeant Craig Carter, my boss and key individual over your ex-husband's murder. Andrea Jackson, same thing, plus he is overseeing your daughter's disappearance. He came here tonight to let me know he was personally joining us to serve the warrant for the video of Tom's call that night."

Ros stood and walked over to him. She hugged him deeply without words. When she pushed away, she said, "I have met you several times but only in passing. Tom spoke very highly of you, as least as highly as anyone would of a sergeant. I know he did not report directly to you being in Vice, but I am glad to know you are helping with the investigation."

For the first time in my life, I saw Sergeant Craig Carter speechless and choked up. He nodded appropriately before Ros continued. "My two sons are

Jamie, the boy at the end, and the little one is Marcus." The boys waved and again Carter just nodded.

Andrea and Jamal Jackson both also stood and walked over with outstretched hands. Andrea fought through tears and a broken voice. "Sergeant Carter, it opens my heart to know my husband's case is important enough for you to be involved. Detective O'Malley has been doing a great job along with Detective Sullivan, but if you can provide any assistance, we would forever be in your debt."

Jamal then added. "We know nothing is going to bring my father back, but having some peace that the person responsible can't do this to any other family does hold great value to us. And if we can find my sister, then the gratitude we would feel toward you would be unmatched."

Sergeant Carter had heard all the words and felt the hugs and handshakes and only now was he beginning to compose himself. He turned from directly facing the Jacksons to address the whole table. "Let me begin by saying I am very sorry for your losses. I cannot imagine the pain you are feeling, and for you to have all your hopes and prayers resting in the hands of others to bring about closure is so hard to comprehend. I can tell you that my team, which is much more than just Detectives Sullivan and O'Malley, will do everything in our power to bring about justice to those responsible. We lost more than one of our own when we lost Detective Clark and Malcolm Jackson. We lost a father, a leader, a counselor, and a friend, and I mean that about both of them."

There seemed to be a break after his words where silence engulfed the room. I knew Carter would be going home to an empty house, or more likely heading back to the station until I called to let him know we were headed to the Chop House. Therefore, my next comment was simple. "Franky, pull up a chair for the sergeant. Let's all eat tonight together. We will head to our next stop on full bellies."

We did just that. I believed the best I could have hoped for was to help Jamal, Andrea, Ros, and her two boys take their minds off their losses for a short period of the night. Once Sergeant Carter arrived and he started telling stories about Clark when he first started on the force—and Franky and I could go back even further—the smiles began to grow. Jamal and Andrea shared memories of Malcolm and Jessica and even their pain seemed to subside. It became a dinner of appreciation for who they had been, not of discussion of their loss or finding their killers. When Carter stood and said he was going to make a quick stop before heading to serve the warrant, I wondered what had changed that had become so important.

"No problem, Sergeant. We will be about ten minutes before leaving as I want to make sure everyone is set here. The Clarks are staying and the Jacksons need to be safely on their way. We can meet in twenty-five to thirty if that works?"

Carter shook his head. "Sounds good. I just want to take a few minutes to call my kids, something I should do a lot more than I have been doing."

•   •   •   •   •

As we drove up to the Chicago Chop House, the valet was ready and waiting. I am sure he does not get the chance to drive a 1974 brown Chevy Camaro every day, so I was pleased to give him the thrill. Right behind us, Sergeant Craig Carter pulled in. With his three-year-old Pontiac Bonneville quieting in the background as the engine shut down, he rose, tossed the keys to me as if I was going to park it for him, and proceeded inside. I quickly handed the keys to the valet and followed in behind. As I entered, I noticed the security camera placed in the open for all to see taping every patron that entered the restaurant. Check box number one in the investigation, I thought. We were greeted at the door by a young and shall we say beautiful woman who served as our host. Her face went straight to a frown when we asked to speak with the manager rather than requesting a table for dinner. Showing our badges at that point was a formality as the activity needed was already in motion.

The Chicago Chop House is a staple restaurant from the Chicago of old. Photos on the walls depict numerous famous people who have passed through its doors. They included but were not limited to: Bogart, Capone, Michael Jordan, President Bush, Sinatra, and just about anyone else who had some notoriety. The food was not good, it was great. I had eaten there a handful of times for special occasions. I never planned on less than $250 for two people, but I also never thought I overpaid for what I got. The restaurant is divided up into many sections and many levels. As we walked in, I noticed the phone by the host's desk and asked if I could use it. When I picked up the receiver, the number was written on the inside of the handle. The last three digits were 638. I remembered what Officer Calvin Call had told me in IT. The main number ended 636, the call came from 637, and another number at the restaurant was 638. Check box number two.

I hung up the phone when a tall and professionally dressed man and woman appeared in the host area. They introduced themselves as Keith Kaplan, Chop House General Manager, and Tammi Julia Hutchin, Assistant Manager, and all I can say is Tammi Julia Hutchin was gorgeous.

Sergeant Carter took the lead holding the warrant out for both to see. "We have a warrant to obtain any video surveillance you have from the times listed at the bottom. It is critical we obtain the footage as soon as possible as a murder has occurred and the deceased spoke to someone at this restaurant from the phone number ending 637 prior to his death. The only information we will take from that video will be related to this murder investigation, as the warrant defines. Is there someone who can help us with this?"

Mr. Kaplan took the lead. "Absolutely, Sergeant Carter. Let me run this by our attorney who happens to be dining with us tonight just to be certain we are handling it correctly. Assuming all goes as planned, TJ here will be glad to get you all the video you require. She is our resident expert on our security system so the timing is very good that she is here."

Ms. Hutchin nodded. The delay with the attorney would be a slight annoyance we did not actually have to allow, but in this case it sounded like they were going to be very accommodating and simply wanted to cover their bases. I nodded to Carter who exchanged the glance saying we would let this play out for a short while. Within five minutes, the attorney, a Mr. Andrew Carpenter, arrived. He demanded assurances that we would restrict our search and seizure to the limits of the video and that anything found on the video had to be related to our case. Once everyone was satisfied, Ms. TJ Hutchin escorted us to the back offices. Franky said he was going to scout around the bar area and talk to the bartenders while Sergeant Carter and I stayed with the video.

"Mrs. Hutchin, can you tell me which phone extension you have here that ends 637?" I asked.

"Please, it's *Ms.* Hutchin, but everyone calls me TJ, or worst case, Tammi. I believe 637 is the downstairs bar phone. Is that where the call came from?"

"Yes, it came from that extension," I answered, also subconsciously pleased that she said it was Ms. Hutchin—like I had a chance.

She made a face that told of disappointment. "That is too bad. We try to keep people off the hostess phone, though on occasion if that is what is available, we do allow its use. We typically have patrons use the bar phone if they don't have a cell or their cell is dead. It happens a lot when people don't want to drive home after sitting in our bar after dinner. There are a lot more calls from down there, so it could have been anyone."

"Do you have a camera at the bar?" asked Carter.

She smiled. "Sergeant, we have one of the most sophisticated camera systems found in any restaurant in the Chicago area. There are only about four corners of this building not under constant surveillance, and you have to walk through multiple cameras to get to those corners. Whoever made the call, we will have them on tape for you."

Both Carter and I smiled in return.

She walked through the main office and into a back room that consisted of one monitor larger than any TV in my house, or any cop's house, with about six other monitors along the sides. Video was constantly streaming and on one of the smaller screens, I saw Franky at the bar, most likely the same bar where the call was made. He had a phone from behind the bar in his hand and was smiling. "Your picture clarity is incredible. It is much lighter on the video than in the room."

"Yes, the cameras we use actually add light by drawing in any light from the area."

I looked briefly at Carter then back to TJ. "How long until you can get us the files?"

She pulled out a memory stick and placed it in the side of what appeared to be the largest DVR I had ever seen. "All I have to do is plug in the time range and specify which cameras and hit "copy files."

"The video files are large so maybe two hours to copy them. You will need someone to spend much more time going through them all. What time range do you want?"

I thought a moment then answered. "Two hours before, through the entire time frame, and include two hours after." Carter shook his head in agreement and pulled out his cell phone as he did so.

After punching in a number without actually speaking to me, I heard him say through his phone, "Officer Call, it's me, Sergeant Carter in Homicide. I need you to meet me at the station in two hours." He paused as I assumed Officer Calvin Wayne Call on the other end of the phone was protesting that it would be past eleven p.m. at night if he were to do that. Carter then continued, "I don't give a rat's ass what time it will be, goddamnit. You get your ass to the station and plan on deciphering some video. I want a full report on my desk by seven a.m. for

Detectives Sullivan's, O'Malley's, and my review. I will give you more information when I see you in two hours."

"CW pleased to be coming in tonight?" I asked sarcastically.

"He was happy to," Carter replied, causing a small smile to curve on TJ's lips as well.

Ms. Hutchin continued with her work and within five minutes she said, "They are all downloading. I included our camera on the street that shoots both directions so you might be able to see if they got in a car or cab as well. It will just be a matter of time now. Can I ask you both to join me at the bar and I will get you a few appetizers while you wait?"

Although Carter was going to say no, the subconscious which Ms. Hutchin had tapped into previously took over and I answered first. "That sounds very nice, TJ. We should gather up Franky and grab a table for four."

Carter shot a glare at me which I ignored and I folded my arm out to her to walk her back through the office to the restaurant floor. Mr. Smooth, I thought. Carter held his glare with each step.

"Hey, Franky, Ms. Hutchin has the video downloading. It will be awhile to complete the download if you want to grab a table with us."

"Sounds good," he replied. As we walked to the table TJ had the waiter clear for us, he continued, "The bartender is Mark Selbee. He worked a double yesterday and remembers several people using the phone. He said there were several businessmen he called 'in no condition to drive,' a black woman who was polite but quiet, and a few younger women and men. He believed all were calling for cabs but he did not listen to the calls so he can't be sure."

"It doesn't sound like mob bosses or people discussing possible hits."

Franky nodded agreement. "That is just what I was thinking. To his credit, however, he said there may have been others. Those were just the ones who asked him to use the phone. He worked with another bartender for the busiest part of the night."

"Did you get the name of the other bartender?"

"Yes, it is in my notes. He won't be in for several days. He is off on vacation."

As we moved toward our seats I whispered, "That doesn't sound good. Vacation? Right now? Pretty suspicious to me."

"You think the bartender could be in on it?" he whispered back.

I nodded. "I don't think anything yet, but I also know we can get his number without a problem. Hopefully the video will tell us what we need to know and we don't need to worry about it." We noticed the others were looking at us leaning close and whispering, and we quickly moved to join the group at the table.

Franky picked up the water glass that had been placed before him. I sat next to TJ with Carter on my other side and Franky across from me. Franky asked, "What is the timing to get the video looked at by IT?"

I smiled broadly and turned to Carter to see if he was going to answer. When he just smirked, I took the lead. "It seems Sergeant Carter believes Officer Call should come in tonight and go through all the tapes for a seven a.m. briefing with all of us."

Franky smiled. "I'll bet he loved that idea."

I was about to comment but TJ cut me off. "Speaking from someone who only heard one side of the conversation, I believe it is safe to say he wished he was not in IT tonight."

At that point a plate of calamari and steak bites was dropped on our table. Although three of us had already had a great dinner, and by great I mean burgers slapped on plates, oven-baked straight-from-the-freezer French fries, and premade store-bought dinner rolls, we were not about to pass up the food at Chop House. TJ had already said that the food and drinks were on her while we waited, so to leave it uneaten would simply be rude. Part of me wished E.Z. Zimmerman was with me tonight as this type of restaurant seemed more like his cup of tea compared to Flapjaws, but truth be told, he'd probably fit in either place.

We finished our appetizers and had a very polite conversation. After about an hour, TJ excused herself and in very short order arrived back holding a memory stick. "Well, gentlemen, here you are. One memory stick filled with five hours of video from about sixteen different cameras. Tell Officer Call to have fun tonight. The way the system records them is not by time, but by camera number, so he will have to open every file and scan through it to find the right time on each camera."

Carter shook his head. "Sounds perfect." Turning to face Ms. Hutchin, he said, "Thank you, ma'am, for all your support in this. And please thank Mr. Kaplan as well."

"I will, Sergeant, and no problem. I hope what we provided helps."

She bid Franky farewell also and then stopped with me. "I enjoyed the brief food and conversation. Thank you for your generosity," I said.

"Nonsense," she replied. "It was my pleasure, and I enjoyed the company as well."

Boom, I thought, she was flirting. "Well, here is my card. If you see or hear anything you think is worth discussion, please don't hesitate to call."

She smiled. "I hoped I would end up with your card. I will call you if I think of anything."

We shook hands and then departed. Franky had ridden with me so once the valet returned with my car, we were off. Sergeant Carter was heading back to the station to meet Calvin Call and start the tape inspection. My gut told me Calvin would not be the only person working through the night. Carter would be no help with the video, but losing a cop hit us all hard. The further up the food chain you were, the more responsibility you felt. Carter wanted the guy who killed Tom, and he believed this video was going to get him that person.

As we drove, Franky sat silent smiling. After several minutes, I even heard him breathe heavy as if he was holding in a laugh. I pulled to the curb. "All right. Let's have it. What has got you so pent up you can't even speak?"

He burst out as if he had been holding in the most difficult information and was thrilled to be able to let it out. "You were pathetic. Laughing at everything she said. Telling those stupid stories. Do you even know how to date anymore, or flirt, or appear interested?"

"No!" I answered, peeling out from my spot without another word.

•   •   •   •   •

Seven a.m. came earlier than normal. It was now Thursday and moving into the weekend usually meant cases went a little dead. A detective's job does not stop on the weekends, but what he accomplishes on Saturday and Sunday usually slows down. I wanted to find this person today. I did not want Friday to come without a solid lead. I wanted to see the video, recognize who I thought it was, go to the Red Carpet, and pick up his sorry ass. I may only be able to hold him, but even that would give me pleasure until I could build an ironclad case. The first thing I needed was to see him on the video on the phone. Whether it was Polino or Moretti, one of them must have made the call. I was sure of it.

I walked into the station and saw Franky eating what was at least his second donut. I knew it was at least two because I am one of the greatest detectives Chicago has ever seen. Also, he had chocolate frosting on the corner of his lips and he was eating a sugar twist. I grabbed a donut of my own and was about to ask about the status of the video when he preempted my question.

"He is not done yet, but he says he is close. Says he has video at the time of the call and outside the restaurant that will be of value to us. Says about fifteen minutes more and that was ten minutes ago."

"Great, who brought the..."

"Carter went out and brought back the donuts. I think he was here the whole night."

Suddenly, I heard my sergeant's voice hollering throughout the mostly empty desk area. "Goddamnit! Where is that idiot with the video? I might as well have reviewed them all myself if it was going to take this long."

The yelling continued but the words became less distinct as he turned away from our direction. Franky continued in a softer tone, "And I think he is a bit moody so I hope the video has what we need."

Officer Call appeared around the corner carrying a different memory stick and instantly sported a smile when he saw us, or should I say, when he saw the box of donuts. Being well into three hundred pounds, there was rarely a donut box he left unvisited. He came by our desk, recovered three donuts holding them pinched between his arm and his side, and took a bite of one before talking. In a muffled, food-filled voice, he said, "Here is your tape. I labeled them all. They are called Bar 1, Bar 2, and Street. That is all you will need to see who made the call and who else was involved after the call was made." He paused, took another bite, and then continued with parts of donut falling onto Sullivan's desk as he talked. "The girl who made the call appeared to be ready to leave, then the bartender went back and told her she had another call. It does not appear she spoke. She took the call, then looked around and headed out immediately. She was followed. She only got a short way down the street before she was picked up."

I looked to Franky and then back to Officer Call. "A girl made the call?"

Franky added, "Picked up? By who?"

The same guy who made the second call. He made it from the bar right next to her. You can see it on the video. He had been tailing her. When she made the call, he waited for her to finish then called the restaurant back from the corner of the bar. He said something which appeared to scare the crap out of the girl and make her leave. When she did, he tailed her and arranged a grab and go."

Without another word, Franky and I hurried into Sergeant Carter's office to view the tape, leaving Call at the desk guarding the donuts. It was exactly as Call had described it. We watched the tape and immediately two things became very clear.

"Can you fucking believe that?" asked Franky when he saw the man who made the call back at the bar.

I did not speak as I was frozen with what I saw. Carter was not as limited in his speech.

"What! What the fuck do you see, Sullivan?"

"We just met that guy. That's Steve Jewel. He is the plant manager at the uniform plant where Malcolm Jackson worked. He's the jackass who called Malcolm for a security issue the night he was killed. Tommy interviewed him. He was a real slimeball."

"Is that right, O'Malley?" Carter asked.

Again I did not answer. I was glued to the screen watching the woman get forced into the car.

"But who is the girl?" Sullivan asked. "Do you think she is some hooker with info on the murders?"

I did not answer, resulting in total silence in the room. Carter grabbed my shoulder. "Goddamnit O'Malley, what is it?"

I turned to them. My voice was soft and shallow. "I know the girl."

Franky smiled. "Really? Great. Who is she? Is she linked to Clark?"

"She is Malcolm Jackson's missing daughter." I paused. "That was Jessica Jackson."

9 STEVE JEWEL LIVED in Tinley Park which was a solid forty-minute drive from downtown. We were not sure what to expect with Jewel's house as neither of us knew much about this area. To us, this might as well have been Indiana. To say Mrs. Jewel, Deborah as we learned later, was not what we expected would be an understatement. It was before noon and she was well into her third martini. The house they lived in was very nice, but upon entering and being escorted into the main living room, it was clear she lived there alone most of the time. I did not know the salary of a general manager of a uniform plant, but it was clearly more than a twenty-year detective's. This house had to go for at least a cool million and most likely several hundred thousand more.

Debbie, as she asked us to call her, was very beautiful but it appeared she had not worked in a long, long time. Perhaps at one point she was a businesswoman, but now the money her husband made more than created the life she wanted. She had to be well into her fifties, but she looked to be twenty-five. Her nicotine-stained fingertips spoke of a long life of cigarettes, but the only way to describe this marriage from appearances was that Mr. Steve Jewel married up.

Steve Jewel was not there, but Debbie was and the martinis she was sucking down like candy made the visit most enlightening. To use her words, she had not seen her "worthless husband" in two nights. "The fucker" had not come home nor did she hope he did tonight. In her words, "I hope he's in somebody's trunk right now." He very well could be in somebody's trunk. I would have asked her to call if she saw him, but there was no way she would. I was not even sure she would remember our visit.

I called Carter when Franky and I made it back to our car, and he sent a team to keep an eye on the place. Franky had already started a background on Jewel after our first visit, and now Carter got it pushed to the forefront. The video of the car that picked up Jessica Jackson was not the same car we had seen Jewel drive at the laundry. We checked the plates on the video car, but they were stolen. Finding a late model Ford Taurus in Chicago probably was not going to happen. We did peek through Jewel's garage before we left and saw nothing but a red Corvette convertible. We guessed that was Debbie's. Therefore, until we found Jewel, our leads were stalled.

As we hopped back on Highway 294, Franky and I were both at a loss as to the next best step. Breaking the silence, he asked, "Are you going to tell Jamal and Andrea?"

"I don't know," I replied. "If I tell them, their hope level goes up two thousand percent, but for all we know, she was alive yesterday but could be dead now."

"I say don't tell them," added Franky. "Let's find her, or not find her. Don't give them new hope only to crush it later."

I was not sure how I felt. I know that if it was my daughter, I would want to know. I was not playing God, but close enough so that I was uncomfortable with the situation. I did not want to ever mess with being God.

Franky then continued, "We need to find Jewel. Everything still points to those strip clubs and that slimeball." He paused as if in deeper thought, then added, "I have another question that needs to be answered. Jessica has been alive since her disappearance. Yes, she appeared out of it on that video, but not so much that she should not have called home. Why has she not contacted her mother?"

It was now my turn to think for a minute. "A better question is, what brought her out now? She has been completely hidden for weeks. What made her reach out to a cop and call now?"

"Her father's murder." We both said it at the same time.

I pulled the car over right on the side of the tollway and looked toward Franky. "Let's say Jessica is involved in something bad, prostitution or drugs or both. She gets in over her head and gets caught. She somehow survives but does not escape. She gets sucked in even deeper or does something that forces her to feel like she can't get out. Then something happens. Malcolm sees something or learns something or whatever. He is always going to the strip clubs. There is nobody more entwined in the underground of old Cabrini Green Chicago. He learns that Jessica is alive."

Franky stared back at me. "Right. He can't tell his wife. He can't tell his son. He has to prove it. He has to come up with something to bring the police into it."

I looked at Franky. "Enter Steve Jewel, his boss and known slimeball. Malcolm went to Jewel and asked him about it or asked him for help. He probably looked up to Jewel. The big general manager. Money. Power. Whatever. Andrea did not bat an eye when Malcolm told her he was going to the plant to help Jewel. He trusted the man."

"There is no accounting for taste, I guess," added Franky.

I nodded but continued with my thought. "But what Malcolm didn't know is that slimeball Jewel owed money to who he was asking about. Slimeball sees a way out. He tells, no he *warns,* this guy that Malcolm saw something. He uses that to either get money or get his debt reduced. The result..."

"They have him removed," he completed for me.

I nodded. "Yep, Malcolm is a problem so they devise a way to get him out and then take him out."

Before he replied, I could see in his eyes he was buying it. "But what happened to Jewel?"

"These guys don't need Jewel. Jewel is a loose end. If he is not dead already, he is in hiding to avoid it."

"Nope," Franky replied, now shaking his head. "Too far. There is nothing linking them. Nothing making them do anything. You may be on the right path, but we are missing something. What is Jessica's role? She is in this. She called Tom to get out. After that call, he called you and questioned Malcolm's reputation. What did she say to implicate her father?"

"*Crap!*" I yelled, slamming my hand down. "I hate this."

"You and me both, partner. You and me both."

I put the car back in gear and proceeded down the tollway. As I passed the fly-through lane, suddenly I remembered. "The f'ing tollway. We have to check out Jewel's story. Maybe that night he went somewhere else. Jewel is the key."

"I already pulled his records. They should be on my computer now. Let's go back to the station. I will get those records and we will track his phone also. Maybe his phone is still active and we can find out where he is. Maybe we find him, and we find Jessica."

"Do you see what is happening?"

Franky looked puzzled. "What do you mean?" he asked.

"That damned Polino and Moretti. They have layers. Layers of people doing their dirty work. They are untouchable."

"Nobody is untouchable, Tommy. You just need to know where to touch them."

"I don't think so, Franky. We are going to get dirty on this one. I can't stop, but if you need to back away, you should do that. These guys play for keeps and they are protected. The worst part is they know it."

"Hey, Tommy, I am just trying to find out who is killing hookers. Your case is not my priority."

I reached over as I was driving and put my hand on his shoulder. It was not a big move and I said nothing, but he understood. As a homicide detective, you always run the risk of being scared. I had been fortunate and rarely ever felt that fear. This time, however, everything in me told me to get away. This one was bigger than me. It was bigger than Sergeant Carter. It was bigger than the father of a high-profile basketball player, possibly an overall number one pick. That was what everyone seemed to forget. Come the NBA draft, nothing got more publicity than who would be number one. These people did not care. They were not trying to blackmail or use Jamal. They simply killed his father and let everyone know they did it. They executed him as a message to anyone else involved as well as the police. They raised a giant middle finger directly at me and the entire Chicago Police Department. Yep, I was scared. It did not happen often, but it was happening now.

Franky interrupted my thoughts. "Let's find where Jewel went. Let's visit the Red Carpet and Rick's tonight. Everything centers on those places. Everything centers on Jessica. Let's follow her trail. She left some bread crumbs."

I pressed the gas and moved back into the lane. "Where does this one stop, Franky?"

"Who cares?" he replied.

We did not speak for the rest of the drive.

•   •   •   •   •

Franky moved over to my desk with a piece of paper hanging from his fingertips.

"What?" I asked.

"Guess who was about to lose his house?"

"I don't know, Bo Jackson?"

"No. Does a general manager of an industrial uniform plant ring any bells?"

"Jewel?" I answered, some excitement building in my voice.

"Yep. And guess who had almost $2,000 in charges at the Red Carpet and Rick's over the past two months?"

"Jewel," I said again, this time not as a question.

"Yep." Franky's voice became lower. "You know, if he was charging that much, how much was he using cash for or getting comp'd for later. How deep was he into them for?"

"He was their lackey."

"That is what I think. He got into them for some money. He is under pressure from his wife because she won't be able to live in the way she is accustomed. He knows he will never land anyone as hot as her again. His world is caving in around him." Franky was speaking with confidence, not his typical "drawing a theory" voice.

I nodded agreement and added, "Then go with our idea that Malcolm comes to him with something harmful to them. Instead of helping Malcolm, he sees it as a way out and goes to tell them. To win their confidence."

Franky smiled shaking his head. "They say, 'Hey Steve, partner, we can make all this go away if you can just get Malcolm Jackson alone somewhere.'"

I continue, "He sets up the bogus security issue. Malcolm shows and the rest is history. The loose ends are tied."

"Except for the new loose end of Steve Jewel," added Franky. "What did his toll pass say?"

Franky could see I had forgotten what I had found out in light of this discussion and instantly the smile turned back on my face. "The slimeball did drive up here that night, and he did not lie about the time. It matches almost to the minute of the alleged security issue. However, his return time is just shy of four hours later."

"What did he do in all that time?" Franky asked.

"And where did he go and was Malcolm with him?" I added.

Franky shook his head. "So Jewel is now this nasty loose end just hanging out there. He is most likely clueless that these guys don't actually value him."

"Yeah, and how hard is it to make something you don't value disappear?"

Franky raised his finger. "But what is the deal with Jessica and the Chop House and Clark? How does that all play into it?"

I stared at Franky without an answer, and then, like a light, I got it. "*Malcolm.* It all comes back to Malcolm. Something went wrong. He set some chain of events in motion that complicated things. He saw something. Something that affected him, Jessica, the strip clubs, and Clark."

We looked at each other in silence.

•　　•　　•　　•　　•

"Jamal, where are you going so late?" Andrea Jackson was not pleased to be awakened by her son slipping out when it was past eleven p.m.

"I told Tiny I would come visit him at work before he got off. Just go back to sleep, Mom. I will be home later."

"You are not going to that strip club."

"Mom, I am not allowed in. I will just hang out with Tiny at the door. The owner said it was fine as long as I did not go in."

She looked at her son questioningly. His smile always made her melt. "If you end up in jail, so help me I will not come to bail you out. You can sit there all night thinking about the girls on those poles."

Jamal walked over and kissed her cheeks. "No girls on poles, Mom, and no jail."

She smiled at the soft kiss. "Very well, but you be home before one or you will wish you were in jail." She paused and then a sadness came over her as she spoke, "Remember, your father's funeral is tomorrow morning, please be up early for me?"

"Sounds good, Mama."

Jamal drove the family car toward the old Green and the two strip clubs. Although Tiny had asked him to stop by, his goal that night was actually to make his way into the clubs and see if he could learn anything. He was going to start by asking for another interview and job. There was no reason O'Malley had to screw this up for him. He could be the guy on the inside and with Tiny on the inside at the other club, they could have eyes in both places. He could pretend to be onboard with Polino or Moretti and then when the case was closed, he could be gone. He would not owe those guys anything. If they were in jail, what the hell could they do to him? His reasoning was solid but even he did not believe it completely. He also did not care.

Tiny had told him he would be working at Rick's again that night so Jamal headed directly for the Red Carpet. He was certain that Mr. Polino would take him on. When he saw the red neon glow in the sky, he knew he was getting close and his heart started to beat more rapidly.

"Are you sure this is smart?" he said out loud, though nobody was in the car to hear.

Jamal parked, got out, locked his father's car, and then proceeded toward the door. There was a large man guarding the door. He was easily 250 pounds, Hispanic, with a shaved head and sunglasses.

"What are you doing here, boy? Twenty-one and over." His voice was deep and hard and the English was perfect, although it had a Latino accent.

"I would like to meet with Mr. Polino if he is in. I spoke to him previously about a job and I wanted to follow-up. I am friends with Tiny. My name is Jamal. I am certain he will know me."

Big Latino sized him up a bit without speaking. Jamal was not anywhere near the size of this man or Tiny for that matter, but he still was a blue chip college basketball player. He worked out daily including lifting for both mass and tone. He was in great physical shape and could outrun most anyone if needed. Big Latino may not have been overly impressed with his total size, but he definitely saw the inherent muscular tone. He pulled a radio from his belt and said a few words into it. Jamal could not tell if he was speaking Spanish or just muffled English. Regardless, with the radio now being held to Big Latino's ear, he began to nod.

Big Latino put the radio back down to his belt. "Come with me, boy. Mr. Polino will see you tonight but he is currently busy. You need to wait in our chicken coop."

"Chicken coop?" Jamal replied questionably.

"The room I take minors to when they need to understand why we have rules."

Jamal nodded but his subconscious wondered if he was being escorted to this room to be taught to understand the same thing. He was banking on being seen as an investment, and therefore worth being protected. He hoped he was right.

Big Latino pointed to a chair. "Sit."

Jamal sat and when Big Latino left the room without another word, he shook his head with a long sigh, relief showing clearly on his face. *What have I gotten myself into?* he thought.

At least forty-five minutes passed without another person entering the room. Jamal could hear the music playing, the deep beat of the stripper songs pounding through the walls, and the occasional sound of someone being questioned at the door by the Big Latino's deep bellowing voice. Other than the sounds, he was in complete solitude in the room. His mind wandered to the unknown, and when the mind does that, it usually goes to the worst places first. He wondered if he would ever see another human or if he was going to be forgotten and left for dead. What would his mother think? On that thought he actually talked out loud to himself. "Oh shit, if this goes much later, I will not only not have time to see Tiny, but I may not be home by one a.m. The last thing I want to do is worry my mom right now."

As if someone was listening, the lock popped and the door swung open. Through the door walked Joey Polino and the big gorilla from Rick's. "Hello again, Jamal. After your friends were here I assumed our business together was done, unless you have other reasons for wanting to come to work for me?"

The last line caught him. "Other reasons?"

The big gorilla was cracking his knuckles to the side but pretending not to be doing it to intimidate. He was acting like they hurt and this was his way of stretching them to relieve the pain. Polino moved closer and took a seat in the open chair. "Don't play dumb with me, Jamal. Two detectives were here. You are here. Your father was recently murdered. The detectives believe my business is involved. They can't prove anything or get a warrant so they send you in to work." He paused, glanced to the big gorilla who continued cracking his knuckles, and then finished. "Undercover work, so to speak."

"No, Mr. Polino, I am not trying to do anything like that. Tiny works for you and speaks very highly of you. With my NCAA scholarship, I can't work or I lose the money. I need to help my mom right now while I am back, but I have to be paid in cash. Tiny said you might be able to do that."

Polino's eyebrows raised. The response was one Jamal had planned since the beginning, but it appeared Polino did not expect to have such a viable reason for Jamal's request. Just like when solving a crime, Jamal needed a realistic motive to need a job. He hoped he had found it. Further, it was actually true. With his father's death, his mother's source of income was gone.

"Jamal, if I do this, both of us would get in trouble if the NCAA finds out.

You could lose your scholarship." Translation for Polino: *"I have the blackmail material I need to keep you under my control throughout your college. We will own Kansas basketball."*

Jamal did not smile nor turn his eyes from Polino. "I know the risks, but my mom needs help."

Polino stared hard into his eyes and then swung his head back to the gorilla. "Marco, take Jamal here to the back and show him around. Have him work in the kitchen tonight and then tomorrow we will prep him for front door with Ricardo."

Hesitantly Jamal spoke up. "If it is okay, sir, I would like to start tomorrow. I did not tell my mother I would be out late tonight and with the recent death of my father, she will worry greatly."

Joey Polino smiled. "Yes, we can't have a worried mother now, can we? Very well, be here tomorrow at four-thirty p.m. We don't get busy until after ten so that will give you plenty of time to get oriented. Ask for Marco, and maybe I will have Tiny work first shift with you."

"Very well, and thank you," Jamal replied starting to stand and walk to the door. Polino nodded to the gorilla.

Marco placed the back of his hand against Jamal's chest blocking his passage. Polino stepped up behind him and whispered in Jamal's ear, "I don't want to start this arrangement off on the wrong foot, but I need you to understand one thing. If I even think you are fucking with me, you and your mother will learn how much I do not appreciate that." Marco took his free hand and pinched his thumb and four fingers to the front and back of his neck near his throat. The pain was intense and sent Jamal to his knees in seconds. Polino continued, "That nerve goes directly to your spine and brain. By applying pressure directly to that spot, you can totally incapacitate a person. If the force is continued, the person will lose consciousness."

Marco released his hand and went back to cracking his knuckles. Jamal rested like a dog on all fours on the ground at Polino's feet. He pushed himself up and stared at the man. "I just need a job for a while. Then I will go back to college. I have to help my mom get back on her feet."

Neither replied. They left Jamal in the room stretching his neck in a rolling motion. The door was left slightly ajar. The teenage side of him wanted to take a look at the girls dancing, but the fear he was now feeling made him make a beeline for the door. The big Latino whom Jamal assumed was Ricardo was waiting for him with a big smile and an open door. "See you later, Jamal. I guess we will be working together after all."

His tone was not that of an employee excited to meet a new employee. It was sinister, as if there was some big plan Jamal was not part of, or maybe he was the main part of it, he just didn't know it.

•　　•　　•　　•　　•

Franky and I pulled up in the Camaro to the Red Carpet parking lot . It was about midnight on Thursday, and we opted to go there first and then Rick's for the "wee-hours-of-the-morning" crowd. Our only goal was to find out if anyone knew Stephen J. Jewel. We would not go in undercover. We would enter as patrons. That meant we would fulfill the drink minimum and see what happened. I was dressed in my normal jeans and long-sleeve shirt and Franky was, you guessed it, cowboy'd up. He was complete with a hat, Wrangler jeans, belt buckle, Western shirt, and bolo tie. His snakeskin boots were almost too much but I let it pass.

We were about to head in when Franky said, "Would you look at that?"

"Damn kid, what is he doing here?"

"Do you want to me to go grab him?" asked Franky.

"No," I replied. "I am sure they are watching him. If we show up, it will put suspicion on him. It looks like he's headed out."

"More suspicion," he added. "We can't go in now. It will look like we are working with him or up to something."

"Yep," I replied. "We need to head to Rick's tonight. We will check out this place tomorrow. Let's let the Jamal dust settle."

It doesn't look like Tiny is working the door here. He may be at Rick's. We might be able to at least get the lay of the land from him as we enter."

Franky was better than me at planning ahead. But I was better at the impact versus intent of our actions. Anything we did to bring Jamal or Tiny into the fold of this investigation put them at risk, regardless of our intentions. They were in deep enough and Jamal was digging himself even deeper. "No, if he is working, let's just walk in without additional comment. Maybe we can even suggest he let the manager know who we are so they build trust with him. I don't want the boys involved."

He understood. We watched Jamal start his car and head out. I feared he may be going to see Tiny at Rick's, but he went in the opposite direction so maybe this meant Tiny was off tonight. That would be the best case. I started the Camaro and headed out making a path directly to Rick's Cabaret.

Unfortunately, when we arrived, we did see Tiny standing right outside the door in his Rick's black button-up shirt and black slacks. They fit loosely on Tiny's big frame. He did make a powerful site, albeit you could easily see his young age in his face. The gorilla we met the last time we were here was not present at this time. I thought about him. He was big, strong, and confident. His face was weathered and mature, and that maturity was carried into his speech and actions. He did not scare me, but I also recognized his talents, and I do not think I scared him either.

We got out of the car and began walking toward Tiny. His eyes met ours, and he was not pleased to see us. Instead we saw apprehension.

"Detectives. I can't really help you with anything. Do you want me to get my boss?"

"No, Ty," I answered. "We are here as patrons tonight. Just want to have a few drinks and visit."

He nodded hesitantly and reached to open the door. "There is a twenty-dollar cover charge at the door. There is also a metal detector as we have a 'no firearms' policy. I don't know if that changes for police or not. Truth is, we don't have many police come through these doors."

I had not thought about the firearms policy. There was no chance I was going in without my gun so this area of discussion may require some additional conversations. Franky was obviously thinking the same.

"Hey Tiny, you need to tell your boss we are here. I don't want him thinking there is anything under the table or that you are protecting us or hiding us or anything."

"Will do, Detective O'Malley. I will call it in right now. I am sure they already see you on the monitor though."

We passed through the door and I heard Tiny calling in on his radio that the same two cops from before were back. I wondered who was there tonight that he would be talking to. Would Polino be there from the Red Carpet or just Moretti? I would bet money that one of them was there, even though it was so late.

We paid our cover charge and arrived at the security window where we were instructed to place any metal items in the dish. Right below the window was the sign forbidding firearms. Franky and I both removed our badges and placed them in the dish. "If you are not going to let us pass with our weapons, then you better go get your boss."

As if on cue, the door behind us opened and in walked the big gorilla. "Saw you at the Red Carpet. Thought you might be coming here when your mole left."

"Hey, I don't know anything about Jamal. Whatever he was doing there, he was on his own."

The big gorilla did not answer and only smiled his pearly white's right at me. "Going to be tough for you to get in with those firearms. Everything needs to be checked."

He was enjoying our exchange as he felt he held all the cards. "Unless you are here on legal business, in which case I assume you have a warrant?"

To his credit, the big gorilla was fairly smart, or I suppose he had just been through this a ton of times. I glanced at Franky who gave me a short nod. Before I could answer, the gorilla added, "We have several safes behind the counter where we can secure your valuables. I am sure your firearms fit that definition."

"I'll tell you what..." I paused and changed my tone. "You know, I don't even know your name."

"I am Marco. Marco Filini II."

I reacted immediately and quickly recovered, but I know he caught it. He was trained to catch it. Marco Filini was a well-known enforcer for hire. He had bounced around and had a rap sheet longer than the Cubs winless World Series streak. I had never met or seen him, but if rumors were true, he was truly dangerous. "Well, Marco, don't take this wrong, but we are not going to leave our firearms under your control. We will enter without them, but we will secure them in our vehicle."

He smiled and it was clear he saw my initial response, no matter how hard I tried to cover it. "Whatever you want to do, Detectives, just know you are not bringing them in these doors unless you are here with a warrant."

We returned to the car and Franky and I had a very quiet discussion about who we had just met. We both knew how big this guy was in the crime world and very few even knew what he looked like. If half the stories about him were true, he was one of the most dangerous men in Chicago history. If all of them were true, he was the deadliest. There is nobody he would not kill. Within moments we were passing by Tiny again exchanging only nods. As we passed through the door, Marco was standing by waiting for us to go through the metal detector.

"After you, Detectives," he stated.

We entered one at a time with neither of us setting off the dreaded beep. I glanced back through the detector to see Marco very pleased with us passing through, sans guns. I also saw Tiny staring back through the slightly opened door, his face showing no signs of smiling.

"That guy means to kill you someday, Tommy," stated Franky as we approached the bar.

"Yes, he does," I replied. "Let's hope he is not successful."

"Don't take this lightly. Guys like that don't forget. It may not be this case. It may in a different city or years from now, but that guy does not mess around with the noise. He simply does it."

I heard the seriousness in his tone this time. "I know, my friend. I pissed him off last time we met. I did not back down. I did not respect who he was. In his mind, I should have known who he was."

"Just watch out."

"I will," I replied, taking a seat at the bar.

The bartenders consisted of another big thug and two bartender/strippers who could mix drinks. Each drink cost fifteen dollars and it was encouraged to buy the bartender one to drink with you, the suggestion that you might end up in bed with one of them always on the horizon. Therefore, I chose the bar thug for my drinks so the bed option was off the table. Franky, however, took Star as his choice and was sixty dollars into the night after twenty minutes of service.

A few girls approached us offering table dances or VIP room action. That was the last thing I wanted knowing how the one-way mirror worked in Moretti's office. I thought for a minute that Franky was going to accept a dance offer from a very pretty young girl who could have easily passed for his daughter, but he refused. We knew the girls were most likely being sent to see what questions we were asking. Therefore, through mutual understanding, we did not ask any questions for a while. Not that we thought they would give up sending girls over. We just thought if we waited, we might get lucky and catch one disgruntled employee or someone not so tight to management. Usually the best-looking girls had the most freedom. The clubs needed them to bring in the clientele. I thought I would start there.

"Hey, Ashley, was it?"

Hot blonde stripper girl smiled and moved closer to me. "Absolutely Ashley is my name. Are you interested in a private dance?"

"Only from you," I replied, trying to sound sincere. "However, before you do that, can you sit down for a drink?"

"I would love to. Can you buy one for my friend?" She waved brunette hot stripper girl over. "This is Taffy. I am sure she would love a drink also."

"Oh, I would," she said as she arrived and took a seat on my leg.

I nodded approval and four drinks appeared before us, covering two strippers, Franky, and me. They immediately started talking about all the detailed things that could take place in the private rooms before Franky simply cut in holding up his phone. "We are looking for a friend of ours. His name is Stevie. We want to party with him. If we can find him, I will buy us all an hour in the VIP rooms with you girls. Have you seen him?"

They were torn between instant interest of the VIP visits being booked, which totaled more than $600, and the red flag of asking the whereabouts of someone. As he hoped, the $600 won out.

"I know Stevie," hot brunette, aka Taffy said.

Both Franky's and my eyes opened as I took a sip of my drink. "How do you know him?" I asked.

"He is one of my regulars. He was here an hour or so ago."

We looked at each other. Probable cause, I thought. "Is he still here?" I asked, but the words seemed to fade as I spoke them. I glanced toward Franky and it looked like he was swaying from side to side.

"Are you okay, sir?" Taffy asked.

•　　•　　•　　•　　•

Friday Morning

A sound of banging echoed through my head. I was confused on where I was or what I was doing. The banging occurred again and then the brightest light I had ever seen struck my face. I was sure I was staring directly into the sun. I squinted and raised my hand. I heard voices but I could not make them out. Again the banging. I heard some rustling off to the side of me and by my cramped neck, realized I was in my Camaro. I tried to open my eyes but it was as if some weights were holding them closed. Again the banging and the voices.

"Open your door, sir, and let me see your hands!" a voice now shouted.

The flashlight was so bright and my head ached. "What?" I said. "I am a police officer."

"Sir, open your car door. Keep your hands where I can see them. Step out of your car and immediately lie on your stomach with your hands above your head and your legs spread. This is the last time I am going to ask."

I was moving into consciousness now. The person next to me was moving also. I reached over to nudge Franky to wake him and saw the blood on my hands. I held them up to my face and the light from the flashlight outside met them in the air. Immediately the voice outside grew louder.

"I've got blood on the driver. Sir, I am going to break the window and unlock your door. Do not lower your hands."

I turned to the window. "No, wait. I will get the door. I am a police officer. Detective Tommy O'Malley."

"We know who you are, Detective. Now I am going to count to three. You will open the door and lay on the ground. Any deviation from that path and I will shoot you."

It was then I noticed he had his gun in hand directly next to his flashlight. "What the hell is going on here?"

His voice answered my question. "One. Two. Three."

Before he could strike the window, I opened the door slowly and as instructed lowered myself to the ground. Franky was still not moving but the police officer outside my car was quickly on top of me with a knee in the center of my back. I had no idea who this officer was or where I was. I could not even remember what happened. Other officers opened the passenger door and began yelling for medical. Franky? What was the matter with Franky? Was this his blood? I tried to think but came up empty. I could not remember anything.

My hands were cuffed behind me and two police officers lifted me from the inside of my arms to stand. I was starting to get more of a grasp of the environment, and it appeared my car was on the side of the road. The Camaro trunk was open and some other police officers were taking pictures. My clothes were torn and disheveled and I had a raging headache. There were at least four police cars in the area with lights on. Yep, this was a big deal.

"Why am I handcuffed? What is going on?"

The two officers by my side did not answer. One of their radios went off, and they were instructed to take me to one of the cars. As we walked by the back of my Camaro, I peered inside my open trunk. Inside, folded over in some bent mess of flesh and bones was a blood-soaked body. I could not see the face initially but as we continued walking, I saw Steve Jewel lying dead in a fetal position. A gun lay on his corpse and the amount of blood clearly showed this man had been shot several times. All I could think about was Deborah Jewel's words, *"I hope he is in somebody's trunk."* Little did she know it would end up being my trunk.

After leading me past the trunk, one of the police officers asked, "Any other questions?"

"Where are we?"

He did not answer but as we approached the police car, I read the name on the side. Joliet Police Department. Joliet? That is fifty miles out of the city. Upon seeing Jewel's body, however, things started coming back to me. I remembered going to the Red Carpet and then onto Rick's. What happened at Rick's? Marco. Marco happened at Rick's.

"Call Sergeant Craig Carter with the Chicago Police Department, Homicide. He can help straighten this out. I did not kill Mr. Jewel."

"A name. He said the victim's name is Jewel," he hollered to those back at the car. He put his hand on the back of my head to guide me into the car without striking my head on the doorframe. "Get in and shut up. I would suggest you don't say anything else. We have already talked to Carter."

Three hours later I had learned that an anonymous tip placed a car off a side road with suspicious activity. That was at three a.m. It was now rolling on seven a.m. and Sergeant Craig Carter was at the Joliet police station. He walked into the holding area where I sat with bottled water and a headache the level of which felt as if shrapnel was lodged inside my skull.

"How you holding up, Tommy?"

"I don't know, Sergeant. I got taken. I let my guard down not expecting anyone would go to those limits and they stung me."

"This is pretty serious, Tommy. Unless I can get some semblance of why you are innocent, they want to throw the book at you. They have your gun as the murder weapon. They have the body in your car and gunshot residue on your hands. What the hell happened, Tommy?"

"Franky and I were just going in to try to locate our suspect, Steve Jewel—the general manager of the uniform plant who lured Malcolm out the night he was killed. It was a long shot but we knew his credit cards linked him to the clubs. We went there to stir things up. While there, we learned that Jewel had just been there. We met Marco Filini but everything after that is a blank."

"How'd they get your gun?"

"We had to be drugged. They would not let us take our guns in so I locked them in my trunk safe."

Carter shook his head. "Key or combination?"

"What?" I asked.

"Was the lock box in your car under a key or a combination?"

"A key," I replied.

"So whoever took your car also had the keys to your gun?"

I shook my head.

"They are going after you on this one. We need a witness other than Franky."

When he mentioned Franky's name I instantly changed the subject. "Where is Franky? How is he?"

"He is as hungover as you. What the hell were you guys doing drinking that much? The bartender, owner, and your credit card show a $700 tab. Hell, two strippers said you paid them an additional $300 each in cash. Internal Affairs wants to look into your finances and everything, not to mention the dead body in your trunk."

"Jesus, Carter, it is a setup. Moretti, Polino, and Filini are all involved. They drugged us, killed a witness we were looking for, and now they are trying to pin it on us."

Carter's tone was clear. "Well, they are doing one hell of a good job on it, aren't they? They are having drinks at the fucking signature lounge and you are rotting in a Joliet holding cell." He paced around, turned back, and put both hands on the table in front of me. "Let's hope your fucking tox screen comes back with something on it."

"When will we have the tox screens back?"

"Any time now. That is the only reason you and Franky are not booked and already sent out. If the toxicology screens are positive for something, then we have a case for the setup."

At that point, an officer I did not recognize stuck his head in the door and called Carter out. I got up to go with him and he turned back without speaking which told me to sit my fat ass down and let him get this cleared up. He was gone for over thirty minutes before he returned with a pissed off Frank Sullivan by his side.

"Franky."

"Tommy," he replied. Both of us carried some level of embarrassment for being caught in this situation.

"Well, Detectives, I am pleased to say you are free to go. Your tox screens not only came back with Rufilin in them at near comatose-inducing levels, your blood alcohol was almost zero. You did not drink $700 worth of liquor nor did you have anything to do with the dead body in your car, at least consciously. The DA is willing to give you both the benefit of the doubt when the entire situation is considered." We both felt instant relief as Carter continued speaking mostly to me. "Your Camaro is going to remain impounded for a few more days, and I just got off the phone with one Ross Moretti who was so concerned when he heard about this ordeal that he made sure all charges to your card were waived. Both your names are on the guest list at the front door for a complementary entry should you wish to return."

"That gloating son of a bitch," I exclaimed. "I am going to fu—"

"You will do nothing of the sort," interrupted Carter. "Goddamnit. You are two of the best homicide detectives I have ever met, but you are thinking with your heart and not about the facts. Clark is dead. Everyone you find linked to this case is dead. You are both coming down to the station and we will go through this entire case together. I want to know everything. I don't want to ever get another four a.m. call that two of my detectives are knee-deep in shit again!"

Carter had a way with words. I still felt like hell and I thought Franky felt the same, though neither of us mentioned it. The worst part of the whole ordeal was the ride back. When your car is impounded, you have very few options other than catching a ride with someone. In our case, that meant riding with Sergeant Carter. If we thought his tirade in the Joliet station was something special, he let it all flow freely in the car. The first rule of being a detective is never make your sergeant look like an ass. The second rule is never make your sergeant have to bail you out. The last rule is never get caught in your sergeant's car for an hour after you did one or both of these.

I turned to him. "Sergeant, Malcolm's funeral is in one and a half hours. I need to be there."

"Goddamnit, O'Malley," he replied. "We have got to solve this case." His voice softened just a bit. "Fine, we will all go and then head to the station, but you both need to get cleaned up first and Wyatt Earp back there needs to get some new clothes. He is not going to a funeral dressed like a cowboy that just got thrown from a bull."

●　　　●　　　●　　　●　　　●

We sat in the back of the church, which to Malcolm's credit was packed. I assumed he had attended this church his whole life, not to mention most of his customers over the years were also there. The respect level for this man was unsurpassed. I saw Jamal and his mother up front. I also saw Ros Clark and her two kids sitting with them. The service was moving, and the eulogy, given by Jamal, brought tears to everyone in the room, even the ESPN reporter in the back row. What in the hell made this a sports news story?

The service lasted for just shy of an hour, and then we followed the hearse to the Oak Woods Cemetery. From there, it was simply a matter of watching the coffin as it was lowered into the ground, with Andrea and Jamal visibly collapsing inch by inch with each foot it dropped. I was there not to just give support. I was also there to see who else was in attendance. Very often killers came to funerals. I have heard a variety of reasons for why they do this, but all of them are bullshit except one—to prove they can. To gloat. I was also looking for Jessica. If my theory was correct, she knew her father was dead and would do whatever she could to be there. She would do it without being seen. I checked everywhere. Every car, every tree, every person who might be in costume or hidden under a hood. Nothing. I left Oak Woods with two questions that morning. First, where was Jessica and why did she not try to come? Secondly, if Tiny was so concerned that he had to visit Jamal and his mother yesterday, where was he today? I became worried for both of them, and more suspicious about one.

Franky, Carter, and I left the cemetery and headed to the station. We did not speak. On the radio, the story about the unidentified man found in the trunk of a car in Joliet was all over the news. I wondered who would be delivering the notification to Deborah Jewel. I was somewhat relieved that it would not be me. Seeing as it was my car he was found in, that would probably not be the right message to send.

10

FRIDAY AFTERNOON

I obtained a car from the station lot and was now cruising the streets of downtown Chicago in a dark brown Oldsmobile. It was whatever the new version of a Delta 88 was but I was so appalled at having to drive it, I did not even look. It may have gone zero to sixty in about two minutes, or it may never have reached sixty, I couldn't tell. Franky had headed home to get his crap together. It was rolling on the weekend now, and we were going to drive this investigation forward. It was nearly three p.m. when we finished going through everything with the sergeant. He had agreed with the path we had followed to date and supported our continuance. We decided on a few key directions.

We were pretty confident that the guilty parties had a plan going into the night for Mr. Jewel. It was too professional and too sophisticated to not be well thought out. We made their job easy by visiting their establishment, but had we not been on the premises, we would have found Mr. Jewel dead today just the same. However, by going to the club, we may have changed their time frame and direction merely due to their pompous nature. They wanted to prove they could do anything they wanted. By doing so, did they make a mistake? Could someone have seen something? The girls or the bartender had to be in on it, or both of them. Moreover, did Tiny see something? He could be the key to this. I wanted to talk to Tiny and Jamal, but I could not risk meeting Jamal first because I knew Tiny would be heading to work. I needed to speak to him away from the clubs. Therefore, I was heading to meet Tiny, and after Franky had run by his home to take care of his enormous dog, he was going to talk to Jamal. We decided that he might handle the fact that Jamal was at the strip club better than I would. He feared I would ring the boy's neck, and he was spot on. The two boys lived right by each other and had done so for their whole life, but I had called Ty's house and learned that he was at the River Court shooting baskets. I headed that direction.

When I got to River Court, I did not see anyone at first. Nobody was shooting but there was a ball there. I scanned the area and that is when I spotted the young man. I was about to call his name but something just did not feel right, so I opted to take the "wait and see" approach. I have been a cop a long time, and I could already see where this was going.

Tiny was not alone. Around him were a few other boys. All African-American and none of them were the normal River Court kids I had heard about. The guys were dressed in hoodies, baggy pants, and sunglasses, and all had cell phones permanently attached to their ears. If I were not a cop, I would have stereotyped them as drug dealers. Because I was a cop, I knew they were drug dealers.

I estimated they were about seventy-five yards away when one spotted me over Tiny's shoulder. There seemed to be some commotion in the group and Tiny turned, met my eyes, and turned back to the group. Some of them seemed jumpy. I envisioned them shooting me. I was well within range for some of these guys who had carried a gun in their hands for most of their lives. Shooting me from this range would not even make their top ten most difficult shots list. I slowly reached down to unsnap my holster. Unfortunately, along with my car, my gun had been impounded as well. I had been fast-track cleared and fully released during the investigation since the medical examiner determined I was unconscious at the time of Jewel's death and could not have pulled the trigger. My gun, however, as the rules were, was not released. Fortunately, I was issued another gun. I had no idea I would consider using it just an hour after its receipt.

I can't believe Tiny could have seen me unsnap my gun, but he raised his hand to me in a form of a wave which was more of a Heil Hitler salute than a wave. The little voice in my head told me his wave meant, *"We will talk about this later. Do not come over here now."* As always, I should listen to that little voice.

I took a step closer to the group and with that first step, I saw one of the hooded figures drop his hand to his side and in it, I saw the sun glisten a quick reflection off the surface of a barrel. As a cop, you make choices, and all I can say is today is just not my day. I could have turned and walked away and been just fine. I could have met up with Tiny in ten minutes and nobody would have been worse for the wear. Alas, that is just not me. I could not let this crime continue.

I pulled out my gun and lifted my badge. "Everyone freeze right there."

Hoodie with the gun lifted it directly toward me. Tiny grabbed his arm and pushed him back. I pulled my gun and took aim. From this distance, I too was automatic, but on a moving target there was too much risk. The boys scattered. The shot echoed across the area, but the direction due to Tiny's grab was straight in the air. I ran toward where they had been, but by the time I arrived, a car was pealing out with all of them inside. No Tiny. No drug dealers in hoodies. Nobody.

•   •   •   •   •

My heart was racing, and I was pissed. I got on the phone with Franky to let him know what happened. I told him that I would meet him at Jamal's, then we would visit Steve Jewel's wife again. Then we were going to pick up Tiny at the damn club. Franky agreed. We compared locations and both guessed we would be at Jamal's in less than fifteen minutes.

I pulled the Olds up and saw Franky already walking toward the door. The shit with Tiny had changed my mind on how to handle Jamal and his presence at the club last night. He was going to stay away, and I was going to make damn sure his mom knew and was involved to keep him there.

"Hey, Tommy. You okay?"

I stared at Franky and he knew I wasn't. "No, Franky. I am pissed. I feel like crap. In less than twenty-four hours, I have been framed, arrested, berated by my boss, been to a funeral, and had a gun pulled on me by a gangbanger."

"And it is not even dinnertime yet," he added.

I raised my hand and pounded on the door. "Jamal. Andrea. It's Detective O'Malley and Frank Sullivan."

I heard some footsteps in the room and then the door lock popped open. The door swung open and Andrea Jackson stared back at us wearing a not-too-often-seen smile. "What can I do for you, Detectives?"

"Good afternoon, Mrs. Jackson," I began. "I would like to speak to your son if that is possible."

She opened the door wider for us to come in. "That would normally be fine, but he is not here."

We entered behind her and Franky shut the door in our wake. "What do you mean? I thought he was going to stay here with you." I was surprised that he would be out at this time of the day.

She held her smile. "Well, he is staying here but he also wants to help me get back on my feet. With Malcolm gone, it will be tough to make ends meet until everything is settled. He got a job making a little cash on the side."

Instantly I knew what was coming next. "Where?"

"That same club where Tiny works." She saw my face drop but not for the reason she thought. "I know what you are thinking. What is a nineteen-year-old doing at a gentlemen's club?" I smiled internally at the ironic description of a gentlemen's club. No gentlemen works there or goes there as a patron. They were all slimeballs like Jewel. She continued, not noticing how my thoughts affected my face. "Well, he will only be working the door and they will pay him cash so it won't be flagged by the NCAA."

"Andrea," my voice sounded much more pleading than it should have. "He could lose everything. His scholarship. His college education. He could end up like Tiny. You have got to stop him. That is no place for a boy."

Her face showed concern but she still defended his direction. "He met with the owner. Tiny vouched for him. That place saved Tiny's mom from being evicted."

Franky could see I was going to blow so he took over. "At what cost, Mrs. Jackson? Tiny will never play football again. That owner will use Tiny for everything he can. He will keep using him until there is nothing left for him to get from Tiny, and then he will spit him out and find some other kid to use. You have to get Jamal away from that man and that place. We can help you, but we need to be sure you understand."

It was as if she only heard one thing. "Tiny *is* going to play football again. He is clean from drugs and getting set to play in junior college in Kansas."

"He is not clean, Andrea. I caught him today dealing drugs. There is an APB out for him for the drugs and for a connection to another set of crimes that took place last night and this morning. Tiny is probably not involved in anything but the drugs, but we need to talk to him."

She still looked hesitant but the facts were starting to wear her down. "He is working with Jamal tonight, at the Red Carpet I believe it is called. Jamal told me he was supposed to meet Tiny there at four-thirty."

I checked my phone and saw it was already 4:35. "So they are both there now," I said to Franky. "We should go, but we need to call Carter and let him know. He may want to send backup. I don't think he wants us going in there alone again."

I took Andrea's hand in mine. "Don't worry, Mrs. Jackson. We will find Jamal and bring him back home. We will also get Tiny out. It's not too late for him. He saved my life today by preventing someone from shooting me. It won't be for nothing."

After we exchanged good-byes, Franky and I turned and headed back to our cars. We considered leaving one car at the Jackson's but changed our minds. I placed a call to Sergeant Carter. He decided to send two teams to meet us at the Red Carpet at 5:45. Our current schedule would put us there in fifteen minutes or so, but Carter made it very clear we were not to go in alone. I called Franky and explained the timing. He said one simple word that turned my steering column sharply—Dagwood.

We hit Mr. J's in plenty of time. After twenty years, I no longer had to order, and in most cases I did not have to wait in line. When they saw me, they nodded me over and the Dagwood was waiting at the end of the line. I usually threw an extra dollar or two their direction to keep that level of service coming, but even if I didn't, they would keep doing it. That business thrived on regulars, and Franky and I were as regular as you could get.

We pulled into the Red Carpet lot at 5:35 p.m. To my displeasure, Jamal was working the door. Also to my displeasure, Tiny was not with him. Instead, Marco Filini stood tall and proud. They showed no recognition when I pulled in but for this time of day, the lot was actually busy. Maybe the weekend night or the unseasonably warm weather just brought the slimeballs out. Whatever it was, there was actually a line at the door. Jamal was being shown the ropes and Marco was the teacher. I did not like Jamal that close to this killer, but for the time being, there was nothing I could do about it. *Your time is coming, asshole,* I said to myself. *I am going to nail your ass to the wall, and your fucking bosses with you.*

My car door opened abruptly causing me to just about crap my pants. "Sorry, Tommy, I did not mean to startle you. I guess you are a little jumpy after that park incident." Franky paused and when I said nothing, he added, "Are you ready for this?"

"We are just picking up the kid. I don't know what all the fuss is about." My tone was cold and my eyes were still locked on Marco Filini.

"Nope. Carter called me back. Said he couldn't get through on your phone. He wants to send a team in first as patrons. Wants them to start asking questions, stir things up a bit. See what happens." Franky used the time to slide into the passenger seat and position himself beside me.

"To what end?" I asked.

Franky turned his head as he shifted in the seat. "They proved they could fuck with us last night. Sergeant wants to fuck with them tonight."

"What about Jamal?"

"Sergeant says to leave him. They need him."

"Filini will kill him to prove a point to me, and he won't leave a single bit of evidence."

"When Carter gets here, let's confirm the plan."

As we finished speaking, two black Bonnevilles pulled into the parking lot. I could see Carter in one of them, but the other passed by us too quickly. Marco also took notice of the two cars. He smiled and disappeared inside.

I left my car and walked to where the two had parked. "Jesus, why didn't you just drive here in black-and-whites with sirens going? Filini knows you are here."

Carter looked disgusted. "Shit, now what?"

"Now we get the boy out and come back to fight another day on this one. There is nothing for us today."

I thought Carter was going to agree, but he did not answer when he saw the other two officers going inside. His response turned instantly to a question of understanding. "Hey, I thought you said your murder victim's son would be working the door? That looks like a big Latino to me."

I followed Carter's gaze to the front door where Jamal was nowhere to be seen, and a large Hispanic man stood checking who entered.

"Goddamnit," I replied. "I am going in. I'm not sure they know the other officers are with us. They are probably only looking for Franky and me. I will go in and you follow. Let Franky come in shortly thereafter. You will have to leave your gun in the car or come in as a cop. Your call."

Carter did not like that part of the plan. "Which one are you doing?"

"My firearm is already locked up." Before he could comment, I continued, "And yes, I picked up a combination lock."

I walked toward the front door and the big Latino man did not even ask me a question. He simply moved to the side. Evidently, I was expected. At the counter, the girl who would normally take a cover charge and explain the metal detector did not ask anything about cover. She only pointed to the metal detector and said,

"Did you leave your firearm in your car?"

"You mean like last time when I was drugged and framed, and someone killed a man with the gun I locked in my car?"

Without missing a beat, the girl replied, "Yes, just like that time."

Trying to not miss a beat in return, I said, "Then yes, it is locked in my car just like last time."

I walked through the metal detector intent on finding Jamal. I located the VIP room and the triple-locked door next to it that I knew was Polino's office. I tried the handle, and of course it was locked. I banged on the door but with the loud music, even if they were not ignoring me, nobody was going to hear it.

"Do you need something, Detective O'Malley?"

I recognized the voice immediately. I turned to face the pompous ass. "No shitting around, Marco. I am here for the boy. I am here to pick up Jamal Jackson."

"Is there a warrant for his arrest?" Marco said with sarcasm. "I have not seen anything on the news and nobody has called us looking for him. He is a brand new employee. I would hate to see him in trouble. Is there anything we can do?"

"Cut the crap, Marco. I saw him working the door not five minutes ago. Now he vanishes?"

Marco took a step closer and lowered his voice so there was no chance anyone but me would hear. "Listen, Detective O'Malley, at this stage I don't really mind you. Sure, you were tough with me when we first met, but since then you have been more respectful. I admire that. If you don't give people time to learn how to properly act toward others, then how human are you really? That being said, just because I have started to like you better, it does not mean you can come in here and take our employees away. We have a business to run. We will not be turning over our employees or patrons to the police without a judge-signed warrant. As you have made no effort to produce one, I must assume one does not exist. With that, get out."

"Interesting that you use 'human' to describe yourself. Where I come from, humans value life."

Marco smiled that same damn smile. "I value the life that has value to my boss." He stepped closer so that we were just inches apart. "I have asked about you. Heard you are a fourth degree. That should make it very fun when we actually do meet."

I did not back down or even flinch. I stood, locked in a stare. "Where is the boy?"

"I am here, Detective O'Malley, and you need to go, and please take those other policemen with you." To his credit, Jamal's voice was very strong as he spoke.

"Jamal, you need to come with me."

Jamal walked up and stood directly next to Marco who had taken a step back from me since Jamal's arrival. "No, sir. I am working here now and I'm fine. Mr. Polino and I have reached an agreement and I intend to honor it."

I became very agitated and it showed. "That is bullshit and you know it. There is only one person who will honor anything and that is not Polino. Your mom instructed me to bring you back and that is what I am going to do." I am not sure why I played the mother card, but I hoped it would strike some nerve with him.

"My mother? Seriously? I am nineteen years old, and I do not need my mother to tell me when to come home."

Nope, no nerve struck.

"Well, here is something that will tell you when you have to leave," issued Carter from the side. "I have a detain warrant for Jamal Jackson as a person of interest involving a warrant on drug trafficking for one Tyrone 'Tiny' Nielson."

Jamal stepped forward and got directly in my face. "Now who is dishing out bullshit, Detective? Tiny didn't do shit and you know it."

"Yes, he did, Jamal. And his buddies pulled a gun on me when I broke it up."

"And here is a warrant to search the premises for said Tyrone Nielson," interrupted Carter again. "So move over, big fella, before I have my friend here move you over."

Marco stared hard at Carter then back to me. His face was locked in a scowl, then all of the sudden it changed to that same f'ing smile, and he stepped aside throwing his arm forward in a "come on in gentlemen" pose. As I passed, he again placed the backside of his hand on my chest stopping me briefly in my tracks. "Like I said, it will be fun when we finally meet."

"I don't think you will be saying that when it does actually happen, but I guess we will have to wait and see."

He smiled wickedly and removed his hand.

I am not sure how Carter produced the warrant so quickly but evidently Polino's attorney, Staci Lambda, was tearing through the warrant with a fine-tooth comb. I don't think Carter anticipated having an attorney onsite when he served the warrant so he pushed us along quickly. The warrant was limited to a search for a person so even if we found two kilos of cocaine, it would not stand up. We would have to produce another warrant and so forth. The Chicago laws were horrific when it came to personal warrants. We did not have probable cause to link the club to Tiny's sale yet, so as of now, all we could do was find Tiny.

The officers that had entered initially met Carter at the front while Jamal had been escorted out to one of the unmarked police vehicles in the lot. He was being watched by another officer so I did not feel he would run. However, I was sure he could outrun the cop in charge of his holding. One officer was whispering to Carter at a level I could not hear but I already knew what was being said. Mr. Nielson, aka Tiny, was not here. Polino emerged from his back office and approached.

"Detective O'Malley. My, aren't we getting cozy, meeting so many times over the last few days?"

The sarcasm was loud and clear. "We are."

"I was so sorry to hear about that awful predicament you got yourself into last night. I can't believe you were drugged in one of my clubs and assaulted as such. I hope you got my message that your tab was cleared, and you have a complimentary entrance anytime you want." He paused and then with a smile added, "We won't count today."

I stepped toward Polino causing both Carter and Marco to also take a step closer. "Joey, may I call you Joey?"

Polino smiled. "No."

"Well, Joey, I have some information for you about last night and today that may be of interest. You made a huge mistake last night."

Polino put his hand to his open mouth in a look of intense surprise. "Oh, do tell. Whatever could I have done that was in such error?"

"You should have killed me last night, Joey." I glanced to Marco who, like Joey Polino, had not expected me to say those words.

Polino held a noticeable pause while he contemplated his next comment. "I don't know what you mean, Tommy. That horrid thing which happened to you last night was an unfortunate random act of violence. That being said, you did just improve yourself in my eyes. I thought you were just another dumb cop. It appears you might on occasion be right about certain things. Although I did not make a mistake, had you died it would not have broken my heart. I shall have to rethink that."

He stepped slightly to the side to where he could see out the front door that was propped open. He picked a time when the music had ended and the dancers were making a change and yelled to his new employee outside. "Jamal, come back as soon as you clear this up. I will send my lawyers to meet you at the station."

Jamal waved that he understood, but the officer watching him slammed the door shut so no words could be exchanged. Polino smiled at me and saluted Carter and then disappeared back to his office. Marco paced back and forth in the front area as if he did not know what to do next. He wanted to screw with me some more but there was really nothing more for either of us to say. We had both postured, threatened, and stood our ground, so the line was drawn in the sand. I did not know when or if we would meet. Part of me wanted to find the evidence to nail the asshole, but the other part wanted to meet him in an alley with no weapons. I wondered which side of me would win.

Our exchange ended when Staci Lambda emerged and said, "Your warrant is over. We have provided sufficient time to search the site and since your search is limited to locating Mr. Neilson and since Mr. Nielson is not here, you may be on your way. I also would like to confirm where you are taking Mr. Jackson as I will be his counsel."

"Mr. Jackson is not under arrest, Ms..." Carter began, waiting for her to introduce herself to him.

"Why don't you forget about calling me by name and gather your troops and exit this location? Your business here is done. If you are taking Mr. Jackson to any location other than the downtown police station, you need to inform me immediately. You are not to talk to my client until I arrive. Furthermore, in an effort to save us all some time, we could meet in my office here, but I don't suppose you, Sergeant..."—she paused imitating Sergeant Carter's false act of caring about her name—"would consider that option."

"It's Carter, ma'am, and you are correct, we will be taking Mr. Jackson to the precinct. I suppose we will see you there."

She turned and walked away with a powerful step and demeanor. She was something impressive all right, in a don't-mess-with-me-bitch sort of way. I had to give her that. All the officers, Franky, Carter, and me met outside the door. The commotion of the police had driven much of the clientele away but they would all return when the coast was clear. In my mind, the losers did not have anywhere else to go. We talked briefly and I thanked Carter and the team for their work.

Although we did not find Tiny, we did get Jamal out of there which was one of my primary goals. One thing that worried me was if Polino did not have Tiny now, he would be looking for him as hard as we would. Either Tiny split when we got there or he was already in trouble. Tiny might be the key to nailing this guy. We may not be able to get Polino on murder charges, but drug charges can put a stop to him just the same, and Tiny might be able to provide the evidence we needed. We had to find Tiny before Polino did. In Polino's eyes, Tiny was a loose end.

•   •   •   •   •

We hit the road with Jamal sitting in the back seat with me, Carter driving, and Franky riding copilot. There are many ways I could describe Jamal that would not do him justice. Aggravated. Annoyed. Upset. I guess the best way would be to say he was pissed beyond any level of understanding. He would have rather been caught naked with a farm animal than repeat what just took place. I was not sure where I came up with that reference, but I had never seen a black man's face completely red.

"What the hell are you doing, O'Malley?" shouted Jamal.

"Saving your ass, kid."

"Screw you. I didn't ask you to save me. They had let me in. Despite all your interference, I was on the inside. Now they will never let me come back."

"You don't know what you are getting into, Jamal. These guys play for keeps. Your friend Tiny knows that now. He is missing. They may have already killed him. He is a loose end. How long, do you think, until you become a loose end?"

"That is bull and you know it. I just talked to Tiny. He said he was not going to make it in tonight because he was doing a special security deal for one of Polino's parties. He is not missing."

I looked at Carter and Franky and then back to Jamal. "Where?"

Jamal was still pissed but he did notice the change in my tone. "Where what?"

"Where is Polino's party?"

"I don't know. I have never been to one. Tonight was my first night."

My voice turned to a higher pitch stressing the importance. "Think, Jamal. You talked to Tiny a lot since you have been back. You know he has said things about what he did. Where are these parties? A hotel? Another property? What has Tiny said?"

"I don't know!" he yelled. "And if I did, why would I tell you?"

Carter slammed on the brakes sending everyone forward until their seatbelts locked, an action he was hoping would have the effect of creating importance and bringing all attention to him. "Listen here, Jamal, and no more pussyfooting around. Your friend is in trouble, big trouble. My gut tells me he knows something about Polino, something Polino does not want him to talk about. Whoever gets to him first controls his life. Do you want his life in the hands of that behemoth Marco or one of the other Polino gorillas?"

Everything was silent. At times I did not care for Sergeant Carter. This was one of those times I understood why he was sergeant. Jamal looked toward Carter and then back to me. Turning back to Carter, his voice was humble and soft. "At one point, Tiny mentioned some hotel that Polino owns. I don't know if that is where the party is. Tiny just mentioned that he could stay there if he wanted to move out of his mom's."

Franky picked up his phone. "I'll check it out."

Carter smiled and turned on his blinker and edged his way back onto the road. Jamal reached out and tapped my arm. "What happened with you and Tiny?"

"Like I said, I was looking for him to talk about what he saw or did not see last night at Rick's. When I found him, he was selling what appeared to be drugs. The guys he was with saw me and pulled a gun. I believe they would have locked on me, but Tiny intervened by lifting the shooter's arm. Then all of them fled. I have not seen him since."

"So you did not see any drugs?" replied Jamal, speaking with inflection like a question but not actually asking anything. "The truth is, you don't know what he was doing."

"Jamal, I have been a cop for over twenty years. Furthermore, you don't have to be a cop to know what was going down. If you'd read a J.A. Jance novel in the last ten years, then you are smart enough to know what was happening."

"He is clean! He told me, and I believe him."

"Great, then he should not have any issues with coming in." My tone was smug and gave the needed impact. I decided not to pull any punches. "What if I told you he might know something about Jessica?" I had no proof or link, but I needed Jamal back on my side. I needed him to consider Tiny was involved in some bad things. Not his father's death or Jessica's disappearance necessarily, but letting Jamal know that we saw proof Jessica was alive lent credibility to my concerns with Tiny. The two were most likely not related, but if Jamal came to see Tiny a little less "clean," it would be to my benefit.

As expected, that stopped him cold. "What do you mean? He knows something about Jessica?"

"We have proof she is alive. Video from this week showing her making a phone call."

"What? Why didn't you tell me? Why didn't you tell my mom?" Jamal was more pissed than relieved—an understandable reaction—and immediately after speaking, I could see the emotions changing. "Alive," he repeated softly.

"Why do you think we have been looking for you?" I said. "You have to start trusting us."

"Where is she now?"

As I paused, weighing my words, not knowing exactly how much to say, Franky interjected. "Our video from the night your dad was killed showed Jessica getting into a car. I should say *forced* into a car. The individual who forced her was found dead in our trunk last night. Someone at Rick's drugged our drinks, killed the man who kidnapped your sister, and tried to frame us with his murder. So you still think Polino is on your side?"

"You have to find her."

I took over again. "We are doing all that we can, Jamal. We can't have you involved. You become a liability if you get caught inside. He will use you as a get-out-of-jail-free card."

"It's too late, I am already involved. He paid me cash up-front. If he leaks that to the media, I will lose my scholarship. He told me after about ten minutes of me being there. He has video of me accepting the money."

"Are you f'ing kidding me? Can you believe that guy?" asked Franky rhetorically.

"Don't worry about that, Jamal. One video is not going to get you kicked out of the NCAA, especially since you were asked by the police to gather info. I still have your back if it is just this one time." It was my turn to place my hand on his arm.

"Why would you do that?" Jamal asked me.

I smiled. "Because your dad would have done that. Because nobody should fall prey to that asshole. I only hope it is not too late to help your friend Ty."

Franky's phone rang. "Sullivan." There was a pause while the person on the other end talked. "Yeah. Yeah. Okay." Again a pause then a long "Okaaayyy? Send me the address. We will be at the station in five and then we will head over."

He pressed his call off and turned back to me sitting in the back with Jamal. "I think we have something. Polino owns some extended living property just south of the Cell." The Cell is US Cellular Field where the White Sox play. "A patrol car was in the area and swung by and matched up plates of a car which shows the ownership as Rick's Cabaret. Someone from Rick's is there. Secondly, there was a noise complaint entered for the property. Someone reported loud music and what sounded like fighting. Because of the location of the hotel and the frequency of complaints, it was, shall we say, not followed up on."

Carter turned and asked, "What is the address? We will head there now."

"No," I stated. "We have Polino's lawyer headed to the station. Let's keep her there. Drop off Jamal and provide him some support. Jamal, I need you to stall the attorney. Keep her there. Ask tons of questions. Do whatever it takes. I don't want her showing up at the hotel."

He nodded as I continued speaking now to Franky. "Franky, how far is the property from the station?"

"Ten minutes. We can drop off Jamal and still be at the hotel in fifteen."

I looked at Carter who shook his head in agreement. For the first time since this case began, the jazz was starting. The jazz was something I stole from the A-Team, a TV show from my childhood starring of all people, Mr. T. "Jazz" by the A-Team's definition is that feeling when a stone falls into place. TV folklore aside, I believe only two groups of people in the real world can feel the jazz—attorneys in court when they know they just took the step to win a case, and detectives when things suddenly start to make sense. It was still early, but I could feel the jazz starting.

11

THE NOISE COMPLAINT came from suite 200, and I use the word "suite" lightly. It was the largest room on the second floor. The person who complained was in the room below. We met with the complainant first and got the layout of the rooms. We made the assumption the floor plans for the second floor were the same as the floor below. Despite the outside of the building, the rooms were not bad. You walked into a good-sized open sitting room with a large, flat-screen television. To one side was a small conference table and office area, and in the center was a fireplace and door to a bathroom. Through another door were two bedrooms and a kitchen. It was really a small apartment, perfect for the "extended stay" person or business traveler who was stationed in South Chicago for several weeks.

We checked the guest register and nobody named Polino or any other name associated with either strip club or either man had ever checked into or out of this hotel. Because it was owned by Joey Polino did not mean anything. He did not manage it or by all accounts ever stay or live there. Basically, unless we caught him or something directly tied to him on this visit, there would be nothing we could bring back against him. The man in room 100 stressed he did not want anyone to get in trouble, but the noise upstairs was just too loud and distracting. It started as fighting with some screaming and then loud music. Franky and I knew what that usually meant. Because the person was screaming, they needed the music to cover it up.

We had police stationed at all the exits but the other critical piece of information we learned was that the noise had stopped forty minutes ago. Our car had only been here for twenty-five. That left fifteen minutes for those involved to get the hell out. Franky and I took the stairs while Carter remained at the elevator on floor one, shutting it down on that level. Management was not thrilled so we put them under watch to ensure they did not call and notify the owner of our presence. There would be no early alarms for those involved.

When we arrived at the door, we listened intently for any sign of life behind its wooden barrier. Nothing. I looked to Franky and he nodded. I raised my hand and knocked three times.

"Open up. Police," I stated in my most authoritative voice.

No reply and no sound.

I knocked two more times. "Open up or we will come in. We have a key."

Still no sound. We both had already pulled our guns. Franky held the key card. We both moved to the side of the door and Franky reached his arm over and slid the key card into the lock. The latch turned green releasing the handle and lock. He turned the handle downward and the door cracked open.

There are two ways you can play this: Bull rush through the door with guns ready or continue talking to any people inside identifying who you are and slowly breaching the opening. I preferred the bull rush, but Franky made the call to enter slowly. I pushed the door open while we both remained on the outside on either side of the doorway. The door had an automatic closure so we only got a brief look before it swung back toward the lock. I blocked it from closing and locking again which would have just been pathetic. I pushed the door open again and used my free arm to hold it open. When we saw the inside, we immediately froze.

"Use your radio. Call for backup, now!"

Franky grabbed his radio and called down. I motioned with my fingers no longer talking out loud. I burst through the door and quickly moved behind the sofa. My feet made a crackling sound as they walked across the plastic and had I not been a cop looking to avoid disturbing evidence, I would have surely slipped in the blood pooled across most of it. I motioned to Franky who had been joined by two other policemen, all with guns drawn. They filed in and spread to clear the room. Within moments, we had heard the "all clear" from each person, and we lowered our weapons.

"I am not sure I have ever seen this much blood," one of the younger officers said.

I glanced at Franky. We had seen thousands of crime scenes but to be honest, I was not sure I had seen that much blood in one scene. "I need only essential people in this room until we have collected all the evidence. I want Dr. G here immediately and her assistant. There are at least two dead girls here."

"Do you see what I see, Tommy?" I looked to him and then followed his eyes to one of the dead girls. "I recognize her."

I looked closely. "Ashley. The blonde stripper from Rick's." I would not have recognized her without Franky pulling her out first.

Franky pointed toward the other body. "Is that brunette Star?"

"Impossible to tell," I answered. As we spoke, the young officer who had commented on the blood vomited in the corner.

"Hey!" shouted Franky. "Get out of here if you are going to contaminate this crime scene."

I grabbed Franky's arm. "That's it!"

"What?" he asked.

I put both my hands on his shoulders. "You have been trying to find a link between your dead hookers. The strip clubs. Something Jamal said just slapped me in the face."

"What do you mean? The strip clubs are the link?"

"All your dead hookers worked at the strip clubs."

He pushed my arms away. "No, they didn't. I checked it out. I traced all their jobs. The few that had family members confirmed where they worked. Other prostitutes confirmed where they worked. Pimps, everyone. I checked it out. None of them pointed back to the clubs."

"Cash. They were paid with cash, just like Jamal. Under the radar. My credit card was charged and credited but the sergeant said the girls got $300 cash. Jamal gets paid in cash. Polino has a handful of girls that he keeps off the books. He makes them expendable."

Franky's eyes widened. "We need to prove it."

"Detectives?" issued a voice from one of the bedrooms.

We carefully walked over the plastic to get to the smaller of the two bedrooms. It too was covered in plastic and had some blood on the bed. It appeared some of the initial torture took place in this room before moving to the main room. The plastic was going to make the cleanup quick and easy. I assumed we must have foiled that plan when the noise complaint came in.

"What is it?" I asked the crime scene investigator.

"When I lifted the sheet, I found this under the pillow." He held up a photograph with an X written across the person in the photo.

"Jessica," I said.

"Do you know her?" he asked.

"Do you think we are too late?" Franky asked, ignoring his question.

I nodded. "It means one of two things. Either she is dead and that was notice of the job being completed, or she is the next target."

"Let's hope it is the latter."

"Let's allow the crime scene guys to do their thing. I want to talk to Carter. We need to get a warrant for the strip clubs. With these two dead strippers from one of the strip clubs and this building owned by the strip club owner, I think getting a search warrant will be easy. I also want to talk to Jewel's wife again. She should have been informed by now that her husband is dead, so I am open to go back to her as part of the investigation. I want to know what his routine was. I want to know why he was killed."

◆　◆　◆　◆　◆

"You boys again," said Deborah Jewel as she opened the door.

Again she was multiple martinis into the day. It was well into the afternoon, several hours later in the day than the first time we had met her, so she was even now further into the barrel. "Mrs. Jewel, may we come in?"

She did not answer but left the door open as she walked away. She was wearing some sort of nightgown or sundress. I actually could not tell the difference. She swung her arms as she walked almost as if she were imitating an airplane. My fear was she was going to start making propeller noises and if that happened, I would not know what to do. We followed her in and eventually found our way to the kitchen where we sat at a long counter with a granite top.

"Mrs. Jewel…"

I was cut off by her hand. "Debbie. Please, Officer, call me Debbie."

"Okay," I replied slowly. "And please, call me Detective." She smiled but did not speak. I continued, "I need to talk to you about your husband."

"What about him? Did you find him with another whore?"

"No," I replied softly. "Has another officer already been here to talk to you about him?"

She did not provide any signs of understanding the serious nature of my discussion or that anyone had come to visit her since our leave. She made a face that pinched her lips together in an annoyed, "leave me alone" look. She then shrugged and replied, "No, but if someone came to the door I may have missed them. I was in the back working." She motioned through the back door of the kitchen to a sitting room. I glanced inside and there were no papers, computer, or anything that would give the impression of some sort of work. There was, however, an empty liter of Grey Goose vodka.

I really did not have the time for this. I was told officers were dispatched to the house. The problem with that statement was the word *officers*. They knock. Nobody answers. They get the hell out of there. No young cop likes relaying this type of news and they look for any avenue to avoid it. This was the famous and most widely used "nobody answered the door" excuse.

I took my voice even softer. Although he was a slimeball and she was a drunk, he was still dead and showing some empathy was critically important in these matters, regardless of my personal feelings. "I am sorry to inform you but your husband has been murdered. He was found this morning in a car in Joliet."

Her eyes opened wide. "Really? He is dead?"

It appeared she was about to cry. I was going to reach for a napkin when she continued speaking, actually bringing her lips slightly upward. "Nope. I just tried to cry. I just tried to feel something. Nothing. I have nothing to offer." She walked to the far counter and grabbed another bottle of Grey Goose vodka. "Can I get you a martini?"

"No, ma'am." I paused and glanced at Franky who just shrugged. "Mrs. Jewel, are you all right?"

She sauntered back over and sat down at the counter again. "Listen, Detective O'Malley. My jackass husband left me this house. We owe out the ass for it. He let the life insurance lapse because he lost all his money to the whores at those damn clubs. He owed so much he had to go do those jobs for him. He kept saying how those jobs were going to get us out of this mess. By the time he was done we would own this house and everything else free and clear. Now what? He ends up dead and I have nothing. So when you ask me if I am all right...do I fucking look all right?"

"No, ma'am, you look like hell." Franky had been taking notes regarding her previous comments so I was going to keep pursuing it. "Who was he doing these jobs for?"

"I don't know, the horse guy."

She seemed like she was actually becoming giddy over the death of her husband. If she was right and she was going to lose everything, then by her actions it appeared she would rather lose everything than stay married to him. A fascinating thought process. *Horse guy*? I thought. What the hell did that mean? "The guy had horses? What horses?"

"No, silly," she said giggling now. "He was named after a horse."

"You mean like Seabiscuit?" Frank asked.

She glared at him. "No, like the *kind* of horse—Thoroughbred or Appaloosa or something."

Bingo. I looked toward Franky and let him ask. "You mean Polino? As in Joey Polino?"

"Yeah, Joey Polino. That is his name. It is just like palomino." Her voice slurred a bit but she seemed pleased to have discovered the answer.

"Did you ever see them together or meet Mr. Polino?" Franky asked.

"No," she said and yawned. She was literally all over the place. "He only talked about him. Each time Steve did a job, he came home with less and less debt. Then he was going to do it for money. He was going to pay off this house."

"What did he have to do?"

"I don't know. I never went with him. He said it was easy though. He just had to clean up after parties. For the money he was being paid, they must have been huge parties."

"They must have," I replied.

"Is there anything else you can remember about your husband and his work with Mr. Polino?"

"No, I don't think so. Is this going to help find his killer? Because I really don't care if the killer is found."

We asked a dozen more questions, but the information was less and less useful. We believed we had gotten everything out of her but were going to have her picked up to give a sober run-through later. We rose to head out when I opted for one more question. I pulled out my phone. "Mrs. Jewel, have you ever seen this girl?" I held up a photo of Jessica Jackson.

She looked at the picture and recognition showed instantaneously. Debbie's face dropped and her eyes narrowed. "Get that bitch's picture out of my house."

I grabbed her arm when she tried to slap me. "You do that, Mrs. Jewel, and you are going to end up in jail for assaulting a police officer. You have about three seconds to tell me how you know this girl."

"That is the tramp my asshole husband brought home to have a threesome with me. She was blasted on some drugs. I refused but that didn't stop him from continuing with just her. He wanted me to participate with a girl of another race. She was all over him. She can have his rotten corpse now though."

"Are you saying this girl was here of her own free will?" I asked.

She smiled and leaned in close to me as I stood and she remained on the counter stool. "You could say that. She was high but she wasn't tied up or anything."

I was disgusted and by the looks of Franky, I believed he felt the same. We were done talking to this woman. She had given us a great deal of information and in her drunken state, she really was not going to be awake much longer. When we got outside, I called into the station to have a car brought out to pick her up. I told the dispatch officer I would file a report later, but she needed to be booked on accessory to a rape and assault of a police officer. I realized without the testimony of Jessica, if she even remembered, the accessory charge probably would not stick, but if nothing else, it made me feel better.

We got in the car and headed to the strip clubs. We had given Carter about two hours to get the search warrant. I was not sure if he had it already, but I was going to the clubs regardless. Carter was going to organize two large teams to hit the two clubs at the same time. I hoped we would find something to tie them to these murders. The dead girls danced at these clubs, but it was only called coincidence. We needed proof that they were involved.

With the same shock as unexpected thunder, my phone rang causing me to almost drop it as I went to answer. "Dr. G. Do you have news?"

"Hello to you, Tommy. It is good to talk to you too. I am doing well, thanks for asking. How have you been?"

"Cut the crap, Doc. I have had a shitty day that started with a body in my trunk of which I have not heard anything from you, and now I have two more bodies, tied to that same night. You need to give me slack on my etiquette. What do you have?"

"I have a DNA match from three of your cases, all matching."

"*Bingo*!" I said loudly. "What cases and who is it?"

"I have the same DNA in your trunk, in the hotel room, and your APB drug case."

"Wait a minute. My drug case. That was just the DNA I gave you as a match for Ty Nielson."

"Wow, they do call you one of the best detectives in the game." She paused, waited for my rolling eyes to stop rolling through the phone, and then continued unhindered. "The positive DNA you provided for Ty Nielson was entered into the database today. When we did it, we immediately got two hits. The two hits came from these two cases. Your brand new hotel from today and your dead body in the car, oh wait, that is also from today." She sighed. "You sure have been busy today."

"What the hell does that mean?" I said mostly to myself, though I knew Franky was listening.

When I finally hung up, Franky asked immediately, "Where was the kid's DNA?"

"Tiny's DNA was found in my trunk and the hotel."

We were silent for a minute while we both chewed on that one. Franky looked toward the road in front of us. "Do you think it's a plant?"

"The car would be an easy plant for them, but how could they have been expecting us to seize the hotel? I think we surprised them." I thought a minute more. "What, were they just carrying around Tiny's DNA just in case?"

For the next ten minutes, Franky did not take his eyes from the road, and the only sound in the car came from the sound of our heavy breathing. Finally I heard Franky ask, "What are you thinking, Tommy?"

Something E.Z. Zimmerman said to me the other day. "Usually the easiest answer is the right answer."

"Yeah, then what is the easiest answer?"

"Do you think Tiny is more involved than just drug runner?"

"Jamal's place is on the way to the clubs. Tiny lives next door. We have a car parked there now. Do you want to go have a chat with Tiny's mother about her son's activities?"

"Yes, I do. And call the station and have their finances pulled. I want to know what their bank account looks like."

Franky shook his head as he pulled out his phone. "Man, what is the world coming to?"

●　　●　　●　　●　　●

Franky took off with the onsite officer when we arrived at the Jackson and Nielson apartment building. The officers were doing their shift change and I thought it would be better if I talked to Tiny's mother alone. I had met her before, back when Jessica first disappeared. If Andrea Jackson was a ten on the calm scale, Priscilla Nielson was a hundred and fifty. She was a fireball.

I debated stopping in to see Andrea Jackson, but I was short on time, and I knew I had nothing to tell her, other than her missing daughter had been recently seen alive and her son was being held at the police station. Well, I guess I had a lot I *should* tell her. However, there was no way I would tell her either of those things, so therefore, it was just easier to pass right on by.

When I got to the Nielson's door, I thought I heard something out of place so I crouched and listened. It was high-pitched but forceful. I could not place it at first but with one big wave, I got it. *Crying.* Violent crying. Tiny was in there talking to his mother. I pulled my gun and knelt down by the lower corner of the window. It was tough to see inside but I could make out a figure in a chair. Maybe there was another figure on the ground, I could not be sure. If I called for backup, they would not be here in time. If I knocked, the person would flee. Bull rush. It was time.

I stepped back about five feet from the door and gave one forward kick about six inches from the knob. For many police officers, kicking in a door took three to five tries. For a fourth-degree black belt, it took one. The door exploded and I burst through with my gun drawn.

"Police! Nobody move!"

"Goddamnit, just what the hell are you doing to my house?"

Priscilla was pissed, and no, there was not a figure on the ground next to her, but her phone was sitting in her seat and it appeared a call was still open. I raised my hand to my mouth pressing my finger across my lips telling her to remain quiet. I walked carefully over to where the phone sat and on the screen I saw the name, Tyrone Cell. I lifted the phone to my ear and said, "Tiny?"

"Who is this? Who is at my mama's house? I will kill you, motherfucker. I will kill you dead. You touch my mama and I will kill you dead."

"Tiny, this is Detective Tommy O'Malley. Remember me? You saved me when that boy pulled a gun on me." I said this for two reasons. First, I needed his mom to remain calm, and if I was giving him praise, she would believe I was on her and her son's side. Secondly, I needed Tiny to believe I wanted to talk to him about the drug deal. "I need to talk to you about that."

There was long silence on the phone. As I said before, an old interrogator's trick is to get comfortable and wait out the criminal. Guilty guys always talk first. For the first time in my life, I may have met my waiting match. Then suddenly breaking the silence, Tiny said, "I got nothin' to say to you, Detective."

"Ty, I know you think you are in over your head, but there is always a way out." At that point, my phone started to buzz. It was Sergeant Carter calling. I did not answer.

"Not for me this time, Detective. I did some things. Some things I had to do."

"I know, Tiny. Mr. Polino made you do some things. He blackmailed you. You are not responsible for that. We can protect you."

Again my phone buzzed. That was our code. Call once and if you don't answer, we don't call back unless it is an emergency. I could not take Carter's call. Not now. I tried to send a text. *Talking to Ty Nielson on mother's phone. Trace the call.* I hit "send."

"He is not the bad one. Joe Polino cared about me. That other one and his muscle. They are sick."

I already knew who he was talking about but I wanted him to say it. I had to be sure. "Who, Tiny? Who is sick?"

"They made me do things. I saw Jessica. I saw what they were doing to her. I tried to help her."

"You saw Jessica? Where? When?"

Tiny had started to cry. I am sure wherever he was, seeing this big child crying was a site that would have brought Priscilla Nielson to her knees. Instead, she was on her knees in tears without being able to grab and hold her son. Again my phone buzzed, this time from a text but I did not have time to look.

"Where did you see Jessica?" I asked again.

"In the back room. In the back room of the club. I recognized the tattoo on her leg. She was drugged. They had been raping her. I couldn't stop it."

"It's not your fault, Tiny. You tried to stop it. It's not your fault."

"But they saw me."

Tiny was all over the place with his conversation now. He was not using names. Everything was "them" and "they." In his mind his comments made sense.

He was reliving it. This was a confession, and I was taking it over the phone. However, as of now I had nothing.

"Who saw you, Tiny?"

Tiny was still crying. "They made me go in there. They made me look at her. She was alive. She saw me."

"Jessica saw you. Then she knew you were there to help. She knew you were trying to help her."

"They put a gun to my head. I had to do it."

"What did you do, Tiny? What did you do to Jessica?"

12

CARTER WAS AT THE STATION having some screaming fit with Attorney Staci Lambda over proper protocol and illegally holding Jamal for no reason other than he was a friend to someone wanted for a drug crime. Any way he cut it, Jamal was going to be free to go in no time. Carter hoped he had kept the attorney occupied long enough. Things had become more complicated with the news from Steve Jewel's wife. Carter was going crazy trying to get the search warrants for both strip clubs.

When Staci left Carter's office, Franky burst through the doors. "Hey, Sergeant, what's the news?"

"I think that lawyer lady is a bitch. Oh, and we should have the search warrant within the next hour. Why aren't you at the clubs now?"

"I was headed that way but Tommy wanted to follow-up on another hunch on the Ty Nielson kid. We separated and I needed to get another car."

"Take one from the lot." He paused and grabbed Franky's arm turning him to face him. "What's the lead?"

"He thinks the Nielson kid is in deeper than just drugs. He wanted to talk to the mom. Moms protect their kids, but you never know what might slip out. I think he may give a run at Andrea Jackson about Ty as well, but I am not sure. He doesn't want to have to lie to her about knowing anything about Jessica, and he doesn't want to get her hopes up until we know she is still alive."

"Fine," replied Carter. "Jamal is going to be out of here in a few minutes. I have nothing to hold him on, and although between him and me we milked this process a long time, I don't have any more questions to ask and he has no more information to give."

"When he is finally released, we should let Tommy know. Jamal may make a run straight over to find Tiny."

"Will do, but let's try to keep Jamal here even when he is free to go, as long as the bitch attorney doesn't insist on driving him."

Franky nodded. "I will drive him wherever he wants to go, even if it is over to Tiny's or his mom's house."

"Agreed. Now I need to follow-up on the warrants. When you both can get over there, head to the Red Carpet. We are going to serve them at the same time. I have two teams set. I want you and Tommy at the Red Carpet and I will take the lead at Rick's. I have guys watching the places now to see if they are emptying anything out."

"Can you get warrants for both Moretti's and Polino's homes?" Franky asked.

"Already on their way as well."

"Great," Franky continued. "We need to find something that ties those guys to drugs, prostitution, and murder." He paused, thought a minute, and then added sadly, "The trifecta."

Carter's phone rang and he pressed the button to answer. "Carter."

The voice on the other end was muffled and not clear enough to hear but by the smile growing on the sergeant's face, Franky assumed the news was good.

"Great. I don't want any loopholes on this one. These guys have a fireball lawyer and if we screw this up, she will find it. I will pick up the hard copy warrants in person. Do not give them to anyone but me. I will deliver one to Sullivan and O'Malley at the Red Carpet and take the other one directly to Rick's. I want two teams ready to go at both locations at six p.m. We will serve the warrants at six-fifteen." He looked at me and softly asked, "Will that give O'Malley enough time with the Nielson woman?"

Franky nodded affirmatively.

Carter went back to his phone. "Now get the signatures on the home warrants. Those may be more important. They are not going to keep anything at the clubs. We need access to their personal homes, and I want a list of every property these guys own. This all started with the bodies at Polino's hotel. What else does this guy own?"

Just as Carter clicked off his phone, Jamal appeared from the holding room with his attorney at his side. Jamal was about to speak when Staci Lambda inched in front of him. "We will be going now, Officers."

Again with the title, Carter thought. "Sounds good, Mrs. Lambda, and thank you both for your time." He smiled, pleased he had intentionally not used Ms. in return.

"Don't thank us for our time. This useless ploy to waste my client's and my time was completely transparent. You will be hearing from my office. I am not going to waste one minute more and Mr. Jackson and I will be leaving."

Franky smiled Jamal's direction. "Jamal, I have to go to Tiny's house to pick up Detective O'Malley. I know you were driven here in our police vehicle. Would you like a ride to your mom's?"

Jamal seemed to jump at the option. "That would be perfect. Thank you, sir."

"Absolutely not," stated Staci firmly. "I will drive you wherever you want to go, but I will not give these officers the opportunity to ask you any additional questions under the disguise of a ride home."

"It's fine," protested Jamal. "I won't say anything."

She pulled his arm slightly causing him to lean into her so she could whisper to him. When they separated, Jamal appeared like a slightly beaten animal who had just conceded to larger opposition. "I think I will stick with my attorney."

"You do not have to," interrupted Franky. "I promise, no questions, and we can videotape the entire time we are together. We can also agree that if anything is said, it will be considered off the record. He could tell us he murdered ten people and we couldn't use it."

Staci leaned back with a smirk. Jamal repeated, "No, I will go with Ms. Lambda."

The two turned to leave and although Franky tried to throw a few more feelers out to Jamal, he received no response back. When they were out the door, Franky turned to Carter. "What the hell was that? The boy wanted to come with me. What did she say to him?"

Carter pressed his lips together hard. "They already have something on him. He is already in."

"What could it be? The NCAA thing? We can handle that."

"I don't know," replied Carter, "but I am going to call O'Malley. If Jamal is headed that way, he needs to know."

"He pulled out his phone and dialed. "Goddamnit, no answer."

Franky heard his expletive comment and immediately advised, "Call right back. That is our signal that it is important. One call, no answer. Second call, pick up if there is any way you can."

He placed a second call and again no answer. "Shit," Carter replied. "Should we be concerned?"

"I have time to get there and back to the club well before the warrants need to be served. Do you want me to swing by?"

"Yes, head that way now. I don't like it when he doesn't answer. O'Malley always answers."

Just then Carter's phone beeped saying he had a text. Carter read it out loud. *"Talking to Ty Nielson on mother's phone. Trace the call."*

"Holy crap!" stated Franky. "We need her number now."

"I will call Dispatch. They can bring it up. Do you have Jamal's number?"

"Yes, he gave it to me the other night when he found out I was working his sister's and father's cases."

Carter looked at Franky. "Call him. If the bitch lets him take the call, maybe he can give us Tiny's or Tiny's mother's phone number. We need it now. I am sure he can't keep Ty on the phone long."

Carter jumped on the phone to Dispatch and began speaking to someone who was going to try to locate the residence, then the number, and then start the trace. Franky hit "send" on a call to Jamal. On one ring, Jamal picked up.

"Hello," the voice said softly. Franky could hear Ms. Lambda asking who it was in the background but because she was driving, she really could not do anything about it.

"Jamal, this is Detective Sullivan. I am not calling to ask you anything about the case. We need to reach Ty's mom. Do you happen to have her number, and Tiny's number for that matter?"

"Yes, I have them both. They are in my phone." Franky could tell Jamal had lowered the phone because Ms. Lambda's voice was significantly louder, though she was probably talking louder to go along with it. He heard Jamal talking to her as well. "Nothing. No, nothing about the case. He wants Tiny's mom's phone number." He left out telling her we asked for Tiny's number also, either on purpose or it was just easier not to say it.

As they suspected, Staci did not want him to help or provide the information but she knew we could find it on our own in short order anyway. Her voice in the background did not continue which Franky assumed meant she was not going to stop him. Jamal read off two numbers then it sounded like he dropped his phone possibly for more of a diversion against Staci's protesting. Franky jotted down the numbers and immediately clicked off his phone.

"Carter, I got it."

Within moments the trace was on.

．　．　．　．　．

"What did you do, Tiny? What did you do to Jessica?" I said, trying to keep Tiny on the phone and talking but also trying to learn what the heck he was talking about.

Tiny was still in and out of crying and confusion. Although he was not making much sense, I believed he was speaking the truth. I repeated the question. "Ty, are you still there? What did you do to Jessica?"

"I have to go now, Detective. They won't let me go."

"Where are you, Tiny? I will come get you. We need to talk. Think about your mother. Think about your friend Jamal. Think about Jessica. We can still save Jessica just like you saved me."

His crying stopped for a second after that comment. He did care about saving me from the kid with a gun. He had some feelings on that. I thought I would repeat it. "You saved me, Ty, and we can still save Jessica."

His voice calmed now, as if something had changed. "Detective O'Malley, keep looking for Jess. I have to go do something now."

I was losing him. I needed another shake-up. "Tiny, did you hurt Jessica? Did you hurt Mr. Jackson?"

He did not answer. He had heard the questions. The phone was still connected, but he was not going to respond. I heard some broken breathing and then the phone went dead and the call ended.

"Shit!" I said.

I looked down to my phone as a new text came in. I read it quietly but loud enough for Priscilla Nielson to hear. "*We have the trace. Oak Woods Cemetery.* Oak Woods Cemetery," I repeated. "What is he doing there?"

"That is where my father is buried?" Jamal said, as he stood unnoticed in the doorway. "What are you doing here, Detective? What did Tiny do?" Priscilla was crying in her chair, and I am sure I appeared lost and confused.

My voice was soft but not smooth. I was trying to choose my words carefully so they did not come out sounding like a lie. "Just hold on, Jamal. We don't know anything. I am trying to find your friend. That is all."

Jamal turned without a word and ran back toward the road in front of the apartments. I saw a car there I did not recognize but as he flung open his door, I saw the familiar female attorney inside. They took off without any delay.

"Go get my son, Detective. Bring him back safe. Please bring him back safe. He is all I have."

My natural response was to tell her that I would do everything I could, however, right now I was not sure what the hell he was involved in. I was sure it stretched further than drugs, but other than that I did not know. I placed my hand on her shoulder. "You need to stay here, Mrs. Nielson. My first goal is to find your son. After that, we will have some work to do to help him."

I ran to my car dialing Frank Sullivan. My car was started and heading the same direction as Jamal by the time Franky picked up.

"Jesus, Tommy, what is going on? Jamal is on his way to you with that lawyer. What did you find out from Ty?"

"Jamal has been here," I said. "Head to Oak Woods Cemetery. Ty is in bad shape. Unstable and feels everything is over. I don't know what he did but he is involved. Jamal tore off with that lawyer. He overheard the end of my conversation with Tiny. I asked questions about Jessica and Jamal's father. Based on what he heard, he may have taken that Tiny was involved in her disappearance and his murder, but I don't know for sure that is the case. They have something on him, that much I am certain. Ty feels trapped."

"But if Jamal believes Tiny had something to do with his father and sister, he may act on that." Franky was following my train of thought.

"Right. How far away are you from the cemetery?"

"Probably ten to fifteen minutes."

"I will be there ahead of you but I am five minutes behind Jamal."

"Break a few laws then." Franky's voice was stressed and his tires squealed as he rounded a corner causing other cars to honk. "I wish I had your Camaro right now."

"Me too," I said as we disconnected.

•　　•　　•　　•　　•

Jamal walked through the well-manicured grass of the cemetery. He did not know what he was going to do but he finally knew a critical piece of information. As he looked toward his father's grave, another possible answer was waiting. He saw the man kneeling down in front of the headstone holding his head in his hands. He appeared to be crying. *Crying,* Jamal thought to himself. *What a joke.*

He drew within about fifteen feet and said, "Hey."

The man raised his head and Jamal could see tears streaming down his face. Their eyes met, but the man did not speak. He looked away in shame.

"What are you doing here?"

The man did not answer.

Jamal's tone became harder as he held back the anger growing within him. "You killed him. You killed my father. I just need to know why."

The man did not look up, but his hand moved toward his leg where a previously unnoticed small handgun was resting. He picked up the gun and turned back to Jamal. "Let it go, Jamal. You need to let this one go."

Jamal pulled out his gun and pointed it at the still crouching man. "I don't think so."

"What are you doing with a gun, J?" Tiny asked.

"What are you doing crying at my father's grave, Tiny? A grave that wouldn't be here if you hadn't killed him."

"You don't know what you are doing, J. Get the hell out of here while you can."

"Was it drugs? Did you kill him for drugs? And what about Jess? What did you do to Jessica?"

The mention of Jessica had a different effect on Tiny. He looked down in shame and could not even venture a short stare toward his longtime friend.

"You hurt Jess," Jamal stated when he saw the change. "What did you do to her, you asshole?"

Jamal charged toward his friend who lifted the gun and pointed it directly at him. Jamal stopped a few feet from him, the barrel of the handgun pointing a path right to his heart. "Stop it now, Jamal. Stop it now or so help me I will shoot you dead right here."

✦　　✦　　✦　　✦　　✦

I parked my car right behind the one that had just left the Nielson's house with Jamal as passenger and Staci Lambda driving. The attorney stood a few feet in front of her car staring up the hill. When she saw me drive up, she ran back to meet me. "Hurry! They both have guns. They are pointing them at each other. I can't hear what they're saying but they are yelling."

I shook my head at her. "Where did he get a gun?" I asked.

"I keep one under my seat," she replied. "He may have seen it when he dropped his phone."

I followed her gaze until I saw the two boys standing feet apart. I unholstered my gun as I ran. Tiny had his gun locked on Jamal and Jamal was holding his at his side. I ran toward the two.

"You do not know what's going on, Jamal. Turn around and walk away." Tiny's voice was strained, as if he was bound and partially gagged as he spoke.

"I can't do that, T. Tell me what happened. Tell me what you are part of. What did you do to my sister? Where is she?"

"This is the last time I will warn you. Walk away."

"Or what? You are going to kill me too, like you did the rest of my family?"

"Tyrone Nielson," I shouted drawing my gun directly on him. "Drop your weapon and lie down on the ground with your hands behind your head."

Ty turned my direction briefly and then back to Jamal. "You are in over your head, J. More people are going to get hurt. Go back to Kansas. This isn't high school anymore."

"Tyrone," I shouted again taking small steps toward him but keeping my gun locked directly on him. I could try to injure him and save his life, but in his state and still holding a gun, a miscellaneous shot could go off. No, the only option if he did not relent was the kill shot. I held my gun locked on his head. "Tyrone, you need to come in with me. Do not hurt anyone else."

He turned back to me, moved his gun under his chin, and fired.

"No!" shouted Jamal running to his old friend but unable to catch his body before it struck the ground.

As I walked up, blood had covered both Tiny and Jamal and what appeared to be brain matter splattered across Malcolm Jackson's grave site. The irony of Tiny's blood across the marker was something I would have to think about another time. Right now, I only had one goal. Tiny's head rested on Jamal's lap. I reached down to the young basketball star. "Come on, son. This is no place for you to be right now. Tiny is gone."

13

"I AM SURE the attorney let Polino know about the boy's suicide," said Franky.

"Me too," I replied to Franky as we sat in the Red Carpet parking lot. We were several hours late of the 6:00 p.m. raid but the schedule had been pushed back to 8:45 as a result of the situation involving Ty and Jamal. It was rolling on 8:30. We had not seen Polino or Moretti or any of the staple people whose paths we had crossed. I had to believe even for these guys, this situation was getting way too muddy. They were going to be circling their wagons and trying to get away clean now. The "business as usual" mentality they had previously tried to carry was over.

My phone beeped that I had a text come in, and I glanced down to my phone. It was from Jamal Jackson.

Thank you for saving me. Tiny would have shot me. I could see it in his eyes.

No, Jamal, I typed back. *He was going to protect you the whole time. He just did not want you to see him do it. His only way to protect you from him is what he did. Blame him for everything else we learn, but don't blame him for that.*

He typed back one letter. *J*

"Everything all right?" Franky asked.

"As all right as it is going to be. I had a boy that was able to procure and hide a gun and place himself in about five dangerous situations all while being essentially under my protection." I paused and let out a soft sigh. "Maybe I am starting to lose it, Franky. Maybe I no longer have the edge."

"Nah," he replied, the tone much more serious than the word itself. "You saved that boy's life. Had you not been there, Jamal would not have shot Tiny, but Tiny would have shot him. You know that."

"Yep, it was his only escape route. A few seconds more and it would be Jamal's funeral we'd be attending in a few days and a manhunt for Tyrone Neilson would be underway."

"About how long until we go in?"

I checked my phone. "About ten minutes or so. We can start walking now. I see the lab boys at their van starting to rustle."

"We closing it down tonight?"

"Yes, we won't be able to keep it closed, but they won't reopen until tomorrow. We need to make it a big scene and drive some of their customers away for a while."

"Why don't we hold everyone who leaves and run background checks? Maybe we pick up a few on outstanding warrants in the process. Word of that kind of thing gets out, and it can really hurt the customer base."

I liked the plan and radioed it over to my counterpart and Carter at Rick's right as the clock struck 8:45.

Our teams tore through the two establishments like a fine-oiled machine. All patrons and employees were checked out and numerous arrests were made on everything from outstanding warrants, violation of probation, various predator laws, and numerous other illegal issues that without this warrant would have gone unnoticed. What we did not get were any of our key players. Polino, Marco, Moretti, or Brit or Michelle—suspiciously, none were there though they had been present every other time we had entered the establishment.

We also found a tremendous amount of video and photographic evidence that would have to be investigated later. We found several weapons and a room beyond the VIP room that appeared to be more like a prison cell than part of the club. The most telling thing we found, however, was in Joey Polino's private office. Behind his desk and under a large Oriental rug was a door in the floor. We opened the door and found a ladder leading down to a passageway. We sent men through and they emerged outside the grounds on a vacant lot about one hundred yards away. Over the last twenty-four hours, Joey Polino and his guys had been able to move in and out of this club without anyone knowing and remove or add anything they wished. When I saw that, I knew whatever evidence we found would be useless.

I called Carter and explained what we had found. Within minutes, he called back saying because of my information, they focused their search on the same thing and found the exact same type of hidden door and passageway.

It was about midnight when we headed back to the station. All the information and materials taken had been logged but none of it had been studied yet. Carter would put a rush on it but it would still take days. My leads had started to dry up and the jazz was fading. We had put an APB out on Moretti and Polino. They would not be under arrest unless we found something in the evidence collected, but I really believed that was unlikely. The APB was to provide official notification to the owners as to what took place. Because we had received Ms. Lambda's card and she was identified as Mr. Polino's attorney, we placed a call to her as well. Carter and I both assumed she would show up tomorrow in his place keeping him free from any level of interrogation.

"Hey, Sergeant, do you want to start going through this stuff tonight?"

Franky had already headed home, and it was just me and Carter at the station. He looked over at me, and I could see the stress in his face. He had counted on getting something at the clubs. He had placed officers on it since Clark's murder, and the information Franky and I provided linking everything to Polino's clubs sealed the deal in his mind. Learning that those officers wasted their time and Polino could move everything out without us knowing cut him deep. "Get out of here, O'Malley. I know you want to go check on the boy anyway, so go do it."

He could read me like a book. "You don't have to tell me twice. I'll be done at Jamal's by 1:15 a.m. You want to meet me at Mr. J's? A Dagwood sounds good right about now."

Why don't you bring the Dagwoods over to Flapjaws and we close that place down. I could use something stronger than just meat."

"A buddy of mine suggested McNaughton's. It wasn't too bad. I will meet you there before 2:00."

"Whatever buddy of yours suggested McNaughton's, he is a buddy of mine also."

"I can guarantee that is correct, Sergeant."

●　　●　　●　　●　　●

I placed a rose on the doormat of the Nielson's apartment before I walked the few steps over to Jamal's front door. I was hesitant to knock because it was so late, but I also knew they would be up. I could have called, but Jamal and his mom would most likely have told me not to come. Therefore, it was shortly before one a.m. and I was about to knock on the door of a house where the daughter disappeared weeks ago and was presumed dead, the father had been murdered this week, and the son was almost shot earlier that day by his longtime best friend. To say they may be jumpy with a one a.m. unexpected visitor was probably an understatement. Maybe I should have called first, I thought, but why keep thinking about it. I was already here so it did not really matter what I should have done. The horse was already out of the barn on this one.

Jamal came to the door and without even checking the eyehole, he opened the door. "I knew you would be coming by to check on us."

"I just wanted to make sure you were okay," I responded.

"Come on in, Detective," Andrea Jackson said from behind. "Please come on in and join us."

"I can't stay, ma'am, I just wanted to be sure you folks were doing okay."

"Nonsense," she added again. "Jamal told me that you saved him. He also said you tried to save Tyrone. Pity all this tragedy had to happen. I can't imagine how we are all going to recover."

"I can't begin to understand, Mrs. Jackson." I turned to Jamal and placed my hand on his shoulder. "You okay, Jamal?"

He shrugged. "Not really, Detective. I want to know what Tiny knew about my sister and father. He knew something. I am sure of it, but he wouldn't tell me."

"I hope we find something in the evidence we recovered from the raids on the two clubs. The warrants for the houses came through as well. We are going there in the morning. We are watching the homes now. We will find something, Jamal. I have not given up on Jessica." I paused then spoke softer, "Did you tell your mother we saw her in video?"

"He did tell me, Detective. And I must say you should have told me too, but I understand why you did not."

How the hell did she hear me ask that? What does she have, Vulcan ears? I thought. I nodded to her, understanding that she was not mad but disappointed I did not trust to tell her. I slapped Jamal on the back. "You folks need to get some sleep. I will head out as I have an early morning with the warrants and all."

Jamal walked me to the door and reached out his hand. "Thank you, Detective O'Malley. I know you said Tiny wouldn't shoot, but I wasn't so sure. He was not really Tiny at that point, and because of that, we were no longer friends at that point either."

I shook his hand but did not reply. I nodded respectfully to Andrea Jackson and then headed to my car, after hearing their front door shut and latch in my wake.

•　　•　　•　　•　　•

Roy Pura, the Flapjaws' bartender, the same bartender that was there almost every night, came over to Carter and me. "Gentlemen, it is against the law for me to serve drinks any later. This is the final last call of the night."

Carter's voice was slightly slurred. "Then we'll take four more McNaughton's on the rocks."

Roy looked at me, and I nodded. Carter then added, "And that was 'each' boy, not four total."

Again I nodded before Roy slid back behind the bar and quickly produced a bottle of McNaughton's. "There's about six drinks left in that bottle. I am going to be cleaning up for about an hour. You boys can finish that bottle and then I will get you a cab. Deal?"

Carter grabbed the bottle, poured two more glasses, and lifted one. "To Clark."

There was no way I would not drink to that. The liquor was already to both of our heads but we didn't care. Tonight was not about Polino or Moretti and it was not even about Malcolm, Jessica, or Tyrone Nielson. It was about Tom Clark. I did not realize it when Carter asked me to join him, but he thought he was going to solve Tom Clark's murder tonight. When he didn't, it was like being stabbed in the back. Now he was letting the liquor do the stabbing.

"Are we going to get these guys, O'Malley?"

"Polino and Moretti?" I paused. "Yeah, we will get them."

"I don't know," he replied, still slightly slurring his words. "They seem to always be a step ahead. Untouchable bastards think they are so smart. So powerful. F the police. That is what they say."

"No, they are not a step ahead. We just had not started pursuing yet. They had been going behind the scenes. They started with all the cards, and now we are just beginning to be dealt into the game. They are scared right now, boss. They are covering their tracks. That is a sign we are close."

"That hidden passageway was pretty smart though, don't ya think?"

I looked at him. I was feeling the liquor too but not as bad. "Yeah, that one pissed me off. I can't believe they had those built and nobody knew about it. The minute they started to feel the heat, they were cleaning everything out."

"Going to be the same thing at the homes," Carter added.

"I know. Probably even less evidence because they don't want their homes involved at all."

"I don't understand why Polino let Moretti in. He had the whole setup. He had everything. Clubs, money, drugs, laundering—why did he need Moretti?"

"I don't know. Moretti has deep pockets, and maybe Polino was involved in something even bigger than him."

"No," Carter replied. "We are missing something there. Clark may have found it, but we are still missing that piece."

We finished our bottle right on the hour and Roy, true to his word, called us a cab and charged it to the bar. "Take care, Detective. Take care, Sergeant."

We nodded and plopped down in the back seat of the cab. The driver looked back at us and smiled. "Detective O'Malley. Good to see you. Headed home?"

•   •   •   •   •

Neither Carter nor I should probably have been at the homes of Moretti and Polino the next morning. We both took cabs to get there because we suspected that if we had been given a Breathalyzer, we would not have passed. I intentionally left my gun locked in the car so I would not end up having to make a decision to fire it or not.

Carter appeared much worse for the wear than I, but if he felt as bad as I did, how we looked was immaterial. Franky took a leadership role in directing traffic. We were at Polino's house first and then headed to Moretti's. They were only five miles apart in an upper end neighborhood of Burr Ridge, Illinois. I believe Bo Jackson lived here as well. In all my years I had never been to this area of Chicago. It was just off I-55 headed toward St. Louis. They were all beautiful homes in the multimillions. That statement alone probably defined why I had never been there. Twenty-year Chicago homicide cops don't typically have cases that overlap with Burr Ridge.

The warrant was served without issue. Joey Polino's wife was present as was his lawyer. It was a pleasure seeing Staci Lambda again—an absolute bitch but she did know the law. None of us could argue that fact. We collected some files, photos, and other information and video, but as expected, the house was clean. Even what we collected was not going to lead to anything. We requested the location of Joey Polino and were informed if we had a warrant for his arrest, he would be produced but until that happened, he would not be speaking with us. Bitch.

What we did not expect was Joey's eighteen-year-old son, Darryn Polino. He walked around as if his crap did not stink. Entitled kid wearing a St. Louis Cardinals shirt in the heart of Chicago. The type of kid I used to beat up in school, but I am sure if someone beat him up, Daddy would make sure everything was made right. I still could not believe I grew up being friends with Joey Polino. Hell, I defended him.

The story was repeated at Moretti's house. Ms. Lambda met us there and ensured we knew the limits of the warrant down to the period at the end. The limits of the warrant are as follows... Bitch, bitch, bitch. I hate that woman.

We were done at both houses by four p.m. and I realized I had not heard or reached out to Jamal. Instantly that worried me because he had been unpredictable throughout this whole process. Kansas was playing at six tonight and I thought I would swing by and see if he wanted to watch with me. The thing about basketball players like every athlete even after they have given up the game, they still will always watch. It is an escape and that is exactly what I thought Jamal needed.

I called Jamal at his home number instead of his cell with part of me hoping Andrea would pick up. Hearing how Jamal was through his mom might lend some more truth to his condition.

"Hello," a female voice said.

"Mrs. Jackson?"

"Yes, who may I ask is calling?"

"Hello Andrea, this is Detective O'Malley."

Her voice raised significantly. I could not believe how well put together she was with everything that had happened in her life. "Why hello, Detective. Do you have any news on my daughter?"

The question went right to the heart. "No, ma'am, but we are still going through the evidence we recovered from the clubs. We believe she was tied to the clubs at some level."

"Will you keep me informed this time?"

The subtle shot at withholding information was very clear. "Yes, ma'am, I will keep you informed. How is Jamal?"

"I think he is doing okay. He fell asleep on the couch watching Sports Center so I think that is a good sign. Kansas plays Texas tonight so he is looking forward to watching that."

"That is what I'm calling about. I was wondering if you both would like to come back to my house for dinner again tonight and stay to watch the game?"

"I am sure we would love to. The game starts at six I believe he said. What time would you like us there? Jamal went this morning and picked up our car so we can drive over no problem."

"Why don't you come by anytime after five-thirty?"

"Perfect," she replied. "If anything changes, just give us a call."

"You do the same," I added. And we both hung up.

I typically do not get personal with families, but the Jacksons were different. This was not personal, this was protection. I did not know what drew their family into this web of crime yet, but something had. Until I knew what it was, I was going to keep them close.

•   •   •   •   •

I am not typically a Kansas basketball fan, but how can you not be a fan of that team? The tradition. The greatness. I had to live through Northwestern and Purdue and to a lesser extent, Notre Dame. All of them can now and again put out a good team for a few years, but not like Kansas. Every year they kill it. The number one place to play college basketball, and I have their star sitting in my living room while his team blows out the Texas Longhorns. The players dedicated the game to Jamal and his family. Bill Williams, the legendary head coach who visited Jamal and his dad on the River Court, said some wonderful things about his star talent, and even the ESPN announcers bid their thoughts his way. All of these gestures caused Andrea Jackson to put her hand on her son's leg and say five simple words: "You have to go back."

"Not until I know what happened to Dad and we have found Jessica," he replied firmly.

"Jamal, your father would want you to be playing, and so would Jessica."

Jamal stood and paced with a definite hard step. I was in the kitchen putting together some appetizers and his walk drew my attention immediately. "Really! Really, Mom. Let's say Jess is being held in someone's basement. Trapped. Beaten, or worse. You think she would want me playing basketball?"

"Hey, Jamal," I said. "There is no need to speak like that. You don't know what Jessica's situation is so do not speak of the worst case. I saw her on a video and she was dazed and possibly a little lost, but she was not beaten. My gut tells me she is in hiding because she is protecting you guys. Don't even think about the rest until we know more."

That pacified Jamal but Andrea was not pleased. "Now you listen to me, Jamal Malcolm Jackson. I am still your mother and you will respect me. You don't raise your voice to me even when it comes to your sister. When I said your father would want you to play basketball, I meant it. He is up in heaven right now wanting to see you on the floor, and don't you forget it." She stopped talking and fixed her hair slightly trying to appear still in control. In a lower tone, she continued, "Now, I will give you five more days to stay here. On day six, you are going back to Kansas. That will get you back in time for the K-State game, which I will watch with Detective O'Malley right here on this TV, and you will score at least thirty points for your father and sister. Do you understand me?"

Jamal had looked down in respect when his mom responded to the tone he had taken with her. However, even he could not keep the smile completely off his face when he heard the very clear description down to the number of points. He was about to speak when she grabbed her phone and began typing a text.

"What are you typing, Mama?"

Dear Coach Williams, my son Jamal will be returning next Friday. He will be conditioning this week locally so he will be ready to play. I want to personally thank you for the time you allowed him and our family to grieve, but his father would want him on the court as soon as possible. Thank you again, Andrea Jackson.

"Send." She smiled at her son. "Your coach was nice enough to provide me his cell phone number if I ever needed to reach him. I just used it."

I used the break to drop a plate of barbeque wings down in front of them and adjust the TV so everyone could see it better. "Looks like Texas is not going to have a chance to get back in this one," I said.

Jamal still looked at his mom who sat with a satisfied look on her face. "You know, Mom, I can just text him that I need to extend it. It doesn't mean anything."

She did not say it, but the look of, "I dare you to try to extend it, Jamal Malcolm Jackson," was visibly written across her face.

As they were getting ready to leave, my phone began to ring. I looked over to see the number. Unknown. I clicked on the "answer" button and put it to my ear.

"O'Malley."

"Wow, so formal, Detective," returned a woman's voice.

"Thank you for noticing," I replied. "Now who is this?"

"It is TJ. TJ Hutchin from the Chop House."

Instantly my voice softened but that was all that was soft. "Ah yes, Ms. Hutchin, to what do I owe this pleasure?" Jamal and his mother could see the change in me, and they each smiled slightly and gave me a quick wave as they stepped out. "One moment. You both do not have to leave. This is a work call."

Andrea looked at me. "Your voice does not sound like work."

They stepped out and I put my ear back to the phone with a small smile of my own growing across my face. "Okay, I'm back."

"Work call, huh?" she said sarcastically.

"Well, I can't believe a beautiful woman like you would call me for any other reason," I replied, pleased with my answer.

"Nice recovery, Detective." I knew she was smiling on her end of the phone as well. "I took the liberty of reviewing the tapes myself, more out of curiosity than anything else. I assume it's the African-American girl you were interested in who made the call and then was followed and picked up in a car outside?"

I was intrigued. "Yes," I said slowly, not necessarily comfortable talking openly about a case with someone not involved in it, even at her somewhat involved level. "Why do you ask?"

"Well, I assume you saw the man leave the bar behind her and then arrange for the pickup down the street, but I also know you only took the video from the two hours before and after the call. I think there was someone else there calling the shots, but they were patient. Very patient. Stayed till almost closing."

"What? Someone else following the girl? How do you know?"

"No, Detective, following the *man* who was following the girl." She paused which was nice because it gave me time to let that sink in just a bit. "I followed the tape back to where the girl entered followed by the man. What you probably did not see was the man who came in after. He came in well after. He did not ask for a table and went straight to the bar. He spent time before entering, scouting the area with his eyes, and then locked on the man. I don't think he even knew the man was following the girl at first. He found a spot where he could see the man, but it would be difficult for the man to see him. There he waited. In the course of watching the man, he determined the man was watching the girl. That made him nervous. When the girl left followed by the man, this man kept his tab open, left his drink and jacket in his seat, and went outside to make a phone call. Whether he made the call or not cannot be determined on the camera, but he paced around putting on a good show, never taking his eyes off the man and the girl. When the man grabbed her, he pulled his phone from his ear and took a picture. Then he came back inside and stayed for at least three hours before leaving."

"Wow!" I said. "You got all of that from your video just because you were intrigued by us asking for it?"

"Did your IT guy already know all that?" she asked.

"No. As you thought, we stopped with the first man. We did not even entertain the idea of a second. Did he pay with a credit card?"

"No," she replied, her voice dropping a bit. "All cash and a lot of it."

"What are you doing right now?" I asked.

"Changing into something nice to meet you at the restaurant."

Bingo. "Ah, well, I guess that takes my next question off the table. What do you say? Thirty minutes?"

"How about forty-five? I was going to jump in the shower first."

Blackout Bingo. "Okay then, forty-five at the Chop House."

"See you then, Detective."

We hung up. For a very brief moment I felt like a kid in junior high who had just made his first date. I had not felt like this in a long time. Then, reality hit. This woman is in the restaurant business. It is her job to flirt. She has video information for me. That is all. Still, I thought, I might want to shave and put on my nice jacket. I did not want to look like a bum, at least on a first date.

"I should let Franky know about the video and then see if he has any new information on the case." Again I was talking to myself, this time louder than most. I stared back down at my phone, spun through my speed dial list, and hit "Franky." The phone rang.

"What's up, partner?"

I relayed what I just learned from TJ and he, like me, was extremely pleased to hear it. Since the lack of early success from the warrant, leads had been very few and far between so anything new was a positive. "I can be ready in ten and will meet you at the restaurant," he said.

"Whoa, Hoss. I think I will take this visit on my own. I am sure you can follow-up on some of the materials we confiscated from the houses and clubs.

Someone involved needs to be present to look through those."

"Yeah, we are set to go through those tomorrow morning. This is the best lead we have to follow-up on tonight."

"Okay, but I think it would be better if you stayed in tonight and got some needed sleep, focused on going through the whole case, and make sure we did not miss anything."

"Well," Franky replied, "I guess I could do that, but I think I will still have time after the video review."

"And what about all the paperwork we have to complete on this? We are way behind." I was running out of ideas for him, and I knew Franky hated doing the reports.

"Well, I thought tomorrow morning as we are reviewing the documents from the warrants we could knock out the reports together. You have more with the cemetery anyway."

My voice got more firm. "Okay, Franky, here is how it is. You said you can be ready in ten minutes. I will be ready in forty-five. I am going to shower, shave, and dig out my brown sports coat." I paused. "Do you understand what I am saying?"

He did not answer immediately. "You want me to wait for you at the bar of the restaurant?"

"Jesus Christ, Franky. I am going to wear by *brown sports coat*. Do you remember the last time I wore that?"

He thought a minute. "Yeah, I think you wore it when you had that date with the prosecutor you liked so much. Really the first woman you dated since your divorce. I don't know if you have worn it since then."

"I haven't. Do you understand?"

"So you think that prosecutor may be at the restaurant?"

"How have you made it as a detective all these years?" My voice was flat and hard. "Stay home tonight, Franky. Let's leave it at that."

"Tell Ms. Hutchin that I am sorry I won't be able to see her, but my best friend thinks you may fall for me if I am there. He wants first shot," he added with a sinister giggle.

"You are an asshole, Sullivan."

"Don't do anything I wouldn't do, O'Malley."

Click. If it was possible to slam a receiver down with a cell phone, I would have.

• • • • •

I pulled into the valet area exactly forty-four minutes after my call with Tammi. I had to drive around the block seven times to be there exactly forty-four minutes since my last call, but damn it, I made it. To my surprise and pleasure, Tammi pulled in right behind me. The valet drivers ran to her car, bypassing me like I was chopped liver. My police-issue car did not really measure up to her vehicle, a Z5 two-seat convertible BMW. Boy, I wished my '74 Camaro was back. She would have been jealous.

"Nice car," I said, reaching my hand down to help her out.

"This old thing. It's for show. I drive it when I am trying to impress a man."

"How many times have you driven it lately?" I asked.

"Twice in five years," she said smiling.

"Sounds like my sports coat," I mumbled under my breath.

She grabbed the inside of my arm. "How many times have you driven that sports coat in the last five years?"

I was surprised she heard the comment but I did not mind answering. "Including tonight, once."

"I am flattered," she replied in a whisper so only I could hear.

She pulled her arm in tight to mine so the sides of our bodies touched the entire way down. She was wearing an elegant dress that held tight to her body. It was blue, long, and formfitted every curve with perfection. Her jewelry was exquisite and her long hair cascaded down her back and shoulders with the beauty of a movie star. Yes, I was out of my league.

As we entered the restaurant, just like the valets, everyone quickly approached and welcomed Tammi. She was greeted by customers and employees alike. Everyone seemed to like her to the extent that they were thrilled to even talk to her. Keith Kaplan, the general manager I had met the same time I met Tammi, swung by and kissed her on the cheek. "Tammi, tonight is your only night off. What are you doing here?" He turned to me. "And Detective O'Malley, a pleasure to see you again."

She smiled at the greeting, as did I. I was surprised he remembered my name, but I guess in his business, remembering people is a major part of his job. Tammi replied first. "I know, but I had an offer I could not refuse from Tommy, plus there was something on the video I wanted to show him."

An offer she couldn't refuse—Bingo. "I believe the offer not able to be refused was for me, but I couldn't have been more pleased with the opportunity, and it is good to see you again as well."

Mr. Kaplan smiled, almost as if he was pleased that his assistant general manager may be on a date, even if it was under the pretense of something else. He directed his next comments to both of us. "Don't work too long. Come have a drink at the bar with me. Enjoy yourselves. I do not know you, Detective, but I am sure having a night off is rare for you, and I know Tammi never takes one. Therefore, savor this while you can."

"Thank you, Mr. Kaplan, and please call me Tommy. All my friends do, although some call me much worse."

He smiled and nodded at Tammi again. "Not too much work, TJ. Ten minutes, then the office is closed for the night."

"We will see, Keith," she said smiling as she passed by him, still locked in arms with me.

When we got into the back security office, I had the opportunity to really look at Tammi Hutchins. She did not sit in the chair at the monitor station and instead leaned down with her hands on the desk. I was behind her and the view from my end was one I am not sure I had seen before. I knew one thing at that moment. I had no business being with her, but for some unknown act of the gods, I was.

"I left it cued up so we could cut right to it. All I have to do is hit "play." It is going to start when he first comes into the bar area. You will not see either the woman or the other man in this shot because he is so far removed from the bar. This was caught on a second camera that I assume your team did not even scan but for more than a few seconds. If he had not paused so long before entering the bar, I would not have seen him myself."

She played the video and immediately my heart raced. It took less than a second for me to say the name. "Marco Filini."

"You know him?"

"Yes, I know him," I replied.

"Is he related to the case? Who is he?"

I looked at her and all the high school crush feelings were gone immediately. "Tell nobody you have this video. That man is someone who is paid to tie up loose ends. The man who was following the woman was a loose end. The woman may have become one. If he finds out you have video of him, even though this really shows nothing, you could be in danger. Do you understand? This is a very bad man."

She looked back at me with a seriousness I had not seen before. The flirtatious nature she had portrayed was gone, and by looks, she did understand what I was trying to explain. "I won't say a thing, Tommy. I had no idea those kind of people really existed."

I caught my tone and realized that there was no reason to scare her. "Hey, don't worry. He would have no reason to suspect anything here. Just don't tell friends about it at a cocktail party. One person tells another person and then the wrong person hears and then there is no going back. Once he and his boss believe there is a problem, then they only know one way to make a problem disappear."

"They really do that?" She paused and then added more softly, "Kill people?"

"The man who followed that girl the other night was found in a car trunk about eight hours after your video was shot."

She had still been leaning on the counter and now turned and sort of collapsed into my arms. I slowly and a bit uncomfortably, because I was so out of practice, placed my arms around her in return. She whispered, "And the girl?"

"Nothing yet," I replied. "But she was not wanted for the same thing. I think the man was looking to find someone to help him get off the hit list. That is why he was trying to get to her. I think she is on the inside somehow. But she also reached out to an undercover police officer. That was the call she made. I think she wanted out. If they found out about that call, then she was in as much trouble as the man."

"This is crazy," she said. "Undercover police officers, hit men, murdered people in trunks—this can't be real."

I actually curled up my lips into the beginnings of a smile. If she only knew what I saw every day. Thank God few people ever see what haunts me at night. "I know," I replied with care in my voice. Motioning back to the video, I asked, "Can you replay this again? I don't need you to cut a tape of it, just replay what you showed me and then make sure it is saved. I will record a video on my phone of your monitor so I have a record of it."

She replayed what she had before, and I made the video and then took Mr. Kaplan's advice. We found a quiet table in the corner that he had saved for her, or us, as the case was. We enjoyed some special chef-prepared small plates and she had a glass of red wine, which although not my favorite drink, I opted to have with her. The wine paired excellently with our food as we talked and learned about each other's lives. Not much was said about past relationships. I shared that I had not been in one in several years and she matched that almost word for word.

"Why did you call me now?" I asked.

"Because when I work here, men approach me almost every night. They talk to me about their successful jobs, their homes, their lives. Many are married but willing to remove that wedding ring for a night. Some are not married but they are so caught up in themselves, I immediately know why they are not. You were shy. You smiled at me. You are a Chicago police officer who is proud to be one. I don't know. I caught you glance at me once and look away. I liked that. Most men in here stare at me until I catch their eyes then they keep staring harder and harder, like that is supposed to draw me into them or something." She reached across the table and took my hand in hers. "Why did you put on that brown sports coat?"

Without a pause, I replied, "Because I looked away when you caught me looking at you."

She smiled. Her phone beeped. She looked down, and her face turned slightly downward.

"What is it?" I asked.

"That is my work alarm. It signals me I need to start doing the rounds to push people out of here."

"What time is it?" I asked.

"Quarter till two."

She saw my face collapse in surprise. "How did it get so late? I would have guessed it was still before midnight."

She again took my hand. "Will you give me a quick minute?"

I nodded and she rose from the table and walked out of the bar area and back up the stairs. In a few minutes she returned, walking through the room, drawing every eye in the place. I stood as she approached the table. She took my hand. "Are you ready to leave?"

"I am. I will wait with you while the valet brings your car up."

We got outside and my car was already parked in front of the valet stand. The valet tossed me the keys. "Thank you, sir, but I will wait for Ms. Hutchin's car to be brought up."

He looked a bit strangely at me and then to Tammi. Tammi, who was still under my arm, leaned in close to me and whispered, "Why don't you just open your door for me?"

I looked at her, allowed the synapses in my brain to fire a few times connecting the dots, then my stare turned into a smile. "Never mind, gentlemen, I will drive Ms. Hutchin home." I walked to the door, opened it, and she slid in. I came around to the driver's side and climbed in as well.

"Why are you smiling?" she asked.

"That is the first time I have ever opened the front door of a police car for anyone. I almost sat you in the back out of habit."

She leaned over and kissed my cheek. "If you had done that, I would have had to have been in handcuffs. That might be for later."

Bingo! I fired the engine up and headed out.

14

"WHAT ARE YOU SMILING AT, O'Malley?"

"That is the second time in about four hours I have heard that question, Sergeant. Only I will answer you with 'no comment.'"

"He met that lady from the Chop House last night," added Franky from the side. "The pretty manager lady. Tammi, I think."

"O'Malley? For real?" Sergeant Carter was more attentive now.

"Relax," I said. "It's not like that. She had reviewed the video and found something we missed. There was another man at the bar that night. One following Jewel. A man we all know."

That got both their attention, which took the focus away from my rendezvous.

"Who?" asked Franky walking over.

"Marco Filini. I think he thought he was out of camera range in the bar, but they had a second camera that caught him. He came in after Jewel and Jessica and then watched. If you watch the whole video, it appears he was only one tailing Jewel. He was probably going to take him out that night regardless. Then the Jessica thing got in the way. Take a look at the video."

They both watched the video clip on my phone. After it completed, Carter threw his arms in the air and asked, "What the hell does all this mean?"

"I have a theory," I said.

Franky pulled a couple chairs around the desk for them to both sit facing me. "Go ahead, Tommy, let's have it."

"Everything in all the video I saw points to Marco only tailing Jewel. When he realized Jewel was not there for dinner but was himself tailing someone, he had to ask the question—what does Jewel want with Jessica?" They both nodded agreement. "The only answer I can come up with is Jewel was desperate to get out. He had been cleaning up the messes left by whatever they were doing but he really was not getting his hands dirty. When he set up Malcolm and then learned Malcolm was murdered and we came asking questions, he was scared he would be tied to the murder somehow. I think he was going to come to us with information, but he needed Jessica for some reason."

"Trade," Carter said. "He was planning to come here and produce Jessica Jackson in exchange for immunity from his participation in everything else."

"That was my thinking," I said. "But Marco realized he was going to do that and took them both. He probably took Jessica just to be sure they had not talked, or he used it as an opportunity to kill two birds with one stone."

Franky shook his head. "It all depends on Jessica's role in all this. Is she a part of it and also needs out or is she a part of it and would have set up Jewel on her own after they talked? Or was this whole thing a setup to get Jewel?" Franky added.

"Yes, Jessica is the wild card, with one piece of info that pushes me to believe she wanted out," I added.

"Clark," stated Carter. "She called Clark."

"Yes," I replied. "Did she call Clark because she knew he was an undercover cop, or did she call him because she believed she knew his undercover identity?"

"The bottom line," Franky added, "we have to find Jessica and we have to find her alive. If she dies, most likely they all go free."

"My thoughts exactly. That is why I want to change our direction. I don't want to go after Polino and Moretti. I want all our efforts put into finding Jessica. She is the key."

"That is fine," said Carter. "Where do we start? You have been looking for her since she vanished with little to no leads."

I nodded. "First, have all that video we confiscated from the clubs analyzed, and look for anything with her in it. Then, do we have any other undercover agents out there who might be able to help? Anyone else she may have gone to for help, undercover or even an informant that owes us? Clark referenced another person one time but it was not recently."

"I can put the word out on my end," said Franky.

"I will get IT copies of Jessica's picture and get them reviewing the tapes. I will also check with Captain Field. He was Clark's contact while he was under. If anyone knows someone else who can help, he would have been the one Clark told."

"I talked to him at the murder scene that morning," added Franky. "He committed any resources to us to help. I will run by and talk to him and see what he knows."

"I will go back to talk to Rosalyn Clark again. I doubt she knows anything but I want to check in on her anyway," I added.

"Let's get on it and meet back here tonight. We can confirm exactly when as we know better our timing. I will also reissue the missing person's report on Jessica. I am not going to say anything that the media will pick up. I just want it in front of all the departments again. If we go too big, it might put her life in danger. Even if she is on the inside, they may see her as too big a target and need to remove her just to make the noise go away." Carter was already heading back to his office as he finished talking. Franky and I gathered our stuff and headed for the door.

•　　•　　•　　•　　•

Captain Dana Field was a large man. He had grown up a military guy and was a stereotypical cop—shaved head, big build, and hard personality. He fit well in Chicago but might not be as well suited if he ever left the big city. His first name did him no favors. Most people thought he was a woman before they met him. However, once that meeting took place, no one ever told him about their initial mistaken assumption for fear of having their arms ripped out of the sockets. There were stories that Captain Field could bench press more than five hundred pounds. He had those arms that could not hang straight down at his sides when he stood. Regardless, this was the guy we hoped knew someone in the Chicago underground that could help us. If not, Franky would go back to Q, his CI, and try to get more out of him. However, overusing a CI was not good for anyone, and it had only been a few days since we last met with him on Lower Wacker. Using Q again would be Franky's last choice.

"Hey, Captain. How are you doing?" asked Franky.

"Sullivan, come on in." Dana's voice was deep and strong and corresponded perfectly with his build. "What can I do for you? Is this about Clark?"

"Yes, Captain. We have got to find the missing woman who contacted Tom the night before he was killed. We have her on video. Detective O'Malley and I were hoping you might know someone on the inside who might have information on where a person would be hiding if they needed to disappear for a while."

He pushed his lips together and stood and paced in back of his desk. Franky could tell he knew something or someone but was not saying anything. "What is it?" Franky pushed. "Tom was killed because this girl called him. I have seven dead women and Tommy has a dead father. How many people have to die before we make some tough decisions?"

"Damn it, Franky, it is not that simple. You know what it means to be undercover. All your safety rides on the knowledge that nobody will find out who you are."

Franky stood from his chair and moved to stand in front of the captain. "Are you saying there is someone else under? Was there someone else under with Tom?"

Field turned away and stared out his back window which had the shades down. It faced an area of cubicles, not the outside. His voice became softer, almost distant. "I don't know for sure. Information like that is need-to-know, and it was not someone who reported through me. Tom said he saw someone one time. That is it. That is all I know."

"Who could tell me?"

His voice did not change. "Let me put it to you this way. If it were reversed and this other cop was killed and some detective came asking me for information on Tom, my answer would be no. One cop is dead. There would be no way I would risk Tom."

"That's fine, Captain, but let it be his choice. If I talk to his contact and then he tells that person what is going on, then maybe this cop wants to help. Maybe he gives a shit that Tom was killed."

"Are you fucking kidding me? This guy, if he exists, is surrounded by killers. The last thing he's going to do is risk everything before it is time, whether another cop was killed or not. You risk things at the wrong time, and we will have two dead cops real fast."

"Still, Captain, with all due respect, it is not your call to make. It is his." Franky paused and then added, "Let me give you a hypothesis. Let's pretend it was me undercover and I learned another undercover cop was killed. What would be the first question I ask?"

There was a long pause before Field answered, "Do they know about me too?"

"Don't you think whoever is under is scared shitless right now? Don't you think we owe him any information we can get? Even if he won't come out, you have to get word to him about what went down with Clark and why. I can fill you in on everything we know. You plant some seeds in the areas with the best possibility for someone to be in the know with the other undercover cop. Include our need for information on a missing girl and see what happens."

Field stared into Franky's eyes. Then, he broke his stare and began pacing again. He turned back and replied, "I'll do it. One time and one time only. If nothing comes of it, do not come back asking again."

"Understood," Franky replied. "If you hear something, call me."

Franky left the office and pulled out his phone. He sent a quick text to Carter and me and let us know he was going to give Q a run again but it may not be until later, even possibly after we meet at the station. I replied, telling him to head back and see how IT was coming with the video and documents we recovered at the clubs. Carter had told them to target their search on Jessica so if they got lucky, and if Polino and company had possibly missed something or made a mistake, then maybe we might have a lead as to her whereabouts.

•　　•　　•　　•　　•

I made it to Rosalyn Clark's house. I knew this was a waste of time as far as the case was concerned, but I wanted to check on her, and as a homicide cop, I liked ruling everything out in an investigation. Often it was the thing I assumed would not make any difference that came up and tied it all together. After a single knock, she answered.

"Detective O'Malley, to what do I owe this visit?"

"Could I come in, Ros? I don't have anything to report so I don't want to get your hopes up, but I did want to ask a few more questions if possible."

"Sure, Tommy, come on in."

We took seats in her living room, me on the La-Z-Boy and her on the end of the couch. This way we could face each other and still only be a few feet apart. I took her hands in mine. "How are you and the boys?"

She smiled. "We are getting by okay. The funeral is tomorrow so we are preparing for that. Because of his cover, they are not going to do a police burial.

The chief of police told me they will recognize him as an officer when it is safe, probably in three or four months."

"I know about the funeral. We were told not to attend. If police show up, it could alert someone. I think it's bullshit. The chance he was killed because of something his cover did is so small. He was killed because the wrong person found out he was a cop."

"Yeah, but he was so careful. He told me all the time. He never risked it with anyone. The *only* people he ever talked to from his real life were Captain Field, me, you, and Franky. Those were the only people he trusted. He changed phones every week, sometimes every day. You don't stay under as long as he did by not being careful. You said that woman called him. If she did, it was not because he was a cop."

"That is really where my question came from," I continued. "You just mentioned those he trusted. Did he ever mention another cop that was under? Did he ever see anyone else or think there was someone else he could trust?"

"No, not that I can remember." Then she stopped abruptly, and I saw the change in her face. She remembered something.

"What is it, Ros?"

"A hooker. It wasn't even that long ago but he came over one night drunk, and I mean really drunk. It was maybe two or three months ago. He had gone to one of his boss's parties,"—she paused and clarified though I knew what she meant—"the boss of his cover identity. It was at some slimy hotel but he was there to help with entertaining a new client. The party got out of hand and this new client beat the crap out of some hookers. He recognized one of the hookers. He did not come out and say it, but I thought it was somebody else undercover. But she had been drugged and raped. He never brought it up again, and he did not say anything more. He would not have told me that if he had not been so drunk."

My mind was racing. What if the other undercover person was not a man but a woman? A vice detective or special victim's detective that got in over her head. Maybe that is why Franky said Captain Field had to be pushed so hard. What if Clark saw her and could not do anything, then could not find her again? What if, what if, what if...

"What is it, Tommy? Is that important?"

"Ros, you may have just given us a whole new direction. The job your ex-husband did was incredible. A real hero."

"I am sure Jamie and Marcus would like to hear that. It will mean more coming from you." She smiled and grabbed my hand. "Tommy, I know you will solve this one, but I also know you can't promise me anything. But when you do, will you come back here and tell my two boys about their dad? Tell them in a way I can't so they understand."

"I absolutely will, Ros. I absolutely will." I got up to leave and then turned back as I reached the door. "Franky and I will see you at the funeral tomorrow. We may be in the background, but we will be there."

She smiled a sad and lonely smile as I walked out.

I started to text Carter and Franky when my phone rang. "What's up, Franky?" I said.

"You better get back to the station. We found some video with a few people we know on it, and one of them is Jessica."

"No shit? Does it show a crime being committed?"

"Just get back here, Tommy. I'm not sure what we want to do with this one."

15 I PULLED INTO THE STATION at three p.m. I don't know where the day had gone. I had woken up with a naked, beautiful woman under my arm but had been on a roller-coaster ever since. Any way I cut it, I did not like the tone of Franky's phone call or the fact that he refused to tell me what the hell was on that tape. I got off the elevator on the fourth floor and saw both Carter and Franky through the windows in our open interrogation room. This was the room everyone could see into. We used it when we wanted partners or other suspects to see their counterparts talking to us. It didn't even have one-way glass like so many of the rooms. It was a regular window, a fishbowl. We wanted both sides to see what was going on. It was only useful in about ten percent of the cases, but when it was, oh my, was it powerful.

Carter saw me first and waved me in. As I entered the room, I could tell by their faces that I was not going to like what they found.

Franky started. "Tommy, I'm just going to warn you, this is not what anyone thought we would find. We are not sure what it means, but Sarg and I are tossing around some theories. We want your opinion before we taint your perspective."

Again with this bullcrap cloak-and-dagger stuff. "Fine, Franky, just play the tape."

There was a monitor on the wall. Carter lowered the blinds on the window so nobody walking by would see—another sign this would not be pretty. I saw Franky move the mouse over the "play" button and from that point on, I was near vomiting.

On a couch, bound at the mouth and tied down was Jessica Jackson. The sound was distorted and no words could be heard but she was moaning in what had to be pain. She was naked and there was a tremendous amount of blood on the mattress. I did not recognize the room she was in but it appeared to be a hotel room. All I knew for sure was it was not the same hotel room we had been in the day before. She was moving but not naturally. Without any more than these first thirty seconds of video, I would say she was drugged. Severely drugged. There were others in the room, other than just the one shooting the video because you could see shadows. However, none were in the range of the camera, most likely on purpose I assumed. Someone walked across the camera blacking out the entire shot and then passed completely by. I heard talking but it was not clear. The voice was male, and by his shadow he was large. Not fat, but large. The person next to him was fat. That shadow took up half the mattress and some of Jessica. There seemed to be some discussion but nothing could be discerned. Then, it happened.

The fat figure came onto the screen. I no longer needed to call him the fat figure because I knew him. It was Tyrone Nielson, aka Tiny. Nobody else entered the picture but Tiny. He walked slowly up to the bed, and it was clear even in her drugged state that Jessica Jackson recognized her brother's best friend. I had no idea what was about to happen, but if I were a writer, I would never have been sick enough to write this.

Tiny undid his pants, dropped them to the ground, slapped her across the face when she began to squirm, and then raped her until he finished. It was the single worst video I have ever seen in my life. The camera shut off when he finished and turned to face it.

"What in the hell did we just watch?" I asked, still trying to keep my lunch down. "Now I know why you couldn't tell me."

"The time stamp on the video is one week ago, just before Malcolm was killed," stated Franky.

There was a pause while we all just sat in silence. "What do you think, Tommy?" Carter asked, breaking the almost morgue-like moment.

I did not know what to say. I could not think straight. Tiny raped his best friend's sister. Hell, she was his friend too. This was not a disturbed rapist who could not control his urges and succumbed to the girl next door because he had some fantasy she was in love with him. This was a girl drugged, bound, beaten, and then raped by her longtime friend. In my life I had vomited once because of something I saw. This was going to be number two if I did not get it together.

"I don't know," I finally said. "I don't know what to say."

Franky pushed. "Just come up with whatever is on the top of your head. We need a third perspective."

"There is no coercion that would make me do something like that, but Tiny is not me. I would take a bullet to the back of the head before I would rape a woman. I would take a bullet in the back of the head before I would stand by and let a woman be bound and gagged and raped by someone else, but Tyrone Nielson is not me. I talked to him on the phone. He said he did something but wouldn't tell me. I assume this was it."

Franky and Sergeant Carter nodded but did not speak.

I continued. "Polino is all about control. It is what he was trying to get set up with Jamal. What if this scene is all about control? They videotaped it. It would appear he was not the first to have raped her but they videotaped Tiny. With a video like that showing no coercion forcing Tiny to do it, they could make him do anything. He was theirs. He would be theirs for the rest of his life."

"What about the girl?" Carter asked.

"Jamal and his mother probably don't want to hear it, but she was a drug user. She got mixed up with drugs at one of the clubs. Polino had girls that were for show on the stage and girls that were for other activities. She got mixed up in the other activities. She was drugged and used as needed."

Franky nodded. "Good theory, and it matches ours."

I pressed my lips together and continued, "However, if that is the case, what do we have on Polino without Jessica alive?"

"Squat," replied Carter. "We got nothing but a nineteen-year-old drug-using kid raping his best friend's sister and having his buddies tape it. With Tiny dead, we don't even have an avenue to his buddies."

"That video was left at the club on purpose. Polino set up Tyrone as the fall guy and left irrefutable evidence to that effect. When Tiny killed himself, it basically was Polino's get-out-of-jail-free card. One huge loose end tied up."

"Not tied up," added Franky. "Gift wrapped with a big bow."

"So where does that leave us?" Carter asked. "Assuming that is true, does Polino just walk on this one?"

"We need to find Jessica Jackson or we need to find the undercover vice officer who got drugged as well."

"What!" stated Carter.

"I don't know for sure, but Captain Field told Franky that he thought there was someone else undercover. He did not know who and did not think he could find out who but said he would try." I looked toward Franky to confirm I had restated it accurately. When Franky nodded, I continued. "I found out from Clark's ex-wife that he mentioned the same thing, someone he recognized under, but it was a woman and she had been caught. Not necessarily discovered as a cop, but caught in the same game as Jessica. Drugged and used. She was probably posing as a stripper or hooker and did such a realistic job, Polino started using her at his parties. Drugged her and used her. For all we know, she is so far under now she doesn't even know she was a cop."

"*Is* a cop!" Carter corrected sternly.

I nodded an apology as Franky continued with another question. "If that was the case, why wouldn't Clark have gotten her out? Told someone? Something?"

"I'll bet he did and she either did not want to come out at the time or they couldn't find her. We won't know until we talk to her handler, and that rides with Field."

Franky paced a bit and asked, "Does Polino have any more loose ends?"

"I don't know," I said. "I have pondered on that, but I don't know. Maybe Moretti. I don't know what their relationship is, but I believe Moretti is the source of the parties that get out of hand and Polino cleans them up. Moretti has something on Polino."

"What about Marco Filini?" added Franky. "He never leaves witnesses. Until now, I never knew what he looked like. He is on video at the restaurant. Would Marco consider that a loose end?"

That one caught my attention, but I had my answer ready. "Only four people know about the restaurant video and three of them are in this room. The other is the one who let me know about the video in the first place, Tammi Hutchin. I can guarantee she is not going to tell anyone."

Franky mumbled under his breath and then went quiet. "What, Franky? You got something to say, then say it." I did not like his current direction, and I felt like I was having to defend the woman I had just spent one of the best nights of my life with.

"It is not about her, it is about the evidence. We processed two murder scenes including your car and the hotel. I know the forensics team captured more than one hundred fingerprints and as many DNA samples, but what information did you receive?"

I looked toward him, although he was not facing me, he was looking away as he talked. Carter had not moved. "I got a call that they matched up DNA from Tiny at both scenes and the drug bust sample I provided."

"Right, but who made that call?"

"Dr. G. You are not implying that Elise had anything to do with this, are you?"

Franky turned now and faced me. "No, not at all. She only entered the DNA information into the database you recovered from the situation with Tiny and the drugs at the basketball court. The match came from who entered the information from the crime scenes."

"Calvin's team?" I asked.

"Not Calvin's team. He insisted on handling it all himself. Came in that night, all night. Protested a little to show his position, but Carter said he worked like a dog and would not let anyone help. He reviewed all the video but somehow did not catch Marco stalking our guy. A professional in the evidence world missed something a restaurant manager found?" He paused while he let that sit. "It just seems to me the evidence we are seeing is filtered."

I pulled out my phone, scanned a few names, and hit "send." The phone rang and was answered almost immediately. "Detective O'Malley, are you calling to ask for results before they are ready again? Oh wait, I don't have any cases in process with you right now so you must not be questioning my results this time."

"Nice, Doc, but I have a question on process. When you called me the other day with the DNA match of Tyrone Nielson to three scenes, where did that information come from?"

She could tell in my voice that this was serious so instantly her tone changed as well. "The lab runs the tests. The results are kept on paper backup and e-mailed to Calvin's group where they are verified and entered."

"So the information that gets entered into the database is controlled by Calvin's group?"

She thought a minute. "Yes, and in this case it was done by Calvin himself. He said you told him to personally handle it himself so there was no lost chain of command. The results were too important."

"I never told him that." I stopped talking. "Oh shit! I have to go, Doc. I need you to review everything in those results. Every sample. Every match. Do not tell Calvin what you are doing. Keep it between Frank, Sergeant Carter, and me."

Normally a smartass comment would be the next thing spoken, but she knew immediately there was something serious here and she could tell by the conversation it sounded like evidence-tampering, which would reflect on her work. "I will handle all of this myself. If that bastard did something—"

"We don't know anything yet, but I have to go," I interrupted and hung up.

I glanced at Carter. "You need to put together your plan, if this theory with Calvin is correct. If he filtered the evidence, then he knows the originals are at the restaurant making anyone who saw it a target." I pulled out my phone and dialed Tammi.

The phone rang four times and went to voice mail. "Hey, Tammi. This is Tommy. I had a great time last night, but something has come up and I would like to talk to you. Would you please call my cell as soon as you get this message? It's important."

I clicked the phone off and turned back to the others. "Go," Franky said. "Try the restaurant on your way but go pick her up. If Calvin let Marco know there was video of him, then she could absolutely be in trouble."

Carter slammed his hand down. "Now I am just pissed. Call your friend downstairs and have him check out Calvin's financials, but keep it quiet."

Franky smiled. "You mean Charlie? He is tight with Calvin I think."

You tell that son of a bitch if he breathes a word of this to anyone I will tear him apart, and he will never work in law enforcement again. This is for you, me, and him, and that's it."

Franky nodded. "That should work."

And I want any strange deposits or withdrawals documented back to me within the hour. If he is dirty, I am taking him down today before he can do any more damage."

I placed a call to the Chicago Chop House and asked for Tammi. The host told me she was not in so I asked for Keith Kaplan. After bouncing through a couple people, I did finally connect.

"Keith, this is Detective O'Malley. Have you spoken to Tammi today?"

"Detective," he said sounding very pleased. "So I assume you are the reason she is not here, and I am pleased to see it. She needed a break."

My concern shot up three levels. "What do you mean she is not there?"

I am sure he picked up on my tone as his changed significantly in return. "She texted me this morning and said she would not be in for lunch. I thought it was a little strange because we are not open for lunch today so I assumed she meant dinner. Either way, I was going to be here so I was not worried." He paused. "Should I be?"

I calmed my voice slightly. "No, nothing to worry about now, just have her call me the minute she gets there and if you hear from her, please do the same."

"I will, Detective. Anything else?"

"Yes, have you been in the back security office today?"

'No, but I don't go there very often. That is really Tammi's office more than mine."

"Can you peek back there and just let me know if anything looks out of order?"

He asked me to hang on and in the background I heard him shout something. He returned to the phone. "Detective, the place has been destroyed. All the wires pulled, tapes gone. Everything destroyed."

He sounded worried and at some level mildly hysterical. "Keith, I need you to calm down. I need you to call 911 and tell them there has been a robbery. Have the officer that comes down to do the report call me when he is done. I am going to call my office and we are going to put an APB out on Tammi. If you hear from her or she comes in, then you call me immediately, no matter what. If she comes in, you keep her there."

"Detective, what is going on? Is Tammi all right?"

"Sir, I am not sure what is going on but I think there was something on those tapes that somebody did not want revealed and they used Tammi to get in this morning and take them. My goal now is to find her."

"Thank you, Detective, and I will call you if I learn anything."

We hung up, and I went from extremely worried to extremely pissed. I also knew exactly where I was going. Rick's Cabaret. That was where I thought I'd find Marco Filini.

●　　●　　●　　●　　●

I made it to Rick's and I was pleased to see a few cars I recognized. The large Latino man who had been at the Red Carpet previously was working the door. If memory served, his name was Ricardo. I approached with my badge out and gun holster unbuckled.

"Hello, Detective," began Ricardo. "You know I can't let you in with that gun."

"Ricardo, what does Polino have on you?"

That stopped him. He stuttered a bit, then said, "What do you mean?"

"I mean Polino is all about control. You look like a good kid, strong and well put together. You speak well and I am guessing you are bilingual. You may get paid okay here, but there are jobs anywhere. What benefits do you have that keep you here?"

"I don't know what you mean, sir. I like the job."

"Okay, if you say so. Now back to your other comment. I am going in there. I am keeping my gun. If you want to try to take it off me, you can. Otherwise, step aside."

He thought for a few moments and in his heart he knew he needed to let me pass, but whatever fear Polino had put in him meant he had to stand between me and the door.

"You sure about this?" I said.

He took a step forward and pushed me in the chest. "Put the gun away, Detective, or do not take another step forward."

I smiled. "I am so glad you pushed me." Less than a second later Ricardo was on the ground clenching his throat. One properly placed thumb was all it took. He was completely incapacitated. "I am going in now and if I were you, I would stay where you are. Assaulting a police officer is serious. If you are gone when I return, I will put an arrest warrant out on you that not only includes assaulting an officer but will include fleeing the scene. You will spend quite some time in jail on those two charges. Stay here on the ground and help if you can, and all charges may be dropped."

I walked in and the girl behind the window was about to protest and then just let me pass. Polino must not have much on her, I thought. I entered the main club area and made a beeline directly to Moretti's office. As I approached, the man of the hour appeared from the open door.

"Ohhh Malley," he said slowly as if he were singing.

"Maaarrrcccooo," I replied.

"What are you doing here, Tommy? You have nothing to do here, or are you letting us know you were responsible for the death of one of our patrons who ended up in your trunk, and possibly the rape of a missing black girl? Are you letting us know that you won't be around for a while?"

"Where is she, Marco?"

"Where is who?" he replied sarcastically.

"Where is Tammi Hutchin?"

"Oh, the whore you fucked last night at your place? I don't know. Is she missing?"

I did catch what was meant by the statement. He tailed us last night. I stepped right up to stand inches from him. We were about the same height and it was clear neither of us feared the other. His breath was stale, like coffee and cigars mixed with crap. "You want to try to take me. You want to try here, right now?"

"I could, you know. For all I know, you are a patron who assaulted my doorman and forced his way in with a gun. I may even take your gun, kill my doorman with it, and say you shot him in a crazed rage trying to find me. You have a recent history of questionable activity which also includes having one of your suspects in the trunk of your car. How many people have to die around you before you realize that you need to back down? You cannot touch us. Not Polino, Moretti, and not me. I don't make mistakes, O'Malley. I clean up other people's mistakes."

"Who do I have on video at the Chop House? You make mistakes, Marco."

He smiled. "You mean the shot of me sitting in a bar and then making a phone call. Oh, that is tough to explain."

Again with the sarcasm, but he was right. He did not need Tammi or to ransack the office for that video. Why the hell did he do it? "What did you need her for then, Marco?"

"Questions, questions, questions. You don't know anything, Detective." He took a step back into the doorway of Moretti's office and waved me in. "Perhaps we can give you some answers. It seems my boss does not want the headache of a dead detective so we will make you an offer. If you take it, anything you have lost will most likely be returned."

I entered the office and it was exactly as I had seen it previously. Moretti was inside and behind the desk. He stood when I entered. "It is funny, Detective O'Malley, but you owe me your life right now. My counterpart here believed you were a loose end. I said no, Detective O'Malley has been in this game a long time. He is a reasonable and smart man. He also needs to solve cases to continue to move forward in the world. That is why I think we can work together."

"Work together. You are foaming if you think I will work with you." They looked at me strangely. "Crazy. Nuts. Foaming at the mouth like a rabid dog."

"I like that. I'm going to use that one later."

I smiled at Marco, so pleased he was going to use one of my descriptions. "I feel complete now."

Marco pulled up a chair for me in front of the desk next to a chair that was already there. He took that one and motioned for me to sit. "You might as well sit. You know you're not leaving here until we talk. You know this not because you don't think we can hold you here. You know this because you came here for something, and you don't have it yet. And I am telling you, the only way you will get it is to talk to Mr. Moretti. You can stand and talk if you like, but it is more comfortable if everyone is sitting."

I took a seat. Although I knew at some point Marco and I would meet in a way similar to that movie, *Thunderdome*—two men enter, one man leaves—but today may not be that day. What I just realized is they want something from me. They want the same thing Jewel wanted and Jessica wanted when she called Clark. They want a way out. "Okay, I am sitting. You have my attention. What do you have to say?"

Moretti smiled. I thought for a minute he was going to pull a mirror out from under his desk just to look at himself before he spoke. "You are a good cop, Detective O'Malley. You have a clean record but you do have a history of bending the rules when it serves you. So do I. My rule is never to trust the police. That is a rule I believe has gotten me where I am today. However, our situation right now is, shall we say, complicated."

"Complicated?" I repeated as I scanned the room looking for anything that could be used to my advantage should this go south really fast.

"Yes, complicated. It is funny, you see, I am a partner with a man I cannot trust. I am a partner with a man that owes me a great deal of money. I could remove that man several different ways, but he has many friends who would not like the fact that I removed him. Further, it is much harder to collect from a dead man, but that may be where I am. Polino's usefulness, though excellent for six months, may have run its course. Marco is good." Filini grunted and shifted a bit in his chair. "I mean to say, Marco is great at what he does, but it would still tie back to me. So to make this clean, I need someone else to take my partner down."

I smiled. "You want me to take Polino down so you can take over Chicago?"

He coughed a bit. "Detective, I already run Chicago. I want you to take Polino down because he is a reckless punk who has outlived his usefulness. I need him gone."

"Why would I leave you alone? You are as dirty as he is."

Marco shifted again. I believe he felt I was insulting his boss calling him dirty. I now understood where Marco's loyalties lied. I thought he worked for both of them, but he worked for Moretti. That was clear. "Detective, I am much dirtier than Joey Polino. He has not even begun to touch what I am."

"Then all the more reason I take you down with him."

He smiled. "You still don't get it, Detective. You have nothing on me. I have given you a few crumbs to make everything tie to the boy Tyrone. There is nothing that ties to me. Nothing. And don't think you will be able to pull one of the Capone tax evasion bullshit charges. You cannot even give me a ticket for jaywalking." He paused and pulled out a cigar and motioned to me asking if I would like one. I shook my head no. "I said I would light this when I knew I was moving ahead of Polino." He cut the end, pulled out a lighter, and lit the cigar. "But if you want to have some bread crumbs that will lead to Polino, I do believe they exist. They may even help you find what you are looking for today, if you know what I'm saying." He sucked in deep. "It doesn't mean I would be going away, and Marco here, he would still be around if you ever wanted to come after us. It just means you would only be looking in one place instead of two."

I did not respond. If I understood him correctly, he could give me Joey Polino on a platter, and I would in one stroke take a huge crime boss off the streets. Yes, it would mean Moretti would grow in power, but with Polino gone, the mob bosses would be down by one. "I don't do deals with criminals."

"This is not a deal, Detective. I make no promises on the condition of anything you may be looking for today. It is not in my hands. You can use any evidence found to bring me down as well if it fits. I am only offering you evidence on my counterpart and assistance in finding your missing friends. It would be my request you remember this sometime later, but if you choose not to, so be it."

"And if I don't accept this today?"

"Nothing changes. You may find those you seek today and you may still find the evidence on my counterpart, but you won't leave with it today. I hope your investigative abilities are good."

"Wait a minute," I said. "You said 'those' I seek and 'anything I lost'. What will I find at the end of this riddle?"

Moretti looked toward Marco. He stood and grabbed the inside of my arm to stand as well. Again we were face-to-face. He whispered barely loud enough for me to hear. "We will not speak of this again. If you understand what we are offering, then you will walk outside with me now and we will part ways. I will give you an address. It is a small warehouse owned by someone we both know. In the warehouse are some chambers. There are a few people there. You will be interested in those people. There is also some video that you will find. It will show individuals bringing those people to this area and keeping them there. It will also show some video similar to the video you have of Mr. Nielson."

He stopped whispering and stepped away back to his seat. I looked at Marco and then back to Moretti. "I do not do deals with criminals."

"I am certain you do not, Detective. Mr. Filini is going to escort you out. I am writing an address on this notebook paper. I am then going to burn in my fireplace the rest of the notebook and this pen so your forensics team can't trump up some charges that this paper came from my office. When you get outside this building, you need to tell Mr. Filini if you want the paper or not. If you do, he will let you read it and then destroy it. If you don't want it, he will just destroy it. After that, if you want back in these doors, you better have another warrant."

That was my cue to go. It was also my cue to make a decision. Was I was going to take the address? It was strange when I thought about it, as there were several lines in the sand here. I watched him write the address on a piece of paper. I then had about thirty-five feet to make a decision. Although this was no deal and no promises were made, it was a gray area, and I was not sure I could go there. Once I went down that path, I was not sure I could get back. I stood, stared at Moretti, and without saying a word, turned to head out with Marco right on my heels. I thought about Jessica, Malcolm, Tom Clark, Jamal, Andrea, and finally TJ. As I thought about those six people, I knew my answer. As I was about to exit the doorway, Moretti spoke.

"Detective?"

I stopped and turned. "Yes, Moretti."

"We will be seeing each other again. I promise."

With that, Marco grabbed the inside of my arm and escorted me toward the door. The girl behind the glass smiled as I passed but did not speak. Ricardo glared as I stepped through the door but he also did not speak, most likely because Marco was there. I looked toward the large Latino man. "How's your throat?"

He took a step in my direction, but Marco moved between us. "Are you fucking stupid? You have no chance so back your ass down."

Ricardo did as he was told. I smiled at him. "Can you sit and beg too, or how about fetch?"

I could see he was about to blow and Marco glared in my direction. "Don't make matters worse. I respect you, O'Malley, but even you should know that at some point I will have to stand up for my employees. Let's call this one good for today. As Moretti said, we will be seeing each other again. You and I both know that."

I did not speak but continued to walk toward my car. My phone had been buzzing nonstop so I really needed this to end. I knew there was one thing left with Marco though, and it was not going to be a test of strength.

"Here is your car, O'Malley. So what is it going to be?"

"You already know my answer," I said.

"Yeah, I do." He handed me the piece of paper, let me read it, but left his hand out to have it returned. "I knew you couldn't pass up the chance to get Polino. I also know you believe you can get Moretti also. He wrote that with a pen and paper which will be burned by the time I return inside. He wrote it with his left hand so the handwriting is not traceable. Furthermore, you will not keep it anyway. For you to answer where you got the address will only bring more questions but no answers. You will not find anything linking me or my boss to any crime."

I put the address on the paper to memory and handed it back to him. "Why didn't you kill me the other night? Why all the cloak-and-dagger crap with the drugs and the setup?"

He smiled. "I don't know what you are talking about, Tommy, but if I did, I would tell you that I respect you. That is not how I want to beat you, if in fact I knew what you were talking about. That sounds more like something Polino would want to do, in my opinion."

I understood. Marco Filini was a purebred killer, but he was a killer who followed a code. I understood that code. To be honest, I appreciated the code because it came with rules. I most likely would not find anything to get Filini or Moretti this time, but knowing how they operated still put me closer than I was before. "I'll be seeing you, Marco."

"Same," he replied.

He walked away and I quickly wrote down the address so I would not leave it to my fading memory.

•   •   •   •   •

I pulled up my phone. I had missed calls from Franky, Carter, and Dr. G. Nothing from Tammi or Keith, but I did not expect it. I shot over to my text messages and the same three people had sent texts. All three said the same thing: *Call me.*

I started my car and punched in Franky's name, dialing his number.

"Where the hell are you?" Franky said as he answered.

"I have a lead. A good lead and I need backup."

"Well, that is all good but I have some information. I got a call from Field. You need to meet with us before you go anywhere else. He wants to meet at Flapjaws. How long until you can get there?"

I checked the address Moretti had provided and realized Flapjaws was right on the way. "I can be there in ten minutes. I have an address for you to run before you leave." I read off the address. "I want to know everything about it."

He jotted down the address but did not stop talking. "There is more. Calvin is dirty. We found deposits into some offshore bank account totaling close to fifty thousand. The deposits came from an account tied to Polino."

"Bread crumbs," I said.

"What? Bread crumbs? What does that mean?"

"Nothing. Is there anything else?"

"Yes, the tapes TJ made from the restaurant which Calvin searched are all erased except the ones we had already seen and the one you made. Also, the restaurant was burglarized this morning. All their backups were destroyed." He paused. "And you know that Ms. Hutchin is missing, right?"

"Yes, I know. What about Calvin and the other evidence. Is there anything else?"

"We had one of our guys go through the video from the houses, and there are some shots of Polino. Nothing too incriminating, but if we had something more, it would be great support for it. Photos of him holding a gun on Tiny and some hookers, things like that. By itself not illegal, but if we could find something a little more solid, it would close a jury, no questions asked."

Bread crumbs, I thought. *More and more bread crumbs.* "Okay, what do you know about this meeting with Field?"

"There is another undercover person. A woman, and she has been off the grid for months. We are going to meet with Field and her handler. I don't know who that is as he wouldn't say it on the phone, especially after what we just learned about Calvin Call. Who would have thought he was dirty?"

"You did," I replied. "Great work, Detective, by the way."

"I will run the address right now and then meet you. Carter is already on his way to Flapjaws."

16 I PULLED INTO FLAPJAWS and left my car running out front. There was no parking allowed but one benefit of not having my Camaro was that if a policeman ran the plate of this car, it would come up untouchable. If a tow driver actually towed it, they would end up being reamed by their boss because they would get no charges collected for it. I wanted to meet with Franky, Carter, and Field, get the info, and then have all of them join me at this address. I wanted Franky to tell me it was owned by Polino and that would just be another bread crumb left by Moretti. I think I realized about ten minutes into my meeting with Moretti that he had orchestrated this whole thing. Whatever debt Polino had with Moretti, it was the beginning of this entire chain of events to bring Polino down. However, Moretti had not planned to be so reckless with some hookers and he hadn't planned on Malcolm Jackson's involvement. Those things complicated his plans. However, he still created enough on Polino to drive a stake through his heart.

I walked in and saw the friendly face of Roy Pura behind the bar. "Detective O'Malley. This is pretty early for you, isn't it?"

"Yes, Roy, but I am just meeting someone here. No drinks for me today."

"Very well. Just holler if you guys need anything."

I nodded that I would and took a seat at a table in the corner. Carter and Field arrived at the same time and Franky showed up a few minutes later. We all sat together.

"Okay, gentlemen," I began after introductions. "This is your show. I need to know what the hell anyone knows about Tom Clark's death and if there is anyone on the inside who can help us."

After I spoke, another person walked into the bar and headed over. I recognized him as Sergeant Jeffery Dalponte. He worked out of North Chicago. Previously he worked alongside me and Franky downtown but took the promotion to the north side about two years ago.

"Sorry I am late," he said as he arrived at the table. He looked to me and Frank. "Detectives, it is good to see you again. Sergeant Carter, you as well."

We exchanged greetings and I grabbed a chair for him to join us. Captain Field was first to speak. "I know this is short notice to get everyone together, but Franky convinced me this was important enough to risk the effort. When I asked a few questions, I learned there were other reasons this meeting might be a good idea. But what we are about to discuss is known only to those at this table. To discuss it outside of this table could get someone killed. As long as we all understand that, then we can continue." We all nodded. "Dalponte, you need to tell these men what you explained to me earlier."

"Well, Tommy, Franky, and Sergeant Carter, like Tom Clark, we had someone on the inside as well. Female, deep undercover and working the prostitution side of things. She was not working with Clark, but she was aware of him because she was in first. She was in about six months longer than he was. Then, about two months ago, something happened. She thought she was getting close to some of the organized crime backing the prostitution rings and then we just lost contact. We were talking about trying to pull her out, but then Clark saw her at a party. He tried to get her out but couldn't. He was going to blow his cover and throw away everything to get her out, and then he lost her. We don't think they knew she was a cop. We think they just started trafficking her through drugs. She has been off the grid for six weeks."

"What's her name?" I asked.

Dalponte looked toward Field and then back to me. "Diana Gallows."

No one spoke. We all knew Lieutenant Gallows. I shook my head. "What the hell is a lieutenant doing undercover? I was told she was on leave."

"She wanted the job. She wanted a change, and everyone was told she was on personal leave." He turned directly to me. "We all know what happened to Clark. If there is a chance we can get her out alive, we need to do it. What do you guys know?"

Franky started to replay some of the information we had obtained but after a few short sentences, I cut him off. "Our best lead is this address. I got it through a contact that I believe has a motive to clean up these issues. However, he has his own ideas on how they should be cleaned. We will have to determine if they meet ours when we get there."

"What's at the address?" Dalponte asked.

I handed him a paper where I had transcribed the address for everyone. "It is in the industrial district."

"If we are lucky, we'll find Jessica Jackson, Tammi Hutchin, Diana Gallows, and enough evidence to put Joey Polino away for life."

"Where in the hell did you get that address?" Carter asked.

"From Ross Timothy Moretti," I replied.

Those at the table were silent until Franky chimed in. "If nobody else is going to say it, I will. How in the hell can you begin to trust information provided by that lowlife? He is most likely behind all the hookers' deaths, not to mention Jewel and Jackson. What are you thinking, O'Malley?"

My voice was hard and direct. "I am thinking we have at least three people who may still be alive and two mob bosses that each want the other one gone. If we can take one down and save three people including a cop, then I'm all for it. We can focus on Moretti another day." I stood and walked around the outside of the circle of chairs causing each of their eyes to follow me, but nobody rose. "You guys do not have to agree, but I weighed my options. I made no promises to Moretti or anyone else that we would not come after them. However, I also believe he has kept his trail clean and intentionally dirtied Polino's. If we want to save these people before Polino ties up all his loose ends, our time is now. I will go alone if need be, but for all I know, this will get messy and I would appreciate the support."

I spanned my eyes across the group and really was not sure where this would go. Though it seemed clear to me, I could see a sergeant and a captain thinking this whole thing stunk to high hell.

Then, Carter stood. "I'm in. I don't give a shit if you got the address from the devil himself, and you are sentenced to hell when you die. If it saves our cop and those two missing women, then I'll take that sentence for you."

Franky did not get up but nodded. "I was in from the start, partner. If what I think will be the case, Moretti is setting Polino up which means his case will be ironclad. Who knows, to reduce his sentence, maybe he has something on Moretti and we get them both."

Dalponte and Field seemed to like that and it was Sergeant Dalponte who spoke. "What are we doing here? Shoot us all the address and let's go. I will call in for some backup, but tell them to stay back until we define the scene."

I wanted to say thank you but opted to just nod. You don't need to thank people for doing the right thing and doing their jobs, but I was pleased this did not go the other way. I pulled out my phone and sent a text to each of them whose numbers I had, and those I didn't have were forwarded from there. We left Flapjaws and Franky jumped in the car with me.

"What happened, Tommy? Why didn't you tell me you were going to see Moretti?"

"Because I wasn't sure I would be a cop after my meeting. I did not know what I was going to do."

Franky turned away. "You would have done the right thing, Tommy. That much I know, but next time, call me and we will do the right thing, or the wrong thing, together."

I stared toward the road in front of me almost in a trance by the lines as they moved by. "I don't know this time, Franky. This case got to me with no success finding Jessica, Malcolm being killed, Tiny's suicide in front of me, and then Tammi. At some point, enough is enough, Franky. I thought I would have to go through Filini to get it, but I forgot these creeps are always in it for themselves. This one got everyone dirty and the only one coming out clean was going to be the best liar."

"Whoever had the best get-out-of-jail-free card?"

"Yep, and right now I am betting Moretti is untouchable."

"I believe what I said before though," Franky added. "What if Polino turns some evidence of his own on Moretti? We might be able to get them both."

"No," I said, almost talking to myself but loud enough for Franky to hear. "Polino did not get where he is today by being a snitch. He would be dead before trial."

"Then let's just make sure Polino does not slip through this one."

"Agreed," I replied. "But to be honest, I am more interested in the women. I want them safe."

"I know they all mean the same to you, and I don't want to burst your bubble, but when we do bring them back safe, you may find it hard to get a second date with Ms. Hutchin. Something about armed kidnapping is tough to overcome I would guess."

Even in this time of stress, Franky could always make me smile. "You don't think the 'saving her life hero thing' will add some bonus points?"

"Not for you," he replied.

As if on cue, the GPS interrupted, "You have arrived."

What the hell is this?" Franky asked looking at the building which showed no sign of activity. "When I ran the address, it came up as an indoor batting cage. You know, for junior baseball and such."

"Looks like whatever it used to be is out of business now." I paused. "Out of its original business anyway."

"Let me run it again. I don't remember the specifics." All police cars, even the loaners, are equipped with a sophisticated onboard computer enabling officers to run an address, license plate, or name, and get their entire history. Franky entered the address and voilà, every owner popped up in seconds.

"Would you take a fucking look at this?" Franky said.

"What?"

"This building was bought five years ago by JAP Enterprises and was started as a Japanese baseball hitting instruction center. It closed after three years but is still on record as being owned by them." He was scanning down the information. "It does not list anything more about the company other than their corporate office is also this address. I don't know, Tommy, it looks legit." He paused and then had to ask. "Could Moretti be throwing us a decoy here?"

I picked up my phone without answering and called Sergeant Carter.

"What's up, O'Malley?"

"Did you run the address?"

"I did," he replied.

"What do you think? Do we need to wait for a warrant?"

"I have one in my in-box as we speak. I have about five judges on call ready to find Clark's killer. We have the full run of the place."

"Nice work, Sergeant."

"No problem, Tommy, and I hope what we want is in there."

"Me too, Sergeant, more than you know."

Carter was about to hang up when he added, "Oh, Tommy..."

"Yes, Sarg."

"When you file this report, regardless of what we find, on the warrant I stated this address was an anonymous tip. You may want to go that route, but it's your call."

"No problem, Craig, and thanks."

I turned back to Franky. "We are a go. Carter has a warrant."

"No shit. How did he do that so fast?"

"That is why he is Sergeant and you and I are detectives. We all know our place."

I opened the door as did Franky. We both pulled our guns and began walking to the front door. I pulled out my radio and called to the others. "Franky and I are going in the front. You guys scan the back. Let's cover all entrances and exits and go on my signal. Let me know when you are in position."

This was a relatively small building with one door in or out on each of four sides, and the back included one overhead door. It took only a few minutes for everyone to signal they were in position and I gave the go-ahead.

Franky tried the door and it was locked. He stepped aside for me to kick, and although it was better secured than most, it swung ajar. We decided bull rush today and tore through the door one after the other. We entered a front lobby area that appeared to have been empty for some time. However, through the window in the double doors behind the counter we could see a large open space. It had netting and other structures supporting the fact that it actually was originally set up as batting cages. Japanese batting cages, who would have thought. We ensured the area was clear, signaled as much over the radio, and proceeded through the double doors. When we passed through the double doors it hit us—the smell of death. Rotten flesh is a smell that cannot be duplicated. Instantly my heart sank.

Our eyes scanned around and I do not know whose eyes caught the area first. Deep in a corner closest to the back of the building was a cage. It was not a batting cage like the rest of the space, but a metal-barred and completely enclosed cage. Inside the cage we saw what appeared to be motionless bodies.

Frank grabbed his radio. "Back of the warehouse. It looks to be..."

I am not sure what my ears registered first—the sound of the radio hitting the floor or the bullet penetrating his chest. The cold thud of a bullet impact to a human body is as recognizable a sound as the smell of dead flesh is to a cop's nose. After the crack of the gunfire, the sound was like the back of a spoon hitting Jell-O. Everything was still for just that moment. Then it migrated to slow motion, before exploding into fast forward.

"Shot!" I yelled, diving to the side. "Man down, man down."

Another shot rang through the warehouse exploding at my feet. The shooter was zeroing in on me now. I crawled over to Franky who was motionless on the ground. I grabbed him by the shoulders and pulled him over behind a bench. I dumped the bench over to provide a barrier of protection from the direction of the shot. Depending on the round, the thin wood of the bench may stop the bullet, but if nothing else, it may take Franky and me out of the shooter's line of sight. Several more shots came our way striking the bench and buzzing over the top.

"Have your vest on, you asshole. Have your vest on, damn it!" I repeated louder. I felt his chest and breathed deeper when I felt his vest, but as I did so, I saw the blood coming from his shoulder. "Shit!" I said.

"There is a walkway above the warehouse," issued Carter's voice over the radio. "It has full view of the warehouse. There are at least two shooters up there. I am on the east wall and can see movement. If you are in the warehouse, stay down. We need someone to get upstairs. Who is down?"

My radio had cracked when I dove and it did not appear to be working. I could hear Franky's radio but it was on the other side of my small barrier and I could not risk trying to get it.

"Who is down, goddamnit?" Carter asked again.

I pressed my hands on Franky's shoulder and throat area. "Hang on, Franky."

Field's voice was next on the radio. "I have a twenty on Sullivan and O'Malley. They are pinned down in the warehouse under fire. Looks like Sullivan is hit and both are separated from their radios."

There was radio silence for a while as I scanned looking for Field. Then his voice came back on. "O'Malley, can you hear me? If so, signal." I raised my hand and another shot rang my direction at the movement. "He still has ears. He is in position to cover anyone who can make it to the upper walkway."

Now I understood.

Carter was back on the radio. "I am at the stairs on the east side."

"I am in the west stairwell now."

Field moved around the perimeter. "On my count, I am going to charge the warehouse. O'Malley, open up with everything you have and don't stop. You have to keep those shooters down. Carter and Dalponte, drive the stairwell."

Franky was still unconscious, and although the blood from his shoulder was fairly extreme, he was breathing. I grabbed his gun in my left hand and held mine tight in my right. "Three, two, one..."

I turned and pointed both guns toward the direction of the shots and opened them up. In seconds, shots were coming from all around but none were striking anywhere close to me. I locked in on some movement on the mezzanine and zeroed in. I pulled the trigger and the movement stopped. The radio lit up with chatter and in only a few more moments, the shots ended.

"We are clear up here. Three perps down. Whoever took the third out, you saved our asses. Nice shot. That guy was hidden."

I jumped over my small barrier and grabbed the radio. "I need an ambulance immediately. Franky is down, shot in the neck. Also, can anyone get to those in the cage in the back?"

Field answered. "I am almost there, Tommy. It doesn't look good. Is the rest of the area clear?"

"All clears" came through from everyone as I sat next to Franky. He opened his eyes and looked at me. "So this is what it feels like to be shot."

"Yep," I replied. "Is it all you thought it would be?"

"I'd rather have sex with a porcupine," he said, trying to issue a small smile. "How are the girls? Are they okay?"

"I don't know, Franky."

"Then what the hell are you doing here? Get over there."

I nodded and put his hand up to where it was bleeding. "Keep pressure on it."

I started to leave and he lifted his other hand to grab my arm. "Thanks, partner. I know you pulled me out of there and into safety."

"No, sir," I replied. I tripped and fell, and *you*, even though you were shot, got us *both* over here and behind this barrier."

He closed his eyes. "Fuck you, O'Malley. Did we get him? Did we get Polino?"

"I don't know, but we got three bad guys."

He nodded but it was clear he was done talking. I heard the ambulance sirens outside and although I wanted to go to the cage, I needed to know Franky was taken care of. Medics will not enter a building even in an emergency unless the scene is secure. I ran to the front door and met them with their gurney. "Call for more and a bus. We have three shooters down and one officer. I will lead you in." I led them to Franky and then made a straight line for the cage area. When I got within about ten yards, I had to stop running and slowly began walking, if you can call it that. More like baby steps.

The smell was still what got me. There were at least five dead girls in the cage.

Most of them naked or mostly naked. Some of them appeared to have been dead for many days or even weeks. Tied to the side bars were two women, heads hanging down like Jesus crucified. Their hands and legs were bound. The Caucasian woman appeared in the best condition, but looked to have been beaten and she was unconscious. She was still clothed and alive. Yes, Tammi Hutchin was alive. The African-American woman was not so lucky. She was hanging completely limp on the bars. Her arms appeared to be about to detach from her shoulders. I was in a trance. I did not even see the other paramedics make their way into the cage. I did not see Carter and Dalponte trying to cut the bindings to get the women down. I did not see Field kneeling over the mutilated body of Lieutenant Gallows.

•   •   •   •   •

Three men were killed that day at the batting cages. All men employed by Joey Anthony Polino. Along with those dead bodies, we recovered the bodies of seven women. Six we identified as employees of the Red Carpet and one undercover lieutenant. It sickens me to think about what the last weeks of her life were like, what any of their lives were like. She was doing a job trying to save those girls and played her role so well that against her will, she became one of them. Tammi Hutchin was beaten for information on the video but she will make a full recovery, though I believe Franky was correct regarding my ability to get a second date. Jessica Jackson was going to live, but as far as a full recovery, I doubted it. Still, it felt good to be able to call Andrea Jackson and tell her that her daughter was alive. Perhaps that would give Andrea and her son some peace, or maybe they would always know that I could not save her in time.

Franky was alive and pissed off. Pissed off that he did not get to go with us the next day when we went to Joey Polino's house to arrest him for more than ten felonies—enough to keep him off the streets for good.

At the JAP Enterprises offices, I later learned JAP stood for Joey Anthony Polino and not Japanese baseball. We found an unbelievable amount of videos. Videos that showed Joey beating women, Joey authorizing and discussing the murders of many people including Malcolm Jackson and Steve Jewel, and more—bread crumbs like never before. There were no references to the parties like the one at the hotel where the girls were found or the five dead hookers that were part of Franky's original case, but it was easy enough to tie them to Polino, and we did.

What we did not have was exactly what we feared—nothing related to Moretti. The only document we found that had his name on it was one which a lawyer would present to him at some point in the future. A document by Joey Polino signing his clubs over to Moretti. How he got that is beyond my level of belief, but he did.

Therefore, as we thought, the only way we would be able to get Moretti would be if Polino turned evidence on him, and I couldn't see him doing that, but you never know. The DA can be pretty persuasive at times.

It was about eighteen hours since the raid on the baseball warehouse. Carter had organized about twenty officers to bring in Polino. He was at his residence. Carter had him tailed all morning. He had taken his family to Perkins family restaurant, of all places, for breakfast. I wondered how he would feel about his last free meal being Perkins. Nothing against the place, but if he knew what was coming, wouldn't he have chosen Gino's East, or as my choice would be, Mr. J's?

We did not believe Polino knew we were coming to bring him in that morning. Carter asked me to lead the team into Polino's house. Field and Dalponte came as well but they all let me run the show. We had men around the entire house and when I knocked on the door, I was dumbfounded when Joey himself answered.

"What can I do for you, Detective O'Malley? Here to relive some of our high school days together?" He was smiling as if he still held all the cards. Untouchable? I thought. He was so blind.

"No, Joey, I am not here because of high school."

"Then to what do I owe this pleasure." He paused when he saw the ten plus police vehicles outside. "Oh, do tell, you brought the cavalry."

"Speaking of high school, Joey, I don't remember, did you ever play baseball?"

"Baseball..." he said slowly, "no, why do you ask?"

"Well, I just didn't know why you made a run at a batting cage business a few years ago?" *Bingo*! I saw it. Just a flicker, but still there. That "oh shit" moment when someone who is guilty has to start coming up with what to say next. That moment the *jazz* arrived.

"Save it, Joe. I don't care anymore. Joey Anthony Polino, you have the right to..."

"Proud of yourself, aren't you, Tommy? You were always jealous of me. Always wanted what I had. The women. The money. You live in that small apartment. Even in the end, that restaurant woman, what was her name? Tammi? Yeah, I heard about you and her. How did that work out for you?"

I looked back toward Field, Carter, and Dalponte, who were all standing encircled behind me. Without a word, they all turned to face the other way. Joey's eyes widened right before my fist struck him exploding his nose in blood. His head fell back, and had I not grabbed him, he would have fallen through his open front door.

"I suggest you follow your Miranda rights and remain silent. You will have plenty of time to talk on death row."

Even at this time, he felt he needed to have the upper hand. "Illinois does not have the death penalty anymore, Detective. My good friend Pat Quinn signed that several years ago. So, nice try. Now take me downtown and call my lawyer. I am done talking to you."

I tightened his handcuffs causing him to wince. "I have a message from your lawyer, Ms. Lambda. She informed me that she is employed by one Ross Moretti and no longer represents you." *Bingo*! "Secondly, one of the women you raped and murdered was an undercover police lieutenant. Before she was pronounced dead, she was made a federal agent for the DEA. For your crimes here, you are correct, you will receive multiple life imprisonments. For the murder of a federal agent, you will get the electric chair."

For the first time, Mr. Untouchable's breathing changed. He looked at me and then to the cop cars, and he made a break for it, handcuffed and all. "Thank you," I said as I let him get about five steps back into his house. I lunged forward with the others right behind me. My body blow struck him mid-center of the back and together we went horizontal landing hard on his marble floor entry. The weight of my body crushed him pinning him hard between me and the floor. His arms were already behind him so when I drove my elbow into the back of his shoulder piercing the nerve that ran from his spine to his leg, the shriek he let out was one of the most soothing sounds I had ever heard. I leaned right in by his ear. "Is that the sound Tammi made while you were beating her up? Did that make you feel like a man? Well, guess what's going to happen to you in prison? You are going to be made to feel like a man again and again and again until you have no feeling left."

"What do you want?" he cried. "Moretti had the issues with the girls. That was his deal. I can help you get Moretti. Keep me out of prison."

"What is going on, Daddy?" said a kid's voice from the hallway.

"Nothing, son," Polino said. "Just go stay with your mother."

"Joey?" issued a woman's voice. "Joey!" she screamed.

"It's over, Carmella. Get the kids and go. Take whatever you can before it's too late."

She picked up the boy and ran toward the room she had just come from. I nodded to Carter who waved two officers to go get her.

"You're right, Joey, it is over."

His body went limp. I stood from my position on his back putting all my weight down on his spine. I don't know why I did that, but I enjoyed it. I lifted his body from under the shoulders of his handcuffed arms and escorted him to my car. Typically I would never transport a criminal in a Camaro, but since it had been delivered to me last night following the raid on the batting cage building, I felt like driving him for his last moments of freedom in the car we drove as kids. Getting his sorry ass into the back seat of a two-door vehicle was a chore but worth it each time his head hit the frame.

I was bullshitting about the federal charges. That was not legal or possible, but I liked the fact that he believed it. He was going away for life, that much was certain. If the DA wanted to reduce his life charges from three to two, that would be fine. I was just glad knowing he would not be on the streets again. I don't believe he hurt all the prostitutes. I do think Moretti was the one behind the prostitute beatings and deaths, but I knew I couldn't prove it. Moretti set Polino up and set him up well. We would have to wait to hear what he had to say to determine if it would help us get Moretti. I assumed it would not, but these guys were slimeballs. Maybe he had something even Moretti or Filini did not know about. Maybe.

As we arrived at the station, I took the time to look back at my old high school friend, but opted not to speak. I just watched him as he stared blankly toward the floor of the car. He had changed more than any of us. We had all grown old, but he had done more. He had transcended into something totally unlike his younger self. Too bad it caught up to him. You can't push fate too far. That is what happened to Joey A. Polino.

I parked the car in front of the station. I was looking forward to calling Franky and letting him know. Field and Carter pulled in behind me. They had driven together which was a link between the departments. Both had lost men on this one. Clark and Gallows would be recognized this week, once all was done with

Polino. Once he was booked and the district attorney was onboard and we knew for sure what we were doing with Moretti, then we could focus on the heroes we lost. Somehow I knew, even if we got Moretti, Marco Filini would skate free, and he and I were destined to meet another day.

One thing I had to admit I liked about Filini was that he played by the rules. I could respect that. He could have killed me that night. One of the Polino videos we collected at the batting cage building was a phone recording of Polino telling them to kill Franky and me that night. The voice on the other end was muffled, but I am sure it was Marco Filini. "It is not appropriate to kill while drugged," the voice said. I thought about the code of criminals. Nothing to be counted on, but for some, it was a level of respect in a business that had little respect to go around. He probably would have let Polino do it, I thought to myself, but he would not have pulled the trigger.

I walked around to the passenger side of my Camaro and opened the door. I folded the seat up and reached in to guide Joey Polino out of the back seat for his last taste of free air.

"Suck it in deep, Joey," I said. "You will never taste free air again. From this point forward, you will be behind bars."

He stopped and looked at me. Our eyes locked, and I could see the depth of the loss he was feeling. That was moments before his brain exploded across my face. Everyone in the area dove for cover. I stood, trying to hold up his body but there was no reason. Most of his face was gone. As quick as a stiff wind blew petals from a flower, Joey Polino was dead.

I don't know where the shot came from. The forensics guys said it came from a building two blocks over. It would have made the shot close to 1500 yards in Lake Michigan lake-effect wind. I knew who took the shot. There would be no way to prove it. The forensics guys could not even tell for sure exactly where the shot came from. They determined the trajectory and distance, but when we triangulated that location back to a source, there was no sign of a former shooter. No footprints, no shell casings, nothing. The scene screamed of Marco Filini, but it was a scream with no evidence. It made sense too. Why risk Polino saying something? Let the police get him, compile the proof against him, pick him up, then get rid of him. Moretti was good, very good, and since there was no way Moretti could have pulled the trigger, I would have to agree that Marco Filini was indeed as good as his reputation claimed he was.

17 I LEFT THE JACKSON'S house on Thursday afternoon, four days since Joey Polino was killed. Jessica Jackson was another source that might be able to bring some evidence against Moretti, but the doctors basically agreed that her memory may never come back, and if it did, its accuracy would be blown away in court by any good defense attorney. I knew if Moretti thought she was a loose end for him, he would make sure she also never had a story to tell. I would make a point to stop by Rick's and tell him. I think he will believe what I tell him, though he shouldn't. I think that is where our relationship is now.

Jamal was headed back to Kansas that night. He had a game on Saturday, and ESPN was already reporting his return. How they got their information so quickly was unbelievable. Part of me felt they had his phone or home bugged. No sooner had we discussed it when I was at their house and it was being reported on AM 1000 in Chicago. All I wanted to do was listen to a replay of *Mike and Mike*, and they had to interrupt the show for that breaking news story.

Andrea Jackson gave me the longest hug I have ever received from a woman, and that includes my wife and every woman I have ever dated. I liked the hug. It meant something more than words can describe. Andrea Jackson was on the verge of losing everything. Her daughter had gone missing, husband dead, and son running down a path of destruction. She came out of it with a son back on track, a daughter who might have at least a fighting chance of recovery, and a lifelong friend in Detective Tommy O'Malley.

As I drove down the road past her front door and the door of Tyrone "Tiny" Nielson next door, I could not believe where this case had taken me. I had not gone to see Ty's mother. I wasn't sure if I was going to or not. She did not want to see me. I was not able to save her son. It was not my fault, but she was a mother. She saw what she wanted to see. I knew I had one thing left to do. I had some questions left unanswered and there was only one place to find those answers.

•   •   •   •   •

I pulled into Rick's Cabaret with the engine of my Camaro sounding like a dream. I revved it up to impress the ladies walking in for their night of work. They were not impressed, but they should have been. I knew that was the truth. I got out of my car and began the walk over to the front door. To my pleasure, Ricardo was working the door.

"*Hola*, Ricardo, *Como estas?*"

"Fuck you, Detective."

"Really? Really?" I replied almost sadly. "You really want to go there again."

"You can bring whatever bullshit move you want to on me, but I am ready this…"

Ricardo was on the ground grabbing his throat. I stepped over him, and I believe he reached out to grab my leg, for a moment at least. Then, with a swift kick before walking through the doorway, his unconscious body slumped to the side.

I glanced at the girl behind the mirror. "I need to have a brief word with Mr. Moretti and Filini if they are in. And you will want to call someone else up to be your doorman for about twenty minutes."

She leaned forward so she could see out the door and saw Ricardo lying face-first in the grass alongside the walkway. "Oh my God, what happened?"

"I don't know. He must have tripped or something."

"O'Malley," echoed a voice from the main club area. "Stop messing with Ricardo. He is too stupid for you to waste your time."

I turned and saw Marco coming toward me. You would have thought we were old friends by the way he sauntered up, but we both knew where the other stood. I knew they were dirty. They knew I could not be bought. We were setting the stage for a huge collision, but we were not sure when. He did not reach out a hand to shake, but instead opened his arm to lead me back to Moretti's office.

Moretti was sitting in the same office chair behind his huge wooden desk. Two chairs were in place for us to sit. It gave the impression he just left them there from my last visit, like he knew I would be returning. Moretti wore a big smile and already had a cigar lit filling his office with smoke. The one-way mirror showed significant activity taking place on the other side. I was pretty sure it included sex in one instance, but I did not take the time to inspect that closely.

"To what do we owe this pleasure, Tommy?"

"Please, call me Detective O'Malley."

"Fine, fine," he waved as he spoke. "Whatever, but you can call me Ross. After all, I owe it to you and your team that I have doubled my net worth almost overnight. Marco and I could not be more pleased with how things turned out. You did a great job finding all that evidence that tied back to my partner, Joe Polino."

"Cut the crap, Moretti. I don't have the time and your patronizing demeanor does you a disservice."

He raised an eyebrow. "Interesting, I have never heard that before. I will keep that in mind." He paused, sucked in on his cigar, and then continued. "Seriously, I do feel I owe you whether you think so or not. What brings you here? Would you like a dance? I have some girls that I am sure can make you feel better than the restaurant woman ever could."

He knew he had hit a nerve there, and to my displeasure, I let him know he had hit it. "Knock it off, Moretti," I said. "I want to know about Malcolm Jackson."

He looked toward Marco and moved slightly uncomfortably in his seat. Marco stood, walked over, and ensured the door was locked. When he nodded to his boss, Moretti stood and came to stand in front of me. "Really, Detective, you need to let this case go. Why ask questions that already have answers?"

"Because in all the evidence that was 'discovered' and in all the videos and recordings, there is nothing that specifically said why Malcolm Jackson was killed. What did he do to deserve to be executed?"

"I don't know anything about what my partner did or why, Detective O'Malley. By saying something, I fear it could make me look guilty."

"Goddamnit! Do you think I care about sending you to jail for killing Malcolm Jackson? Joey Polino is going to be found guilty of that murder as far as the City of Chicago is concerned. All I want to understand is what put him on the radar? Why Malcolm?"

Moretti looked back to Marco and then made a slight gesture with his hands like waving a magic wand. Marco walked over to me. "Stand up, Tommy, and put your hands straight out."

I did as he asked and Marco walked over to a cabinet and removed a long, narrow metal board that resembled a cricket bat. He walked over, turned it on, and proceeded to move it across my body. When it sounded at my belt, he had me remove my belt and gun and set them on the chair. I then tossed my phone next to them. He waved it across the rest of my body. Marco returned the wand to the cabinet and nodded to Moretti that all was clear.

Moretti returned to his seat. "Detective O'Malley, I do not approve of this conversation being recorded. Knowing now that you are not interested in recording this conversation, am I to believe you are interested in the truth and not justice?"

"If by that you are asking will I pursue anything regarding the death of Malcolm Jackson, I cannot answer that without knowing the truth. What I can tell you is that I am certain you have yourself well-protected and your comment just now is only to fuck with me. I don't have the time to be fucked."

He smiled as did Marco. "Fair enough, Detective O'Malley. You are correct. Malcolm Jackson was a big mistake. A big mistake on my part. I know you thought Malcolm must have seen something at one of the clubs, but you did not ask yourself what else was on his route. Before we started using the hotel, we used another location for our 'fun times.' It had not been in use for several years and we did not have any towel service but we needed some. Malcolm ran the route when it was in business so Joey asked him to do a few deliveries and charge it back to the club. Malcolm was more than happy to oblige. He was such a good guy."

"The goddamn baseball cages. He delivered to the baseball cages," I said.

"They don't call you the best detective in Chicago for nothing, do they?"

"They don't call me that," I added.

He smiled and continued. "Yes, so Joey has it set up for Malcolm to deliver to the warehouse and he is supposed to go in the front. Joey has the windows blocked and doors locked so he cannot get into the main warehouse. But what does Malcolm do, he goes in the back. Somehow the door is left open and he is able to get in. What he sees there upsets him greatly to say the least. He assumes his longtime friend Joey Polino does not know what his building is being used for because Joey had told him the towel delivery was just for clean-up to sell the place. So what does that man do but run to the Red Carpet to tell him. By some twist of fate, he did not call the police right then and there. If he had, I might be behind bars." He paused and smiled to himself. "You should have seen my face when I saw him walk through those back doors and the cages."

"You? That building was for you?"

"I am not saying anything of the sort. All I am saying is that when you are destroying everything that a woman is about for your own pleasure, you do not want a uniform delivery man talking about it."

He almost seemed proud of what he was saying. "What happened when he arrived at the Red Carpet?"

He burst through the back doors and saw some girls that were...incapacitated, to say the least. He went crazy. Polino finally calmed him down with one promise. Can you guess what he offered?"

"Jessica," I replied. "The only thing that would keep Malcolm from going to the police was a chance at Jessica."

"Give the man a prize, Marco," Moretti said smiling. "Polino said he knew who had Jessica. He would have a mutual contact call him that night and set up the exchange. If Malcolm agreed to forget everything he saw, then Joey would ensure the safe return of his daughter. Can you believe he fell for that?"

I shook my head. "Yes, I believe he did."

"From there it was easy. Jewel was into Joey for thousands. He had been cleaning up after me for months. Malcolm trusted Jewel, so Jewel made the call to have him meet Joey, and from there, no more Malcolm. He never got to see his daughter again, but because of his actions, you got involved and now his daughter is home. From a certain perspective, he gave his life for hers, which I am sure he would have done ten times over."

"What was your part in this?" I asked Marco.

He did not reply. He just stood quietly.

"You don't need Moretti, do you, Marco?" I asked.

He simply replied in an exaggerated, stunned voice. "This is the first I have heard of any of this."

"What is the matter with you, Marco? Where is that coming from?" Moretti asked.

"I don't like it, sir. Something is not right. I suggest you quiet down."

I bent down and picked up my phone that still rested on the chair. Without dialing anything, I simply asked, "Did you guys get all that?"

"We did," a voice said back through the phone.

Moretti smiled. "You are a dead man, you realize that, don't you?"

"I do," I replied. "But so is Malcolm, and I could not live with myself if I did not at least try."

"What charge are you going to hold me on? Suspicion of assaulting a woman? Knowing about Joey Polino's crimes and not reporting them?"

"I think we can make *conspiracy to commit murder* stick for starters, and we will see what the district attorney can come up with in addition to that."

He looked at Marco. "Call my lawyer and have her meet me at the station."

Marco looked down to him. "I think our business together is done, Mr. Moretti. You are a liability." He turned to me. "Detective O'Malley, is it your intention to arrest me as well?"

"Will you confess to shooting Polino from over fifteen hundred yards the other day or any other crime?"

"No."

"Then, unfortunately, our time to meet up is still in the future. I am sure there will be some questions for you now. After that, I would say don't leave town, but you would do it regardless of whether I tried to stop you or not."

"I would."

"Good-bye then, Marco Filini. I will hand you off to the detectives about to come through the door. It would be fine with me if you stayed out of Chicago from this point forward."

"I am sure it would, Detective O'Malley. I do look forward to crossing paths with you again."

"Likewise."

I REACHED DOWN and pulled the small cooler out from under the hospital bed. Just then, the doctor walked in and I quickly pushed it back under. "What are you doing down there, Detective O'Malley?" the doctor asked.

I smiled. "Just kicking my shoes off before the game, Doc." I began to kick my shoes off but one of them pushed forward making a small thud against my cooler. I pretended like I meant to make the noise and continued with my shoe removal effort.

Doctor Bonebreak—yes, that was his real name—turned to Franky. "How are you feeling, Detective Sullivan? How is the movement in your arm?"

Franky lifted his arm to about three o'clock from his body. "The pain starts about there," he answered in a slightly labored voice, the scent of beer pushing forward with each word.

I think the doctor smelled the beer because he took a quick glance toward me and then panned down to my feet, but the bed still separated my cooler from his view. However, if he did, his direction did not give it away or he did not care. He continued unhindered. "Good, that is higher than yesterday. As I said, I think we repaired all the damage. It will hurt to lift anything for some time and your movement will be restricted without pain, but if you keep up with the physical therapy, I'm sure you will make a full recovery."

Franky seemed pleased with this, as was I. I reached over and tapped his hospital gown-clad belly. "You see, you will be lifting that gun again and not shooting it in no time."

He smiled but did not respond. The doctor turned to leave and then stopped when he saw the game. "Hey, my alma mater. Big rivalry game tonight."

"You went to Kansas?" I asked.

"Yes, four years undergrad and then med school. Some of the best years of my life. You guys basketball fans?"

Just then Andrea Jackson and Jessica Jackson tapped lightly on the door. "May we come in, detectives?"

All eyes swung to them and a broad smile crept across my face. "Absolutely, ladies. Please come in." Turning back to the doctor, I answered, "Doctor Bonebreak, please meet Andrea and Jessica Jackson, Jamal Jackson's mother and sister." He did not seem to make the immediate connection so I added, "KU star forward Jamal Jackson's mother and sister."

Instantly his face rose two inches almost lifting his surgical cap off his head. "Oh my, what a pleasure to meet you both."

"The doctor here who fixed up Detective Sullivan is a graduate of Kansas, and clearly a big fan of your son," I added as they each shook his hand.

Andrea appeared very pleased. "Well, Doctor, I must thank you for saving the life of the man who helped save my family. Obviously you are a great doctor coming from such a prestigious school."

Doctor Bonebreak appeared moved as he released her hand. "Ma'am, I don't know what these detectives did for your family, but I was just doing my job. Although I would love to claim being a lifesaver, in this case I think I simply saved some mobility in his arm." He paused, smiled at Jessica who stayed to the side acting extremely shy. He appeared moved by this timidness, but did not add anything and turned back to Andrea. "And for the important comment, thank you for raising such a talented young man and having him choose that same prestigious school to exercise those talents."

She smiled but had noticed the doctor's gaze upon her daughter. She pulled her hand back and reached it out to Jessica to help guide her into the room. I watched her shy walk and knew that every room she walked into must be terrifying. *A lot of damage*, I thought. I saw the doctor's eyes and knew he must see the same thing. He had no idea what Jessica had been through, but with his medical background he probably made numerous assumptions that were spot on. He turned back to Frank and I and acknowledged Jessica and Andrea in the same fashion. Giving us all a small wave, he simply stated, "Rock Chalk," and walked out the door.

Andrea Jackson walked up to me and gave me another long, deep hug. If it had been from anyone else, it would have been uncomfortably long, but from her it was perfect. She released me and turned to Franky. "Detective Sullivan, I am sure you are in pain, but you are not going to get away from taking a hug from me. I promise to be gentle, but I have been storing this up for days so it may get away from me."

Detective Frank Sullivan beamed. I am not sure I have ever seen a smile as large. His head was stuck out on her shoulder, and I was one hundred percent positive he felt more pain at that moment than when the bullet first struck. I also knew he did not care.

When they finally broke, I looked at the two ladies taking Andrea's hand in mine. "What are you both doing here? Jamal is about to play his first game back. You should be at home watching it on a nice TV in a comfortable setting."

Out of nowhere, Jessica answered. Her voice was quiet, maybe half as loud as it needed to be for everyone to hear, but nobody said a word about it. "Detectives, Mama and I talked and we thought there was no better place to watch Jamal's first game back than with Detective Sullivan. I am sure Mama is as pleased as I am to see you here also." She gestured toward me.

We were both dumbfounded. Franky, still beaming from the hug and the appreciation he felt from Mrs. Jackson, broke in with a powerful tone driving his words. "Well then, Tommy, move your ass out of the way and let them sit. Go get another chair. Tip-off is in less than five minutes if they start on time."

"Mama said the food here stinks, so we made you some monster cookies," added Jessica. She pulled out a Tupperware filled with about fifteen monster cookies, large oatmeal-M&M-chocolate-chip all in one cookie. She also said you fancied some place called El Famous Burrito. We picked up these as well."

Jessica Jackson, in her shy, scared voice and timid demeanor, gingerly lifted out a brown bag. I peeked inside and saw a handful of foil-wrapped football-sized burritos. My heart went to a place I am not sure it had been before, only to be met with Franky's. Andrea smiled but when Jessica saw how pleased I was, her expression appeared like a child seeing what Santa left for the first time Christmas morning.

"I don't know how to thank you both," stated Franky, breaking the silence created when I did not speak.

"Yes," I added quickly. "Thank you."

The women nodded and Andrea pushed me aside slightly so she could sit in the recliner next to Franky and still face the TV. "Now, let's all sit down and see if that fool boy of mine will decide to make a few baskets tonight."

That one comment brought us all back to the game. Jessica was still quiet, even when Jamal knocked down his twentieth point before the half. The game was not close, but again, it was Kansas State. Franky and Andrea talked quite a bit, and I just sat back and let it sink in.

With a few minutes left in the game and a thirty-four point lead for the visiting Jayhawks, my phone rang. I recognized the number. "O'Malley."

"Tommy, this is James Esson. District Attorney James Esson."

I don't know why he did that. He did that every time we talked, whether in person or over the phone. I knew his name. I knew his position. Hell, he was calling me on my cell phone which obviously has caller ID so why did he have to do the James Bond introduction—Bond, James Bond. James Esson, District Attorney James Esson.

"Yes, this is Tommy O'Malley, Detective Tommy O'Malley," I added.

To my surprise, Esson did not catch the meaning behind my repeated statement. He continued in a deep, monotone level. "Moretti is being released."

"What!" I exclaimed, moving slightly away from the others when I realized how loud my voice was.

"Yes, you heard me correctly. I wanted to let you know that Moretti is going to be out on bail in a matter of hours. We are going to take the case to a grand jury, but that is still months away and the judge did not feel comfortable with the level of evidence surrounding this case and how it was obtained. He felt that holding him the entire time before the grand jury was not the right choice."

I was steamed and my voice showed it causing the others in the room to take notice. "Goddamnit, what the hell do you mean, how the evidence was obtained?" I shouted into the phone. "I served this guy up to you on a silver platter and you can't even hold him. Screw the grand jury. This guy is dirty, and I am the one who set him up. What do you think, he's going to come over to play bridge knowing I am the guy that did this?"

"That is really the point of my call," Esson replied calmly. "You should be aware that the case may not make it to the grand jury, and even if it does, there's better than a fifty percent chance it stops there. I think your phone tap will be thrown out. Moretti said during the conversation he did not approve of the conversation being recorded. It was not a court-issued wiretap so the law is cloudy at best. You may want to take some time..."

I cut him off with the simple pressing of the red button ending the call. I turned to the others and saw all their eyes on me. "Sorry about that," I stated, looking toward Franky.

"They are letting him out?" Franky asked.

"They are not even sure it will make the grand jury," I replied. "Something about the phone evidence being no good and most likely being thrown out."

Both Jessica and Andrea gasped slightly but it was Jessica who spoke. "You mean he is going to be out there again? Able to come and get me again?"

It was the first sentence she had spoken that was not soft and sounded as if she was hidden in a shell. It was in my face and cut like a dagger. In my experience, she never had a thought of her own. The hard but still broken voice told all what they needed to know. This woman was terrified.

I checked the time on my phone, glanced back to the game that had just ended, and then turned back to the group. "Don't worry. I am going to talk to Moretti. You do not need to worry about anything. I will never let that man hurt you again."

I believed the words right as I said them, but after they had left my mouth and had a moment to ferment in the air, I knew I could not back them up. If Moretti was free, everyone in that room was a target. The only thing I could do was put the target directly on me.

"Just a minute, Tommy," started Franky. "Do not go off half-cocked and do something stupid."

Andrea also started to protest but halted when I raised my hand. "Don't worry. If I pretend I am scared that he is out there, then I will always be looking over my shoulder. I need to confront him, and I can't wait. It has to be now."

Again Andrea started to protest, but this time it was Jessica who placed her hand timidly on Andrea's forearm. "Mama, let him go talk. He won't do anything to Detective O'Malley right now. There are too many people watching the situation. This is the best time for him to talk to him. I don't want to be scared all the time."

Everyone heard her message clearly. She was not telling her mother what to do. She was begging me to go. "I did not answer but looked around the room, and the fact I heard no more protests answered my question for me. Everyone agreed, whether they were willing to say it or not.

As I turned to leave the room, Franky said, "Tommy, wear your vest just the same."

I lightly pounded my chest showing I already had it on. Smiling at my longtime friend, I added, "Keep an eye on my cooler."

"What cooler?" Franky replied.

•   •   •   •   •

I ran by the station and then on to Rick's. I arrived at the club an hour and thirty minutes later. I really did not have a plan, but what I did have was a hard-on the minute I saw the Mercedes. *He is here,* I thought to myself. Part of me did not think he would be here. Part of me wished he wasn't. I pulled out my gun while I sat in my car and ran through a full check. I made sure everything was in order. I had been without a true partner for two years. That was against company policy but Franky and I always stuck together, so although it was not officially on paper as such, we were partners. There is nobody at the department who would accept me entering this establishment alone. Every rule in the book stated I should not. The little voice in my head told me I should not go in alone, but who was I to listen to a little voice?

I opened my car door and began the long walk over to the entryway. Again my good friend Ricardo was manning the front. He did not even look at me nor did he move to step in my path. In fact, I believe he gave me enough space I could have driven my car through between him and the red carpet-lined doorway. I smiled but with my nerves the way they were, I did not even think to speak. I was focused on what was on the other side of the blacked-out glass entry.

I pushed through the door and I think I heard Ricardo let out a short deep breath. There was no girl behind the counter today, most likely due to the time. Any loser coming to a strip club at this time must get in for free. There was a dancer on the stage but the music was half its normal level of blaring loud, and believe it or not, there were about five losers in the place. It is worth noting that I had to do a double take on the dancer. Not that I was a strip club connoisseur or anything, but the woman dancing was disgusting. Not including being overly, what is the word, *humongous*. Her complexion was horrible and above all, she could not dance. A horrible combination. The detective in me immediately asked the question—how in the hell did she become a stripper?

As the thought went through my mind, there was a tap on my shoulder. "It was 50-50 that you would come by," stated Moretti leaning close to my ear. "I can't say if I'm pleased or not."

I turned to face him and was surprised to see he was alone. "No bodyguard today, Ross?"

He shrugged slightly and turned to walk to his office. "It seems not everyone wants to work with someone who was arrested. Something about if they are no longer arrested, they must have done something to help the police to be released." He stopped, reached into the inside breast pocket of his jacket causing me to reach for the handle of my gun. Seeing this, he held his jacket open with his hand revealing three cigars. "Relax, Detective, I am actually glad you came by. It saved me the trip of trying to set up a meeting with you." Pulling two cigars out, he offered, "Cigar?"

I shook my head, though by the wrap, they appeared to be Cuban. *Maybe I could arrest him on import charges*, I thought. "You wanted to meet with me?" I asked, slightly inquisitive.

"Join me in my office?" he asked.

I was hesitant. I did not like the electric lock and bolt from the outside door, but Moretti's demeanor was completely off. If I were going to write down what I expected, this would have been as far from that as I ever would have guessed. He was acting like we were old friends. "Come and sit with me and let's catch up." I did not know if I liked that or not. Regardless, without answering, I followed him in. I left the door open which I think he noticed.

"You can leave the door open," he stated.

Once again, that is why I am the best detective in the city. He sat in his large chair behind his desk and sucked in a few puffs of his cigar. The smell was very good, and it only added to the mystery around what was going on. This man before me was simply a narcissistic asshole. The worst thing that could have happened was I almost got him but missed, furthering his untouchable mentality. He was going to sit in this room in silence for as long as it took for me to say something. He was going to be in control. I took a seat across from him in the same chair I had thrown my phone in previously that worked as my radio tap for our conversation. Today I did not have fifteen police officers outside the doors listening and recording every word spoken. Today it was just me. Again I thought how stupid a move this was. No matter how stupid it was, there was no chance I was going to speak first.

There we sat. I have never watched anyone smoke. I mean really watched them smoke. It was actually disgusting. They put the wet end of a burning bundle of leaves in their mouth, pulled it out, and then back in. My mind thought about dental work and how I could never be a hygienist. I then thought about sex. I tried to think about anything but speaking. I was not going to let this loser beat me. So we sat in silence. He turned his head away from me to stare through the one-way mirror into the VIP Room. I followed his gaze.

Nasty dancer girl was giving a lap dance to one of the patrons. He was smiling broadly and I believe his pants were off but there was too much flab around the sides to determine for sure. Anything to take my mind off the discomfort of sitting in silence.

Then, the silence was broken. "I should take my gun out and put a bullet in your head right now," Moretti stated. "I should have forced Marco to do it before."

Yep, stupid, stupid, stupid for me to be here alone. "You could always try, I suppose." My voice was not nearly as strong as it needed it to be, but it passed.

"I could do it, you know. Kill you right here in my office, and your body would never be found. I guarantee you there would be no evidence and no witnesses. Your disappearance would simply go through as an unsolved cold case. Detective Thomas O'Malley, Never Been Found."

"Again, Moretti, you could try." I sounded much stronger this time.

"Is that why you are here, Detective? To see if I am putting a price out on you?" He waited for me to answer and when I didn't, he continued. "Because I am not."

Again he paused for me to respond. "Should I be happy about that?" I asked.

"Everyone is touchable," he replied. "There is nobody that could not be killed with the proper planning."

"Then why don't you do it, Moretti? Why don't you just kill me?" I actually was becoming pissed now.

"Because I don't need you dead now," he stated flatly. "Polino was stupid and reckless. He had people in his employ who had no idea how a business like this should operate. My business is cleaner and quieter. I own enough now that I can simply hit 'cruise control' and coast. I don't need to kill you or anyone else because I will no longer even be on your radar."

I was growing in anger with each word. "You will not fall off my radar just because you become better at hiding it, Moretti. I can't let that happen because of what you did to all those women, and for what you did to Diana Gallows."

"Ah yes, Lieutenant Diana Gallows," Moretti stammered. "We never had any idea. Trust that had we known, nothing like that would have occurred." He paused, took another puff on his cigar and then extinguished it in the tray next to him. "We would have done much worse."

"Aren't you afraid I am taping you again? Saying things like that will definitely get you in trouble." I was just trying to play with him a bit, the same way he was playing with me. He was trying to get me on the attack, and what he said was bringing my blood to a boil. I hated this man.

He leaned forward and spoke in such a soft tone that even if I was trying to record it, it would not have taken. "Let's get one thing completely clear. I respect you, O'Malley, but I am not stupid. If you ever come after me like that again, I will take you to a place you never believed existed."

He ended the comment there and I was expecting more. I actually did not know if he wanted me to respond or not. So I did, in the same soft, unrecordable tone he had used. "Moretti, let me make one thing abundantly clear to you. If you hurt anyone I know in an attempt to hurt me, I will kill you."

He sat back. Slowly a smile turned across his face. "I get it," he said. "You are not here to get me. You are here to make sure I don't hurt the Jacksons, or Clark's ex-wife, or that bitch from the restaurant. So noble are you. Well, here is what I say to that, Detective. Fuck you."

He leaned back with the appearance that he believed his shit did not stink. From where I was sitting, it stunk like shit. The "bitch from the restaurant" comment seemed to hang in my mind. "Maybe you're right, Moretti," I broke in. "Maybe I am here to simply protect those around me. My question for you is, why would you need anything from them anymore?"

"Only because you want me to not need anything from them anymore."

There was a long pause. I suddenly began to understand that coming here to be so "noble" may have been the completely wrong decision. I was showing my cards. I was showing this asshole where I was vulnerable. And the damage was done. My only direction from here was clear. I stood up, put both my hands on his desk, and leaned in until my face was only inches from his. Whispering, I said, "Let me leave no room for gray area or interpretation. If you hurt anyone to get to me, I will destroy you. I will pick your operation apart piece by piece. I will take down—you, your businesses, your family, your friends—and if you trust nothing else I say, then trust this. You will never see the inside of a prison cell. If you think what you would have done to Lieutenant Gallows was bad, then you've seen nothing yet."

"Take care of your family and friends, O'Malley, and get the fuck out of my office." As I turned to walk out he added, "It does not make business sense to do anything right now, O'Malley."

I did not respond, but if I had wanted some assurance everyone was safe for the time being, I believe I had just gotten it, though I had no confidence it would be upheld. I walked straight through the seating area toward the front entry. I did not look at the dancers or the patrons. At this point, everyone disgusted me. They were all part of Moretti, and Moretti was dirty. I was going to clean all this up. I was sure of it. As I pushed through the door to the outside, there was Ricardo.

"Hello, Ricardo," I said in a cheery voice.

"*Hola,* Detective. *Vete a la mierda*!"

The young man had balls. He is stupid, but he does have balls. He hit the ground, and I believe he was unconscious, but I did not stop to find out. I simply replied, "Fuck you too, asshole."

As I reached my car, I was not sure if I felt satisfied, confident, or played, but regardless, I did believe those whose safety I wanted to ensure were, at least at this point, safe. I let out a deep breath as I sat behind the wheel of my car when my phone rang. I looked down and was very surprised at the number on the screen.

"Hello, Tammi. I am glad you called."

Her voice was faint and distant. Instantly, my mind went back to my previous thought—satisfied, confident, or played. *Played*, I thought to myself. "Tommy?"

"Yes, Tammi, are you all right?" My tone was much more pleading than I thought it should be.

She spoke louder, possibly hearing my tone and realizing how she sounded. "I am fine, Tommy. I am sitting here alone. I have picked up my phone and dialed twenty-five times and then hung up. I don't want to lose you, Tommy, but I am scared."

My heart sank. Here I was, a lifelong detective, a beautiful woman way out of my league actually wanted to be with me, and my first instinct was that my job had put her in danger once and could again. I was torn. I could tell her now that I could not see her anymore. Tell her to go be with someone in her league, someone much better than me. I knew that was the right answer. I knew it was the best answer for her. I knew what I had to say.

"I'll be right over." I figured, what the hell.

Bingo!

•

Look forward to the second book in the series,

NEVER BEEN TRACED

A high school football star is killed in a scene clearly well-planned out in advance. As the mystery unfolds, bullying, parental control, and a high school staff that clearly were more about keeping things under the carpet than facing them bring Detective Tommy O'Malley out of the cold and into a web of teenage and adult mystery. More than five suspects had motives, but all had ironclad alibis. Teamed with his first official partner in years, a young female detective who just moved into homicide from Joliet, O'Malley must weed through the entire disgusting truth to find out who was really behind what eventually grew into a vigilante spree throughout the entire downtown Chicago prep school. Multicity and unbelievable misdirection of evidence leads O'Malley down a twisted path where the only answer is the one he does not want to hear.

ABOUT THE AUTHOR

Born in Topeka, KS, Kenneth S. Kappelmann graduated from the University of Kansas and later Graduate School in Oregon State, in cellular biology and microbiology respectively. He has worked in the Pharmaceutical and food industry his entire life and only began writing books while living in Switzerland. If he could spend his entire year on a lake, he would; but otherwise, he lives in the frozen tundra of Minnesota raising a family of five.

Twitter: kappelmannbooks
E-mail: kappelmannbooks@yahoo.com
Facebook: HiddenMagicReturnoftheDragon
https://www.amazon.com/Kenneth-Kappelmann/e/B00F9F3SSW

View other Black Rose Writing titles at www.blackrosewriting.com/books and

use promo code **PRINT** to receive a **20% discount** when purchasing.

BLACK ROSE
writing™

Made in the USA
Monee, IL
19 August 2021

76036442R20134